Heartstrings AND Helmets

ALEXA ASTON

OLIVER HEBER BOOKS

Prologue

W est Sutherland opened his eyes after the best night of sleep he'd had in months. No, years. Today, his Dallas Cowboys would play the Las Vegas Raiders for the Lombardi Trophy.

And he was going to retire after the game.

He was wrapping up ten seasons in the NFL, where he'd been All-Pro seven of those years. Last year, he had missed the final two regular season games and one playoff game, and the Cowboys had badly missed his contributions. He'd suffered an ACL injury during a catch at the two-yard-line. The infamous popping noise and sensation had been instant the moment he hit the ground. Still, West had made certain his body fell over the goal line, ensuring his team won the game, which had gone into overtime. His reception iced their victory.

Thankfully, the MRI showed only a sprain of his anterior cruciate ligament, which crossed the middle of his knee, and not a more serious tear. He couldn't put any weight on it, though, and had been carted off as Dallas fans cheered loudly, chanting his name. By the time he reached the locker room, the painful, rapid swelling frightened him. West had lived a charmed life on the football field, only suffering minor injuries since his days of playing Pop Warner football. A few sprained ankles. A dislocated shoulder, which still popped out on occasion. A couple of broken fingers.

While his injury had not required surgery, he still put in the hours of rehab necessary to come back and play this year. The exercises had helped him regain strength as well as stability in his knee. The loss of range of motion, coupled with the feeling of instability—as if his knee would buckle—was what the physical exercises dealt with.

Tougher than the rehabbing process was the mental stress. Although his body felt fine, his mind still told him it could happen again, this time leading to a tear and surgery. Because he was so shaky mentally, he'd started seeing a therapist, something he'd scoffed at before. But Dr. Linda really listened. She challenged him. Not just about the injury, but about what he would be doing after football, something West hadn't put a lot of thought into.

Dr. Linda walked him through all kinds of scenarios—ways he could suffer another ACL, especially because he'd hurt his knee once already—and it was more likely to happen again now that he was vulnerable. He mentally walked through pivoting when his foot was planted firmly on the turf. Going up for a ball and landing awkwardly after the leap. Or the worst—being victim to a direct blow to his knee from behind by one of those gnarly linebackers or defensive backs who seemed to have no fear as they flew across the field at breakneck speed, ready to bring down a receiver.

West had an in-person session with his therapist every day leading up to last summer's training camp, fighting through his fears. Then he'd scheduled FaceTime therapy with Dr. Linda during camp and hadn't missed a day. All their conversations had led him to the decision that he was ready to walk away from football after tonight's game.

He showered and shaved, dressing in a crisp, white dress shirt and gray suit. No tie. His cell rang, and he answered it, grinning at his therapist's image.

"Right on time, Doc," he said, sitting on the bed and bracing his back against the headboard.

"Have you made your decision?" she asked, concern in her deep, brown eyes.

"Yes, ma'am. Tonight is my last game."

She nodded thoughtfully. "Tell me why. Walk me through it, West."

Gathering his thoughts before he spoke, he finally said, "It's not fun anymore. Actually, I was feeling this all during last season. I'd always told myself when I wasn't having fun, I would walk away."

"Do you think your injury last year has contributed to your decision?" she pressed.

"Yes and no. I still worry when I go out on the field about getting hurt again. Once I'm out there, playing, caught up in the game, that worry goes away. I don't think I've been tentative on a single play. But leading up to games and making myself hit the field has been brutal."

He paused. "But it's more than that. I've accomplished every goal I set out to do, at every level I've played at. I've been the Golden Boy my whole life, Doc. All-State in high school. All-American in college, winning a national championship. Then All-Pro, with two Super Bowl rings, and the chance at another one tonight. I've always studied the playbook hard. Been a great teammate. Even a leader."

"Yes, being named captain this year in your comeback was quite an honor," she noted.

"I agree. But this whole year, even though I've put forth my best effort, the joy has been missing. I used to play with such abandon. Let's face it. I've been fearless on and off the field my entire life. Never backed down from a challenge. But you've got me thinking about life after football."

He chuckled. "I've spent a lot of hours on that topic, and you know what? I'm at peace. I've had a great career, but it's time to be an adult. Move on."

"To what?"

West grinned. "You never let up, Doc. I like that about you. You're like a female version of me."

Dr. Linda laughed. "Yes, at five-two and just over a hundred pounds, I'm exactly like you, West."

"You know what I mean. You're relentless. Like a dog with a bone." He paused. "I want to coach."

Her expression turned curious. "At what level?"

"Definitely not pro. Not even college. The NFL is a business. That's how most players approach it, and they should. College has become more like a business, with NIL changing the financial landscape. What I want is that sheer happiness and love a player feels for the game. I want to go back to coach high school. And not just any high school."

"You want to go home to Hawthorne," she stated.

"Yes. I want to teach, really teach the game. Get kids to understand it. Like it. Find the pleasure in playing it." West cleared his throat. "And I want a family."

Her eyes widened. "A family?"

He grinned. "I know. Coming from me that's saying a lot. I've dated famous women. Beautiful women. Famous and beautiful women. But it was all shallow. Pretty much all for show. I've never let my guard down around a woman or ever had a serious relationship." Determination filled him. "It's about time I did."

"What kind of family do you envision, West?"

"Like the one I came from. Where I have a wife I love more than football. A couple of kids I'm crazy about."

"Will you push a future son into football?"

"No," he said honestly. "You've taught me enough to know that people have to follow their heart. If my kid likes basketball or baseball—hell, if he doesn't even want to play sports and do marching band or drama instead—that's fine with me. I've come to understand that football isn't the be-all, end-all in life." He smiled. "You've done some good work on me, Doc. The West Sutherland from a year ago would have thought West 2.0 here was bat-shit crazy. But I'm not. I want a relationship that can lead to marriage. I want kids. I want them to be raised in a small town and have good values."

"Is this football coaching position even open in Hawthorne?" she asked.

"Not the head coaching job. And I wouldn't ask for it anyway. I need the seasoning. Besides, my high school coach still holds the job, and he's not going anywhere anytime soon. It would be a privilege to work under Coach Markham. Frankly, I learned more from him than any other coach I've ever had. I still think Coach M has things to teach me."

Dr. Linda nodded approvingly. "You seem to have your head on straight, West. That's a good thing. I don't think we should quit cold turkey, however. Transitioning from a life in the NFL to being a regular guy—wherever you land—will be tough."

"I get there'll be roadblocks, Doc. The work we've put in together has prepared me for them. I agree that we need to continue our sessions. Maybe once a week?"

"I know the next couple of weeks will be crazy for you. Call my assistant for an appointment to FaceTime our sessions. Then once we've spoken, if you feel as if you have a good handle on things, maybe we can go to once a week."

"Sounds like a plan." West hesitated. "Thanks again for taking me on as a patient. I know I wasn't quite into the idea of therapy when we started, but I am stronger mentally because of it." He smiled at her. "And proud of that mental health, too."

She beamed at him. "Go play the best game of your life, West."

Dr. Linda pulled the phone away from her, so that he saw not only her face—but what she was wearing.

A Green Bay Packers sweatshirt.

He burst out laughing.

"I neglected to tell you I'm a Packers fan. My dad was from the Midwest, and he worshipped the Pack. Passed along his love of the team to my brother and me." She grinned. "But I really do hope you play a wonderful game tonight."

"Gig 'em," he said, hearing her echo the same thing as he ended the connection.

At least Dr. Linda was an Aggie. He supposed he'd have to forgive her for the rest.

He tossed his things into a duffel and headed downstairs. Coach Nelson had given West permission to spend last night away from the hotel. His mom had rented a house in New Orleans the day after training camp ended last summer, telling West that she thought the Cowboys would be playing for the title. More than anything, he wanted to break the news to his family about his retirement, instead of them hearing it on social media's post-game blitz. He couldn't announce it, though, because Flint Ferris was here.

West had never liked his sister's husband. Autumn had married Flint during his first year in med school and had worked many a double shift as a nurse, paying to put him through school so he wouldn't be drowning in debt after he finished his residency. They'd been married six or seven years now, and West had never warmed to Flint. He seemed to treat

Autumn too cavalierly, and she always was making excuses for him. Flint was very into appearances. If West told his family now that he was about to play his final game, Flint would splash it all over social media. He'd already asked for pictures with West and posted those. The guy just rubbed him the wrong way.

Because of it, he'd keep quiet now. And hope Autumn would come to her senses and dump this loser.

They were all gathered in the kitchen. He stood in the doorway a moment, drinking them in. Dad was flipping pancakes for brunch. Mom stood behind him, her arms wrapped around his waist, snuggling close. Summer was taking bacon out of the oven, while Autumn poured coffee and juice for the group. Naturally, Flint sat at the breakfast bar, scrolling through his phone, not lifting a finger. The doctor seemed to think he was too good for menial tasks.

"Hey, everybody," West greeted, entering the kitchen.

"I love this suit," Summer declared, coming and wrapping him in a tight hug. "You always dress well, West. Manhattan men have nothing on you."

Summer worked for a publishing house in New York as a book editor and had taken a couple of days of vacation to come to New Orleans. She'd shared with Autumn and him that she was writing her first romance novel, saying she thought she could do better than the manuscripts that crossed her desk.

Autumn said, "My turn to cozy up to the past and future Super Bowl MVP."

He hugged her tightly, wanting to tell her she could do so much better than Flint, but knowing Autumn would never listen. She thought she was lucky to have Flint, who was smart and good-looking. His sister always looked out for everyone but herself.

"You just went and jinxed things. Now, Van Foster will definitely be named MVP."

"Just because he's a quarterback doesn't automatically mean he'll be the MVP," Flint said. "Although the winning team's quarterback usually has the best shot. You were lucky to win it two years ago, West."

He noticed the annoyance flicker in his mom's eyes. She came to him, and he wrapped his arms about her, lifting her off her feet.

"Save your strength, West," she said good-naturedly, brushing a kiss across his cheek.

"Pancakes for you, son?" asked Dad.

"No. I can sit with you a few minutes while you eat, and then I need to head back to the hotel for a team meeting and meal."

"You be sure and thank Coach Nelson for letting you come stay last night," Dad said.

Laughing, West said, "He'd rather me be playing cards with my family than hitting Bourbon Street."

"Well, it was nice of him to allow you to come and be with us," Mom said. "I need to make him some of my peanut brittle."

His mom's peanut brittle was famous, especially among his teammates and coaches. She would send a ton of it to training camp each summer, and guys fought over it.

They gathered around the table, Flint continuing to look at his cell. Mom talked about a new display she would tackle at the public library when she returned to Texas. Dad said the school district was going to hold their job fair next month. As superintendent, he would have a good idea of job openings, but West refrained from asking about it now.

Maybe tomorrow. Or the day after.

He glanced at his watch. "I need to call an Uber."

"I'll drop you at the hotel," Autumn offered.

"Ooh, I want to go, too," Summer said, scrambling to her feet and taking her dishes to the sink.

"I'll clean up," Mom said. "You girls take West."

Finally, Flint looked up. "Guess I can go, too."

West caught Dad's frown. "Since you were too busy to pitch in and cook, why don't you stay and help clean up, Flint?"

His brother-in-law frowned. "I was checking on patients," he said brusquely.

"Well, if they're all fine, you have time to help now." Dad's glare had Flint sitting straighter. "You kids go ahead. Flint and I will tackle clean-up."

He breathed a sigh of relief, glad his brother-in-law wouldn't be accompanying them.

In the car, Summer said, "I miss driving. I can't remember the last time I was behind the wheel of a car."

"You don't need a car in New York," Autumn pointed out. "You've got subways and cabs."

"I do love that about the city," her twin said. "There might be traffic jams on the streets, but the subway can get you across town in minutes."

"I'm glad Flint and I live close to the hospital," Autumn said. "I usually walk since we're only a few blocks away."

West frowned. "You're not in the safest neighborhood. I don't like that. Especially when you pull a double."

She shrugged, changing lanes. "It is what it is, West. Once Flint finishes his residency, we can hopefully buy a house. I'm pretty tired of cramped apartment living."

"I've seen your apartment. And the complex. It's really rundown. You should move. Especially if you're thinking about having kids anytime soon."

Summer perked up. "Are you and Flint talking about kids?"

"No," Autumn said quickly, a blush spreading across her

cheeks. "He needs to finish his residency and then get established first."

"You'll be forty by the time he does that," Summer retorted. "You've always wanted kids, Autumn. More than West or me. I think you should—"

"Mind your business, Summer," Autumn said quickly.

He didn't want the twins at war. Usually, they never fought. West decided it was time to speak up.

"Hey, I have something to share with the two of you. And it can't leave this car. At least until after the game."

"Please tell me you're not going to marry Bianca," groaned Summer. "Yes, she's gorgeous, but she's also—"

"I'm not," he said, shutting down that discussion.

West had made the mistake of bringing the model he was dating to Thanksgiving a few months ago. Since the Cowboys always played on Thanksgiving Day, his mom prepared their holiday feast the day after. He'd never brought a girl home and told Bianca she'd be charmed by his small town and family.

She wasn't.

They'd fought about it the entire way back to Dallas. He'd called her rude. She'd called him and his family boring. They'd traded insults all the way to her condo. When she got out of the car, she had told him never to call her again. He'd shouted that would be the last thing he ever did before she slammed the door.

Her behavior had been something he'd analyzed. Talked over with Dr. Linda. He'd come to the conclusion that he always dated women who didn't want to make a commitment, much less think about settling down, because they were safe. They didn't expect anything from him.

Except great sex, of course.

"Nope. Bianca's not even in my rearview mirror anymore. This is about something else."

"What?" Autumn prodded, glancing over at him.

"I'm retiring after tonight's game."

Silence blanketed the car. Summer was the first to break it.

"Did you say what I think you said?"

"I did," he confirmed. "I wanted to tell you two before anyone else."

"Coach Nelson doesn't know?" Autumn asked.

"No. No one on the team does. But ten years in the NFL is enough. Most wide receivers only make it three or four years. Other than last year's ACL trouble, I've led a pretty charmed life in the league. I want to go out on top. While I can still walk."

Autumn stopped at a light and looked at him. "What if the Cowboys lose tonight? Would you feel right going out on a losing note?"

He shrugged. "Then they lose. I plan to play my best, but this is the last game I'll suit up for."

"Good," she said, accelerating through the green light. "You've had a stellar career, West. I'm glad you're ready to hang up your cleats."

"Will you miss it?" Summer asked quietly from the back seat.

"Maybe. But I've accomplished all I set out to do. I'm ready to go home."

Summer touched his shoulder. "Go home ... as in Hawthorne home?"

He nodded. "I'm tired of the glitz. The travel. I'm like Dorothy because I've finally discovered that there's no place like home."

Autumn pulled up in front of the hotel where the team was staying. She touched his cheek. "I think you're making the right decision, West."

Summer squeezed his shoulder. "Me, too."

"Not a word to anyone," he cautioned. "That means Mom. Dad. Flint. This is between the three of us."

"Agreed," Summer said. "Have a good game, West."

"Enjoy your last time out on the field," Autumn added.

* * *

HOURS LATER, he stood on the sidelines. The fourth quarter had less than ninety seconds to go.

And the Raiders, leading by three points, had just coughed up the ball.

West ran out onto the field with the rest of the offensive unit, adrenaline firing through him. They huddled, arms locked around one another.

Van looked to him. During their two-minute drills, Coach Nelson had entrusted the play calling to his talented quarterback.

"You're up, West," Van said, calling the play, one they had practiced a few hundred times in camp and had executed flawlessly twice during the season.

He lined up, face stoic. The Raiders expected the ball to go to him, so he had double coverage. It didn't matter. Confidence brimmed through him. West could shake the pair.

The center snapped the ball, and West took off, streaking down the field. He cut, his knee holding up, and ran toward the sidelines, cutting again and heading toward the end zone. As he reached it, he glanced over his left shoulder. As expected, the pigskin floated over it and into his hands, Van's timing impeccable. He crossed the goal line without having to break his stride.

Suddenly, teammates were mobbing him. He couldn't wipe the grin off his face. He kissed the ball and then held onto it, running toward the sidelines, where he handed it to Coach Nelson.

"Just thought you'd like to hang on to the winning ball," he said casually.

The head coach bumped his head against West's helmet. They both watched, seeing the kick was good.

"We're up by four," Nelson roared. "Go seal the win, defense!"

The defense dashed onto the field. Van came and slung an arm about West's shoulder.

"Great catch, buddy."

"Greater throw, Van. You've been on tonight. MVP, all the way."

The Cowboys defense held the Raiders, and the game ended. West stood, savoring this moment, knowing he would never have this experience again.

But he was still happy with the decision he would now announce.

He hugged teammates. Shook hands with losing players and coaches. Watched the Lombardi Trophy presented to his team, confetti raining down. Heard the announcement that he and Van were CO-MVPs. Then the team retreated to the locker room, where the trainers tossed ballcaps and T-shirts proclaiming the Dallas Cowboys as Super Bowl champions as champagne bottles were shaken and uncorked, spraying the players and coaches.

West took it all in, satisfaction filling him.

The press was waiting, and he went first to Coach Nelson.

"Coach, I'm retiring."

Nelson looked perplexed, as if West were speaking in Greek to him. "What?"

"I'm done. I wanted you to know before I announce it now."

The grizzled coach wrapped him in a bear hug. "You

deserve it, West. Walk away with your health. But damn, we're gonna miss you."

"I won't pull a Tom Brady on you," he promised, referring to the famous quarterback who retired—and then un-retired. "I'm done."

Van Foster joined them. "Hey, let's go get this over with," he told the pair.

The three men joined other teammates and reporters in the media room. West made certain he went last, not wanting to rain on the parade going on now. He answered every question asked of him, and when no more came his way, said, "I'd like to add one thing."

The room quietened.

"I've loved every minute playing for the Dallas Cowboys, but a time comes in each player's life when he knows it's time to walk away. Tonight's Super Bowl game was my last. I've accomplished everything I ever dreamed of doing, including earning this final Super Bowl ring. Thank you for all you've written about me, the good and the bad. Good night, and God bless."

The room erupted, dozens of journalists calling out his name, firing questions in his direction.

West merely smiled.

And walked away from them—and playing professional football.

CHAPTER
One

DALLAS

Kelby Blackstone bid her assistant goodnight and returned to her office. She tidied up her desk and switched off her computer. Glancing at her watch, she still had a quarter-hour before she needed to leave and walk downstairs to meet Celia and Jessica for dinner. The three had cheered together in college and had also been sorority sisters. Once she moved to Dallas after her divorce, they had decided to meet once a month for dinner and girl talk.

Those women had saved her sanity.

Tonight, they were meeting at a restaurant in NorthPark Center, Kelby and Jessica's turf. Kelby worked for clothiers Wyndham & Warren, running their social media, while Jessica was a buyer for an exclusive men's store. Both businesses were a part of the over two hundred stores and restaurants in the shopping mall, one which had survived the death of malls across America, thanks to its unique, one-of-a-kind, upscale stores which appealed to Dallas shoppers.

She picked up her cell and started scrolling through favorite sites. It surprised her that West Sutherland was still

getting a lot of press three days after his retirement announcement at the conclusion of the Super Bowl. Although she never
watched football anymore, she knew West was one of the
premier players in the NFL. She couldn't imagine why he was
walking away at the height of his career. Then again, they had
lost touch years ago.

West had been her brother Chance's best friend, and he
had been at home visiting Blackstone Ranch. After he broke up
with his girlfriend during their last year in high school, West
had asked Kelby if she would accompany him to the big senior
events that spring. They had gone to prom together, as well as
the senior breakfast and several graduation parties. He had
kissed her—once—after that final party. More of a thank you for
giving him company during the many events. Both had been
surprised by their reaction to the kiss. What had started as a
friendly one had turned steamy. Fast. Thoughts of West being
like a brother to her had fled, replaced by a deep yearning.

When the kiss ended, they looked at one another. Both had
agreed that while something was definitely there, they were
headed in different directions and agreed it would be foolish to
start up something which couldn't be finished. West left a few
weeks later for Texas A&M, while Kelby moved to Austin to
cheer at the University of Texas. They saw one another some
during college vacations but had not seen one another since
graduation, too busy with their adult lives. She knew Chance
heard from West every now and then, but that was it.

Sometimes, though, when she saw a picture on West's
Instagram, escorting another beautiful model or actress somewhere, she couldn't help but wonder what might have been.

Her cell buzzed with a text from Jessica, telling her that she
was heading to the restaurant where they were meeting. Kelby
left her office and proceeded to the first floor of NorthPark,
ready for a couple of hours of Mexican food and girl talk.

Jessica was waiting with Celia in front of the restaurant, and they exchanged greetings.

"I'm so glad to see you two," she declared.

"Well, you saw me Sunday night," Jessica said. "What a game."

Kelby had attended the Super Bowl party at her friend's house, mainly to watch the halftime performance and clever commercials. She had talked with all the women present, glancing up every now and then when the guys whooped, watching the replay. West had been a part of those cheers, catching three touchdown passes, one in the final seconds, the game winner. He and the Cowboys quarterback had been named Co-MVPs, something which hadn't happened since the 1970s, when another pair of Cowboys claimed the honor.

"It was a good game," Celia added, telling the hostess there would be three of them. "But I fell asleep on the sofa and missed the end."

They were taken to their table and looked over the menu. When the server arrived and asked for their drink orders, Kelby ordered a margarita, on the rocks, no salt. Jessica asked for a frozen margarita with salt.

"And for you?" the server asked, looking to Celia. "Another margarita?"

"No, just water with lemon for me, please," her friend said. "I haven't had a margarita since our college days. I got sick on tequila shots and haven't tried tequila since."

"I'll get your drinks right out," the server promised.

Celia looked eagerly at them, and Kelby had a good idea why.

"Okay. I can't hold this in any longer. I'm pregnant!"

They squealed, jumping to their feet and exchanging hugs.

"When are you due?" Kelby asked.

"Mid-August. And no, I don't look forward to being big as a

whale during the heat of a Texas summer. Last time when I was pregnant with Sam, I wound up wearing oversized T-shirts and underwear around the house during all of June and July."

"You're due right when you start back to school," Jessica noted. "How long of a maternity leave will you be able to take?"

Celia beamed. "I'm not. Dan just got a promotion a few months ago. Better title. More money. He said I can stay home."

"That's terrific news," Kelby said, knowing how much her friend enjoyed being a mom.

"Two should be it for us," Celia continued. "The plan is for me to stay home until this one starts kinder." She rubbed her belly. "I'm hoping for a girl this time. We won't tell Sam for a while. I know he'll want a baby brother."

"We'll have to talk about a shower once you know the gender," Jessica said.

"If it's a boy, I know he can wear Sam's hand-me-downs," Kelby said. "But Wyndham & Warren has such cute clothes for baby girls. And remember, I get a huge discount."

Their drinks came, and they ordered appetizers and dinners. Talk ranged from what they were doing at work to the latest books they'd read and movies they'd seen. While they were waiting for the check, Kelby pulled out her phone and brought up a page of baby clothes, which they oohed and ahhed over.

She set her cell down as the server brought their check. It was her turn to pay. They'd found it was easier to simply rotate between the three of them than have separate checks brought to them each time. She handed over her credit card, and the others thanked her as the bill was processed. She signed and added a generous tip.

Then her phone started blowing up. Ping after ping. Frowning, she picked it up, hearing Celia and Jessica's cells also start getting multiple texts. She began reading.

Have you seen the news???

Brace yourself, Kelby. Turn on the news.

Glad you divorced his ass.

That last message let her know something was going down with Bax. A sick feeling washed over her. She glanced up, seeing her two friends looking worriedly at her.

"I need to use the ladies' room," she said succinctly, leaving the table, cell in hand.

She entered the restroom and a stall, locking it behind her. Immediately, she googled Bax Porter's name. The screaming headlines jolted her. Bax had been arrested.

For murder.

Kelby leaned against the stall's door, taking deep breaths. Her ex-husband had turned out to be a horrible mess. In college, he could do no wrong, being named the Heisman Trophy winner his senior year. He was the first draft pick that spring. They had wed after graduation and before he went to training camp.

Then the fall from grace began.

First, he tore his ACL in the last game of the preseason, just as he'd been named the starting quarterback for the regular season. The surgery was complicated, and the rehab was brutal. Bax had verbally abused her, taking out all his frustrations on Kelby. She had been patient. Sympathetic. And never argued back. Football was Bax's life, and he hated sitting on the sidelines, letting down his teammates and himself.

After his return to training camp the next summer, things went downhill. He was too tentative. Bax had been known as a scrambler, leaving the pocket and often running down field when he couldn't find an open receiver. Now, he was afraid to run. To throw. When he did throw, his timing was off. He blamed the receivers. The coaching staff. The plays being called. He lost his starting job to the same quarterback who had replaced him, a guy drafted in the sixth round the previous year. Bax became so bitter and impossible to be around that the Browns had traded him. That meant Kelby had to give up the terrific job she'd found once they'd moved to Cleveland.

The nomadic years began then. Bax bounced from one ball club to another, five teams in all. He only started once when the current starter had the flu and had thrown up so much he was hospitalized. Bax continued to suffer injuries, big and small alike. His attitude went from bad to worse. She had followed him around the country, leaving job after job, until it was hard for her to even find one. His drinking had escalated. Then Kelby had found the cocaine, which was the final straw for her. When she confronted her husband about his drug use, he gave her excuse after excuse. She told him she'd had enough and wanted a divorce.

That's when he'd hit her.

Bax had never struck her before. She had seen other women in abusive relationships and determined never to be one of them. Kelby immediately packed her things and left, contacting a divorce lawyer. They had very little. He had refused to buy a house because he was traded so often. No kids, so no problems there regarding custody issues. She'd later learned that he had a gambling problem, which had also eaten into what money they did have.

Blinking rapidly at the tears forming in her eyes, she continued to read, discovering her ex had shot a bookie whom he'd owed a lot of money to. His booking picture was already circulating online, causing her stomach to cramp painfully. She had taken back her maiden name after their divorce. No one at Wyndham & Warren knew Baxley Porter was her former husband. But it would come out. Already, she was seeing pictures of Bax and her in the stories, mentioning their divorce. She'd lose all privacy in the next few weeks. Her name would be on the internet. Reporters would hound her. She'd had a stable job and life the past five years, but that would be a thing of the past. Being in social media—and knowing how Wyndham & Warren valued their sterling reputation—she knew she was merely part of the fallout.

Should she resign?

Kelby shut off her phone and left the stall, taking a wet paper towel and dabbing cold water on her face. She looked in the mirror. The confident, capable woman she was used to seeing looked hollow.

And scared.

She returned to the table, Jessica and Celia giving her worried glances.

"Are you all right?" Celia asked.

"No. But I'll have to deal with it. I may not be able to eat in public for a while. Let's cancel next month's dinner, and then we'll see," she said brusquely, wanting to hurry home and lock the door and hide from the world.

"Don't shut us out," Jessica begged.

"I just need to be alone," she explained.

They left the restaurant, and already, Kelby saw shoppers looking her way. She held her head high as they walked through the mall.

"Let us know if we can do anything," Celia told her.

Both women hugged her, and Kelby went to her car. She drove home and went inside her apartment, rushing to the bathroom, where she lost all her dinner. She cried as she washed her face and brushed her teeth, wishing the curse of Bax Porter would finally leave her.

She decided to text Chance. He ignored social media and

the news, so he would have no idea of the maelstrom coming. Her brother and the Blackstone Ranch wouldn't be immune. Journalists dug deeply with a story like this one, and they would talk to everyone who had even a remote connection to Bax.

When she turned her phone on, she saw not only a plethora of texts but several missed calls.

Nine of them were from Chance.

Her hands shaking, she listened to his voice mails, wanting to know what he knew before she returned his call. The first two just told her to call him. The next few, she heard the impatience in his voice as he asked her to call him back. Listening to his final voicemail, she heard, "Do you *ever* answer your damn phone? Call me!"

Things must have gotten bad quickly. Kelby touched his picture, and the phone rang once before he answered.

"About time," he said grumpily.

She heard the weariness in his voice.

"I'm sorry, Chance. After the news broke, I just turned off my cell. That's why I didn't get your calls. Everything about Bax is—"

"Bax? What the hell did that creep do now?"

Confused, she asked, "You're not calling me about Bax?"

"No. I don't give a rat's ass about that loser."

Taking a deep breath, she told him, "He was arrested for murder. Already, I'm seeing the story splashed everywhere, along with old pictures of the two of us." She hesitated. "Then if it's not about Bax, what is so important?"

A long pause, then her brother said, "It's Dad, Kelby. He's had a stroke. The doctors don't know if he'll make it."

CHAPTER
Two

Kelby sat at her dad's bedside. He'd been taken to Emory Decatur Hospital, the closest facility to Hawthorne. She bemoaned the fact that the new Hawthorne regional hospital, halfway between Decatur and Gainesville, would not open for another few weeks. That would have been more convenient, having Dad closer to the ranch. Chance would now take on their father's responsibilities at Blackstone Ranch.

She only hoped it wouldn't be a permanent change.

It had been yesterday since she'd even brushed her teeth. After talking to Chance, Kelby had thrown several shirts and pairs of jeans, along with bras and underwear, into her carryon suitcase, shoving toiletries into a bag. She'd driven to the hospital, well above the speed limit, and arrived just a little before midnight. Chance had told her on the phone that Dad was in ICU, and she'd headed there, finding out where Jim Blackstone was located at the nurse's station.

It had been eerie, going down the silent hospital halls, the only noise being the steady beep of machines monitoring patients. When she entered her father's room, Chance had been sitting at the bedside, staring at Dad in the bed. She'd gone to Chance, wrapping herself around him, tears finally spilling down her cheeks. Her brother had told her more than he'd mentioned on the phone. How he'd come across Dad in a horse stall, lying on the hay, his mouth twisted, his body curled in an unusual way.

Not knowing how long Jim Blackstone had lain there, Chance quickly found a ranch hand, and they loaded Dad into the back seat of Chance's truck. Tammy Carruthers, their long-time housekeeper and the only mother figure Kelby had ever known, had come along, Dad's head cradled in her lap. Chance said he'd driven as if the Devil had been chasing him, dashing into the emergency room and shouting for help.

The doctors had ruled it to be a stroke. Ironically, Kelby's mom had a stroke when delivering her daughter and had died two days after giving birth. Jim Blackstone had never remarried, raising his Irish twins on his own, with the help and support of Tammy, who'd managed the household and raised the two Blackstone children as if they were her own.

She glanced over at Chance, sleeping in the chair on the other side of the bed. Standing, she retrieved her bag and slipped into the restroom a few feet away, brushing her teeth and running a comb through her long, raven hair. She returned to the room and pulled her phone from her pocket, ready to send an email to her boss. Because her dad's condition was so serious, she would need to take a leave of absence from work. The timing couldn't have been better, with the Bax scandal breaking last night. Being away from work would help Wyndham & Warren put some distance between the company and her.

Before she could open her work email account to request the LOA, her phone buzzed with an incoming call. She'd kept the ringer off to avoid hearing the numerous texts.

Her boss's name came across the screen, and Kelby stepped outside the room.

"Hey, Reginald," she said. "I was about to send you an email, requesting a leave of absence."

"A dreadful business," he said in his posh British accent. "Journalists were hanging about the moment I arrived this morning. This is a terrible situation, Kelby. Simply dreadful. How on earth could you have been wed to such a worthless scoundrel?"

"It was a long time ago," she said. "We divorced five years ago. I couldn't have told you where Baxley Porter was until the news hit last night. I know it still reflects on—"

"Reflects is not the word I would use," he said crisply. "Wyndham & Warren is an established company with a very specific brand. We simply cannot have any scandal associated with us, and that includes one of our high-profile employees."

A sinking feeling filled her. "What are you saying? Are you firing me?"

"No, no, no," Reginald said quickly. "That would be illegal. What we would *prefer* you to do is resign."

She took in his words, thinking how unfair it was after all these years that Bax was still having a negative impact on her life. Determination filled her. Kelby liked her job. She was not going to slink away, all because of something Bax had done.

"I was about to call you to tell you that I wouldn't be in the office today," she said, trying to hold herself together. "My father had a stroke last night, and I've gone up to Decatur to be with him. I was hoping to take an LOA from the company so that if he makes it, I can care for him. Then I could return, say in a couple of months. I'm certain by then that this situation regarding my former spouse will have blown over."

"That will not do," her boss said flatly. "These things never blow over. We simply cannot have you associated with us.

Think of it, Kelby. You, through our social media campaigns, represent our brand. Our *brand*! It's unthinkable to have your troubles associated with Wyndham & Warren."

"And what if I don't wish to resign?" she countered, her tone sharp. "I have plenty of vacation and sick days I could use up."

"We will pay you for those, as well as give you a glowing reference," her boss said. "But we need you to resign, effective immediately. I want to be able to tell those journalists that you no longer work here and that I have no idea where you are."

Hurt swelled inside her. The past five years had been good ones. She'd grown as a professional and put in great work with a therapist, finally finding herself again. Now, everything she had done was lost. Yes, she could sue for unlawful termination, but Wyndham & Warren had deep pockets. They could find the right attorneys and make certain she never worked again, as well as keep delaying trial dates until her savings dried up. If she rejected Reginald's offer now, she could effectively be killing her own career.

"All right," she agreed. "But I want to be paid for those unused days. And I'd like a severance package, as well as copies of any reference letter you might send out."

Reginald sniffed. "I see you wish to play hardball. You have us in a bind, Kelby, because of your past association with this drug-addled murderer."

He named a figure, which was far more than she would have expected.

"But that is if you do not speak of your time at Wyndham & Warren. Ever. You will be required to sign a nondisclosure agreement. You may list us as part of your previous experience, but we reserve the right not to pass along any recommendations regarding your employment for a six-month period."

She could see the company's lawyers had already told him

what to say. Most likely, one or more of them sat across from him now, listening on speakerphone, passing him notes as to how to continue the conversation.

"As I told you, I'm at my father's bedside. It may very well be his deathbed. Either let me sign electronically or send a courier to the hospital with the documents to be signed."

"It can be done electronically," Reginald said brusquely. "I will forward them to your business email account. Once you return these digital copies, you will no longer have access to your work email account. Already, you do not possess work privileges anymore, so do not try to access the employee website or your created content."

Kelby wanted to protest, wishing she had access to copies of campaigns she'd created, but she didn't want to push Reginald too much. She knew her assistant was sharp and told her soon-to-be-former boss that was who should take over her position.

"I will have my lawyer look over the paperwork once you send the email," she said coolly. Of course, she didn't have a lawyer, not since she'd divorced Bax in Florida.

Silence. Then Reginald said, "This offer is only good for twenty-four hours, Kelby. If I do not have the signed documents by this time tomorrow morning, your employment will be terminated. We will find just cause for this termination. There will be no excellent reference. No package. You will be out of a job. Period. And if you choose to sue Wyndham & Warren, I can assure you that the case will never see the light of day."

"I understand," she said through gritted teeth, not bothering to tell Reginald goodbye as she ended the call.

Slipping back into the room, she saw Chance stirring. Slowly, his eyes came open. His gaze met hers.

"What's wrong?"

He had always been able to read her moods. They weren't

actual twins, but they were close in age. Chance's birthday was September fifteenth, missing the September first cutoff to start public school. With Kelby being born eleven months to the day later, she and Chance had been in the same class at school. Because of that, they had been close growing up, sharing experiences and friends in their small town.

She shrugged. "I just got off the phone with my boss. Five years, down the drain."

He frowned. "They're firing you? Over the Bax situation?"

Nodding, she said, "Pretty much. They know how to frame things and control the narrative. Either I sign the NDA—or I'm toast."

Briefly, Kelby revealed her conversation with Reginald, ending with, "I have no choice. I don't have the money or willpower to fight them in court. They'd probably drag it out and delay, again and again. I need to be here. With Dad and you. So, I'll sign whatever."

"Not without someone looking it over," he said firmly.

"Who? I know you and Dad still use Isaiah Smith, but he's getting long in the tooth, as Tammy would say. He probably wouldn't even understand e-doc signing, much less an NDA."

"I agree. Isaiah is talking about retiring soon. In the meantime, let me see if Sawyer Montgomery would read through them for you."

"Sawyer from Hawthorne? The hot basketball player who was two years ahead of us? Gosh, I haven't thought about him in a bazillion years. He's an attorney?"

"Yes, an assistant district attorney in Dallas." Chance pulled out his cell, scrolling for Sawyer's number.

In the meantime, Kelby opened her work email and found the documents had already been sent to her. She wondered if they had arrived during her conversation with Reginald.

"Hey, Sawyer. Chance Blackstone. Long time, I know.

Listen, Kelby is in a pickle. She could really use your help. The clock's ticking."

She listened as her brother gave Sawyer a quick rundown of her work situation.

"Yes, I'll put her on." He handed his phone to her.

"Hi, Sawyer. Sorry to bother you at work."

"It's not a bother, Kelby. And I'm not actually at work. Yesterday was my last day in the DA's office."

"Really? What are you going to do instead, move to corporate law and make some real money?" she teased.

"I'm going to practice law in Hawthorne. I've been in touch with Isaiah Smith. He was ready to retire and is turning his practice over to me. I'll office where he does on the town square. Hopefully, I'll keep most of his clients and find me some new ones."

"Then I'll be your first," she told him, explaining how Reginald had just sent the email to her.

"Forward it to me." He gave her his email address. "I'll print out the NDA and anything else that comes with it. Read over and see if we want any changes made or if you can live with what they've come up with."

"Chance wasn't kidding. There's a deadline, Sawyer. Reginald gave me until this time tomorrow morning to return the signed docs. If I don't, I'm gone. No recommendations if future employers check with them, which is the kiss of death. And no severance package of any kind. And I'll be fired, not given the chance to resign."

He chuckled. "Well, I guess it's a good thing all I'm doing is boxing up things to move. I'll get right on it, Kelby. Once I'm done, we can talk on the phone, or if you'd like to meet in person, I'm happy to do so."

"I'm not in Dallas right now, Sawyer. Dad had a stroke

yesterday. Chance and I are at the hospital in Decatur with him now."

"I'm so sorry to hear that, Kelby. Jim Blackstone is a pillar of the community."

Her throat swelled with unshed tears at his remark. "Thank you."

"I'll get started now. I know you'll be meeting with doctors and whatnot. I'm home all day. Call any time after noon. I should be able to comb through the files by then. Wherever's convenient for you."

"Thank you, Sawyer. I really appreciate this."

He chuckled. "Wait until you get my bill. Just kidding."

They said goodbye, and she forwarded the email to him, not bothering to read it. It would all be legalese anyway. Hard for her to interpret. Better leave things such as that to an expert. Sawyer would let her know if she should sign or not.

"What did he say?" Chance asked.

Kelby ran through their conversation, her brother nodding, as she spoke.

Then a noise came from the bed. Both Blackstone children said, "Dad?" at the same time.

She took her father's hand, while Chance rang for a nurse.

She squeezed his hand. "How are you, Dad? Chance found you. He brought you to the hospital." She didn't want to say any more than that, not wanting him to panic.

He tried to speak, but nothing came out. Kelby could see the anger and frustration in his eyes. Jim Blackstone was a self-made man, one who never asked anything for himself and never allowed himself to be beholden to anyone else.

"It's okay. Let's wait for the doctor. See what he says," her brother said, their gazes meeting.

A nurse came and checked the vital signs. She tried to get her patient to speak, but even she saw the frustration.

"I'll let Dr. Brock know that Mr. Blackstone is conscious. He should be here shortly. I know he's already in the hospital making rounds in ICU now."

A few minutes later, Dr Brock appeared. He introduced himself to Kelby and greeted Chance, then his attention focused on his patient. He poked and prodded, asking questions, having her dad blink once for yes and twice for no as nonverbal responses. While Jim Blackstone could move his left hand, his entire right side was paralyzed. It hurt her deeply to see such a large, powerful man humbled by this stroke.

"Looking good, Mr. Blackstone. You close your eyes now and get some rest because once you wake up, it's going to be nothing but therapy out the wazoo. You'll have physical and occupational therapists working with you and rehabilitation nurses looking after you. I'll put all that into motion while you get some shuteye."

Her dad blinked once and then closed his eyes.

Dr. Brock asked to see Chance and her outside, and the three of them retreated from the room.

"Isn't it too soon to start therapy?" Chance asked. "Dad can barely move, and he can't even speak."

"Most stroke victims start their therapy within twenty-four to forty-eight hours after their diagnosis," the physician assured them. "His rehabilitation nurses will be specialists. They'll help him with things in his daily routine. PT—physical therapy—is for relearning movements. Sitting up. Walking. Keeping his balance. The OT—occupational therapy—will try to help him become more independent and active. They'll help him relearn how to bathe and dress. Do simple chores around the house. Even learn how to drive again if he's able to do so. They also work with improving swallowing and cognitive abilities."

"It sounds like a lot," Kelby said, trying to hide her worry.

"We've got experts for everything," Dr. Brock assured

them. "Speech and language pathologists will help with language skills and swallowing, which can be difficult for those who've had a stroke. They'll also help with tricks and tips to help his memory, as well as addressing his thought process. What does Mr. Blackstone like to do?"

"Ride," the siblings both replied, with Chance adding, "Boss people around."

"Then if he's capable, we even have therapeutic recreation specialists who could teach him how to ride again." Dr. Brock paused. "Does your dad still work? We have vocational counselors who address heading back to work and any problems that might involve."

"He owns a ranch," Chance said, "The Blackstone Ranch." His brow creased. "But just looking at him lying in the bed, Doc? I don't see how he can be the man he once was."

"He won't be," Dr. Brock said flatly. "Even if he learns to walk and talk again and has most of his faculties, he'll be a different man. A near-death experience does that to someone. Oftentimes, a stroke patient's personality will change. An extrovert will become an introvert. That kind of thing. We don't know what Mr. Blackstone's future holds. As of now, his vitals are stable. I hope he'll regain his strength and the therapists who work with him will be able to help restore him to a full, meaningful life."

The doctor paused. "Then again, he may have been affected greatly by the stroke. He could have limited mobility. Right now, he has no movement on his right side. No reactions to touch or other stimuli. But it's early days. My advice is to keep your hopes up—but temper them some."

"Thank you, Dr. Brock," Kelby said, liking the physician and his approach.

"I'll be back around this afternoon. By then, I'll have discussed Mr. Blackstone's case with our therapy departments.

It's going to be a day-by-day thing." He smiled. "Even miracles can take some time, you know."

"I'll be here every day," she promised. "Chance will have the ranch to run, though."

"I'll come as often as possible," her brother said.

"Good. Having family nearby and supporting him will be the best medicine of all. I'll see you both later."

Dr. Brock left, and she told Chance, "I meant what I said. Obviously, I have no job. I can't even go back to my apartment in Dallas because I'm sure there would be reporters waiting to hound me."

"Or paparazzi jumping out of the bushes?" Chance teased.

For the first time since dinner last night, Kelby laughed. "Bax used to love having his picture taken. I always hated it. I thought the photographers were so invasive. And it wasn't just them. Anywhere we went, people had cell phones, holding them up, recording our every move in public. I got to where I never wanted to eat out or go anywhere."

She frowned. "And with Bax drinking and us being shifted from city to city, team to team, it was no life at all."

Her brother wrapped her in a tight embrace. "Don't worry, Sis. Bax is out of your life. Yes, it's awful now, but you won't have to deal with him again. And I know you loved your job, but you're going to find another one. For now, move back to the ranch."

"Really? I thought I'd just rent something in Decatur temporarily so I'd be close to Dad."

"I'm sure they'll send Dad to some rehab facility after his hospital stay. Eventually, he'll come home. You should be there, already settled in. You know Tammy would love that. I sent her home in my truck, but she's supposed to return sometime this morning."

"Okay," she sighed. "At some point, I'll need to go back to

Dallas and turn in my notice with my apartment manager. I was thinking about moving and was letting my lease run out. I only have about six weeks on it."

"I'll go with you when you do. We can put your furniture in storage. Or bring it to the ranch if that's what you want. We have plenty of room for it there. Nothing needs to be decided right now."

They entered the room again, Dad still asleep. Kelby decided to nap while he did. She brought her chair next to the wall and leaned against it.

She was now unemployed, but at least she had a place to stay. The good thing was that she would be free to work with her dad and his therapists, trying to bring him back.

For now, that would have to do.

CHAPTER
Three

West stood in his Dallas high-rise two weeks after his retirement announcement, looking out the penthouse window at the spectacular view of the city's skyline. It was what had convinced him to buy the unit in this particular building. It had been a bit of a drive to get to the team's practice field daily, but he usually had gone in at odd hours, so traffic hadn't been too bad. He'd also liked having some distance between himself and the other players, as well as being closer to the nightlife and unique restaurants. While he loved the guys on his team, even as a rookie, he knew for his mental well-being, he needed a break from them. Yes, he had been the guy who was always first at a team meeting and last off the field, with many hours of watching film. During the season, it was impossible to do anything but live and breathe football.

Off-season was a different matter. He'd kept in good physical shape, thanks to hiring a personal trainer, but his diet wasn't as strict. West liked to travel and had hit the road once the season ended, usually by himself. He'd been to Tokyo.

Prague. London. Barcelona. Dubai. Now that he'd officially retired, he still wanted to travel, especially more throughout the United States.

Mostly, though, he wanted someone to do it with.

He had been friendly with everyone on the team, especially the other receivers and his quarterback, but he wouldn't call any of his teammates close friends. He hadn't done a good job of keeping in touch with Chance Blackstone, his best friend since kindergarten. They texted occasionally, but West was ready to have Chance back in his life. Probably Jace Tanner, his sports agent and fellow Aggie, was the closest thing West had to a friend these days, which was pretty sad. Not because Jace wasn't a great guy. He was. Essentially, he worked for West, though. And Jace was consumed by his business. He had worked hard, creating one of the premier sports talent agencies in the country at a young age. West felt glad he'd been with Jace for so long.

He turned, glancing about the condo, doubting he'd keep it. Living in Dallas wasn't for him anymore. He was tired of the glitz and glam. It was important to him to get back to his roots, back to life in a small town. Hopefully, life as a coach *in* his hometown.

A knock sounded on his door, and he crossed the wide living room to answer it.

"Hey, Mr. S," Scotty said, entering the condo.

His doorman had to be one of the happiest people West had ever met. Scotty never seemed to be in a bad mood. He decided to ask him about it now.

"Why are you always happy? I don't think I've ever caught you in a bad mood. You have an eternal smile on your face."

Scotty shrugged. "I didn't have a lot growing up. I was on the free breakfast and lunch program. My mom worked three jobs just to keep the electricity on and make sure I had something to wear. But she told me I could dream as big as I wanted and go places through books. She got me a library card when I was eight, and I was off on all kinds of adventures. History became my thing, and Lincoln is the one figure that captured my imagination the most. I can quote you all kinds of things that great man said, but the one which always stuck with me most?

"Most folks are as happy as they make up their minds to be." Scotty paused. "Just think about that a minute. We *choose* to be happy or unhappy. Unhappy takes a lot of energy. It drags you down. You wallow in misery. But happy? That's an energy booster. You're light on your feet and have a smile on your face. You feel good—and you want to make others feel good, too. Being a doorman is a people job, Mr. S. I make a conscious choice every day to be happy and spread that happiness to the lives I touch that day."

The simple philosophy blew West away. "You are a wise man, Scotty. I think I'll take a page out of your playbook and run with it." He looked around. "Let me show you what needs to be moved."

He'd bought a ton of boxes at a storage facility, packing up his clothes, books, and the trophies and memorabilia associated with his playing days. The furniture and everything else would stay behind. If he were ever in Dallas overnight, he would simply stay at a hotel. No sense in letting this view go to waste. It was meant for someone else. West was at a different stage of his life now. Selling would give him a nice nest egg for the future. Especially if he landed a coaching job. His annual salary would be a pittance of what he'd earned in a single game playing professionally.

"Okay, Mr. S. My cousin and I will bring everything downstairs and put it in the small cargo trailer you rented."

West removed a key from his key ring and handed it over. "I'll text you the address. This is the key to the front door."

Scotty looked dubious. "You sure you want to move to the boonies, Mr. S? I follow you on Insta."

He laughed. "I've been a city slicker for too long. Time to get back to who I am underneath the fancy Italian suits and shoes."

It hadn't been a hard decision to leave Dallas for Hawthorne. He wanted to be closer to his parents. His cousin Sawyer was also at a crossroads in his life. He, too, was moving from Dallas to Hawthorne. They would be sharing a three-bedroom, furnished rental for now, one his mom had found and leased for them. He liked Sawyer, who was two years older, and had called him on a whim the day after he'd retired. When he learned his cousin had decided to leave the district attorney's office to open a practice in Hawthorne, rooming together while they both figured out a more permanent living arrangement had seemed a natural fit.

"Should we do any unpacking for you when we get there?" Scotty asked.

"Nope. Any boxes marked clothes go in the primary bedroom. The others can go on the kitchen table and around it. My cousin may or may not be there. Sawyer Montgomery. If he's there, he'll give you a hand. He's already moved in."

Scotty nodded. "Okay, Mr. S. Where should I leave the key?"

"On the kitchen counter is fine. Or give it to Sawyer if he's there."

"If he's not, where should I leave the key after I lock up?"

West laughed. "You don't. It's a small town, Scotty. Even being gone as long as I have, I'll still feel as if I know most everybody there. Kitchen counter will be fine. Let me text you the address now."

Scotty got the text and then told West he would return the trailer once they returned to Dallas.

He picked up an envelope on the end table. "Here. For today. I already prepaid the rental. You can split it with your cousin however you'd like."

The doorman slipped it into his pocket. "Thanks for the gig, Mr. S. Glad we could work it out so you moved on my day off."

Thrusting out a hand, he said, "I'm going to miss you, Scotty."

They shook, with Scotty asking, "You aren't coming back? Ever?"

"No. I'm going to sell the place. My life is changing, and so is my address."

West left, going to the parking garage and claiming his Jaguar convertible. The two-seater wouldn't be practical anymore. He decided to trade it in for a truck, probably a Ford F-150, affectionately known as the state vehicle of Texas because so many Texans drove it. Not only was the Jag too flashy for Hawthorne, but a truck would be more practical. Buckling his seat belt, he left the Turtle Creek area and headed downtown to the offices of TTM, Touchdown Talent Management.

Once inside, he was greeted by Elena Arturo, Jace's administrative assistant, a woman in her mid-thirties, with dark brown hair and eyes. She kept Jace on his toes, and even West found himself standing a little taller around Elena.

"Good morning, West. It's good to see you. You're my favorite MVP of any Super Bowl."

"Co-MVP," he corrected. "Van Foster wouldn't like getting shorted."

He followed her to Jace's office, where she tapped lightly and opened the door.

"Go ahead. He's on a call, but you'll be his excuse to get off it."

West took a seat on the plush sofa as Jace waved at him.

"Yes. It's a done deal," he assured the caller. "I told you to count on TTM. Listen, I've got to head to a meeting. West Sutherland just arrived. Yes, I'll tell him. I'll message the contract to you now. All you have to do is sign and date it. Return it to the messenger, and then sit back and count your money."

The agent hung up. "Hey, West." He tapped a couple of numbers on his phone. "Elena, send the contract. And have whoever goes wait for the sig and head straight back. We're good to go. When will lunch be here? Okay."

Placing the phone in its cradle, Jace came toward him, offering his hand. "I should punch you in the face instead of shaking your hand."

"I knew the announcement took you off-guard. Sorry about that. I should've shared with you beforehand, but it really was a game day decision."

"No, you do what's right for you," Jace said, taking a seat. "I've told you that ever since you became our client. TTM has always done what's best for you. If you think now is the time to retire, then now is right. You're in perfect health."

He laughed. "I'll only admit to you that the knees are a little creaky in the morning, getting out of bed."

"Overall, you've been blessed not to have the kind of injury that could end your career. You're going out on your own terms." Jace paused. "I'm wondering if you're ready to cut ties today with TTM or if you'll let me pitch to you what's next."

"Guiding champions from the field to the spotlight," West quipped, citing TTM's motto. "No, I am happy to hear if you think we can continue our business relationship. If not, I hope I'll keep your friendship."

"For life. But business isn't at the end of the road for us, West. You're still young. Popular. Nice-looking. Well-spoken. I can find products you approve of that you can pitch, in addition to the ones you already endorse. Will some of the current companies you work with want to move on once you've fulfilled the contract? That's a given. But there are still others who will be happy to have their product or services associated with you. I think Nolan Ryan is a terrific example of that."

West knew the former Baseball Hall of Famer turned businessman and entrepreneur had his finger in dozens of pies, most all of them lucrative ones.

Jace rose. "Come down to the conference room. We've got about half an hour before lunch arrives although why you wanted to eat at eleven in the morning is beyond me."

He grinned. "I know you love Italian as much as I do. I thought a last meal from our favorite place would be a nice send-off. I'm going to leave Dallas. Sell the condo."

"I'll buy it."

"Why? You already live in a terrific place."

"The views you have don't grow on trees," his agent said. "Besides, it wouldn't be for me. I'm thinking one of my clients might be interested in it. We have a lot of professional sports teams in this town. Athletes with a whole bunch of disposable cash. I can think of three guys off the top of my head that might like to purchase it."

"Should I just sell it directly to them?"

"If you'd like. But I'll pay you cash. It would be quick and easy."

"And I'm making it easy for you. The furnishings stay. The interior decorator you recommended did a fantastic job. That furniture was meant for that condo and that view, not where I'm headed."

"Where *are* you going?"

"For now, I'm moving back to Hawthorne." He looked sheepishly at Jace. "In fact, I have a job interview at three o'clock this afternoon with the football coach and athletic director."

His agent nodded approvingly. "I can see you as a coach. You've got the smarts. You know the game inside out. You're patient. Dependable. But what about coaching in the pros? Or college? There's a hell of a lot more money in that."

"It's not for me. I'm in a position where money doesn't factor in. Frankly, I could do nothing the rest of my life and be fine, financially. But I want to be where there's still a true love of the game. Where I can make a difference in kids' lives. I want Hawthorne, Jace."

"If there's an opening, you'll get it. You're the hometown hero. The guy who left and made a name for himself, both in college and the pros. They'd be crazy not to hire you."

Jace escorted him to the conference room, where his partner at TTM waited, along with their marketing specialist

"Hey, Mark. Penny."

Steve Butler dashed in behind them. "Sorry I'm late."

"We're just ready to start," Jace told their social media specialist.

Penny Hiller gave her pitch, discussing ways that TTM could market West, now that he was retired from the game. He liked some of her ideas. Others were not his cup of tea.

"Let me make this clear," he said. "I'm not a Peyton Manning. I don't want to host SNL or a quiz show. I don't want to go into broadcasting or be a college professor. I just want to be an average Joe. Coach high school football. Get married and start a family."

He watched a few eyebrows raise, but no one jumped in with an opinion.

Penny cleared her throat. "Okay, then."

She proceeded to focus on opportunities for endorsements, sponsorships, and philanthropical ideas. West passed on most but pointed out the few he liked and was interested in.

"This gives me a good starting point. Jace, too," Penny said. "But can I just say how dismal watching the Cowboys is going to be without Van throwing balls to you, West?"

"You may say it," he said, grinning. "I'm sure you'll find another favorite player, Penny."

"What about your social media?" Steve asked. "You'll be a private citizen now. Do you want to stay high profile or go low?"

"I won't need you to manage it anymore," he said frankly. "You've done a terrific job. You got my face out there. The team's. The messages I wanted to convey." He paused. "And perhaps a little too much of my social life."

"Hell, West, you've dated too many famous people," Steve protested. "I had to capitalize on that. But I get it. I'll email you all your login and password information for your accounts. I can delete the ones you don't want to use anymore, too."

Jace turned to his partner. "Mark, anything to add?"

"No. Just happy you'll still be a client with TTM, West. I would advise you to have an attorney on hand to represent you in other matters. Real estate. Wills and trusts. Or if you decide to pursue any business opportunities beyond coaching."

"My cousin Sawyer will fit the bill. We're going to rent a house together for a few months."

"He's leaving the district attorney's office?" Mark asked.

West nodded. "He's ready for the next chapter in his law career, just like I'm looking to see what West 2.0 will look like."

Elena entered the conference room. "Lunch is here. Shall I have them bring it in?"

They feasted on everything from cannelloni and lasagna to vanilla bean panna cotta for dessert. He would miss the fine dining scene in Dallas, but all good things must come to an end.

West told everyone goodbye, promising to let Jace know how this afternoon's interview went. He returned to his car, heading north, Dallas finally in his rearview mirror for good.

CHAPTER
Four

Kelby woke up, disoriented. Then she realized she was in her childhood bedroom. The sun was shining into the room, and she picked up her phone, seeing it was almost nine o'clock. She couldn't remember the last time she had slept so late, but her body felt good, her mind clearing now.

She had moved from the motel room she had been staying at in Decatur to the ranch late last night. It had been easier to remain in Decatur in order to be close to her father while he was in the hospital. She spent every day with him, observing and making notes of the medications he was given. The various doctors who stopped by. The exercises the different therapists put him through. She had fed him every meal the first few days, but one of the therapists told her to let him try. It had been painful to watch that first time. Dad was right-handed, but the paralysis had remained on that side of his body. He was having to learn how to do everything with his left hand, and she could see the frustration in his eyes.

At least he was eating on his own now, for the most part. Kelby had cut up some meat for him the other day since he couldn't hold a knife and fork. He'd glared at her, so she'd put the cutlery down. Dad simply picked up the chicken thigh in his left hand and ate it that way, giving her a satisfied look as he did so.

He still wasn't speaking. He had difficulty swallowing, as Dr. Brock had mentioned might occur, but his therapists were working with him on it. She hoped he would be able to talk with them soon. It had to be tiring not to be able to communicate, answering yes or no questions with a nod of the head or blink of the eyes.

Thankfully, yesterday's transfer to a rehab center, located halfway between Hawthorne and Decatur, had gone smoothly. Dad would be a live-in patient for an undetermined amount of time. Kelby and Chance had met with the head of the center before the transfer occurred, learning what their father would be going through. They were given a sample schedule, one which applied to patients who had experienced strokes, but Mrs. Paulson said this would change. They would tailor the schedule to Dad's needs once they evaluated him during the next couple of days of therapy.

The director also asked that neither of them come to the facility today, saying that Dad needed time to adjust without either of them hovering over him. Even when they came tomorrow, Mrs. Paulson explained that they wouldn't be allowed to go to the therapy sessions. Kelby had wanted to argue about that, but the director remained firm on this point, explaining that patients did better when they worked with their various therapists in privacy.

Since Dad would be in therapy off and on throughout the day, Mrs. Paulson suggested they could visit him around noon each day. He would finish up a session about a quarter till twelve, and he wouldn't go to another one until one o'clock, at least for the first few days. Or they could wait and come around suppertime, which was between five and five-thirty. Kelby had thought her days would be spent as they had been for the past ten days, but she didn't want to sit in Dad's room at the rehab center all day, waiting for him to return.

Chance had told her after taking off all today, she could go to see Dad at noon each day. If she wanted to accompany him, they could go back together for supper. It would be a new pattern to settle into, after the last ten days of being at the hospital around the clock, only leaving to shower and sleep. At least having somewhere to go had kept Kelby occupied. She had barely looked at her phone. The texts and emails were stacking up.

As for what was happening with Bax, she couldn't care less.

She rose, stretching, feeling a bit sluggish. It had been too long since she'd worked out, and she felt an itch to do so. But her belly growled, so she headed downstairs to get something to eat.

Tammy was in the kitchen, kneading dough. "Hey, baby girl. Did you sleep all right?"

"I really did," she said, turning on the coffeemaker and pulling out a hazelnut pod.

"Can I get you some breakfast?"

"You've got your hands full. Cereal will be fine."

"I've got some fresh blueberries you can put in it."

She laughed. "You sound like Darby. She's the health nut."

"How is Miss Darby? She still with that cheer association?"

Her longtime friend had called a couple of times, and Kelby planned to return the call today now that she had some time to herself.

"She is. Got a promotion last fall. She's hoping she won't have to travel so much and teach camps."

Tammy flipped the dough over and began working it again.

"I suppose I shouldn't bring up work or that lazy ass ex of yours."

Chuckling, she set the pod into the coffeemaker. The instant aroma of coffee filled the air as the hot liquid began dropping into a coffee mug. "You just did. You've never minced words, Tammy."

As she ate breakfast, Kelby explained what had happened with Wyndham & Warren pushing her out.

"Sawyer Montgomery took care of everything for me."

"That basketball player? The handsome one all you girls mooned over?"

"That's the one. He's been working in Dallas, but he's moved back to Hawthorne. Or at least that was his plan when we talked a couple of weeks ago. He'll take over Isaiah's practice. I assume Dad will still use him."

She removed the pod and turned off the coffeemaker, doctoring her coffee with sugar and cream and pouring cereal into a bowl.

"Sawyer read the termination agreement and severance package documents, as well as the NDA. He fine-tuned them a bit and countered. My boss brought in the big guns, and it took a couple of days for the lawyers to hash things out, but Sawyer did well. I have a nice lump sum which will tide me over until things get better with Dad and I can find another job."

Tammy covered the dough with a cloth, leaving it to rise. She washed her hands and joined Kelby at the table.

"You know I've visited Mr. B, Kelby. I know he's improved a lot, but I can't say things will get much better."

"You don't know that for certain," she said quickly, her own thoughts now being voiced aloud by Tammy. "Dr. Brock said we might be surprised by how much movement Dad will recover."

Tammy gave her look which caused tears to spring to

Kelby's eyes. "I know you're hoping for the best, but Mr. B will only be able to do so much. I've talked some with Chance, and we think it might be a good idea to hire a fulltime nurse."

Anger spiked within her. "Why did you talk about this without me?"

"It was just talk, baby girl. One conversation. You know absolutely nothing would be decided without your input. But Mr. B is not going to be able to run this ranch anymore. Chance'll step up. He'll see things get done. Your daddy, however, will need someone to help him. I won't be able to. I've got the house to run and meals to put on the table. Besides, I might be tough, but there's a limit to what I can lift. Mr. B is six-three and outweighs me by a good hundred and fifty pounds. Or at least he did before the stroke," Tammy added quietly. "We'll need someone who can help him address his needs. Bathing and dressing him. Doing all that therapy. You and your brother need to start looking to the future."

That was the last thing Kelby wanted to do. While she'd been at the hospital, she'd been able to remain in a cocoon, unaware of everything happening beyond the doors of her dad's hospital room. Keeping occupied with his health crisis had let her ignore the world outside.

Once Dad came home from the rehab center, however, she couldn't stay at the ranch forever. She would need to see him settled and then get back on the horse, as she'd been taught to do. Big Jim Blackstone expected no fear in his children. He would want her to go back and conquer the world.

"I think I'm going to go for a ride," she told Tammy, taking her breakfast dishes to the sink and rinsing them before placing them inside the dishwasher.

Riding had always been her favorite activity. It was exercise. It was escape. It was freedom. When she was young, it had been the gateway to a new world she created as she flew across the ranch.

She returned to her room and dressed in a pair of jeans and a long-sleeved shirt, placing her hair in a ponytail. She slipped on a pair of sunglasses and took an old hat which hung in the mudroom and made her way down to the stables.

Entering, she saw Dusty, one of their ranch hands, and greeted him.

"Hey, Miss Kelby. Want to go for a ride?"

"I need to clear my head. There's no better way."

"How about I saddle Echo for you?"

"Please do."

Echo looked almost exactly like the horse Kelby had ridden growing up. Dusty had suggested the name since the two horses favored one another so closely, and she had thought it perfect.

Taking the reins Dusty offered to her, Kelby led Echo from the stables and then mounted her. She let the horse become familiar with her again since it had been a good while since she had visited the ranch, much less ridden. Once they'd warmed to one another, though, she let Echo have her head, and off they went, practically flying.

She rode for almost two hours, slowing down after that first gallop, trotting around various places on the ranch. At one point, she saw Chance and waved to him. He looked busy, so she continued on her way, enjoying the feel of the sun on her back, even as the end of February proved cool.

When she returned, she gave Echo a good rubdown and then went inside the house and showered and dressed before blowing her hair dry. She hadn't bothered packing makeup in her rush to get to the hospital, but she did pull out a tube of lipstick from her purse and use it to give herself a little color. Then she tackled all the messages that had stacked up. Although she didn't read the content of all the emails and texts she'd received, she did hit reply and copied and pasted the same message, saying she was doing her best to look toward her future and would be in touch when she could.

She deleted all voice messages without listening to them, only listening to the ones Darby had left. Her best friend had simply given a few words of encouragement and told Kelby to call whenever she had licked her wounds and was ready to talk.

"No time like the present," she told herself, calling Darby.

Her friend answered on the second ring. "How are you? Tell me whatever you want. I'm here to listen."

"Are you busy?"

"Not when you call," Darby said, laughing. "Actually, I'm closing the door to my office. No one will bother us because I've done that. I'll be quiet now. Spill your guts, Kel."

She did, talking for almost an hour. Kelby shared how she'd learned about Bax. The horror of reading about what he was arrested for, as well as the sick feeling when pictures of the two of them began popping up online, accompanying the stories about his arrest. Then she explained how Wyndham & Warren had wanted to cut her loose, fearing she would spot their reputation.

"What did you do?" Darby demanded. "I hope you stood up to them. They can't fire you. That's against the law."

"Long story. Short version is that they did let me go, but I received a nice severance package to walk without a fuss. Sawyer helped me. He read through everything and advised me on what we should ask for in return."

"*My* Sawyer? He never said a word to me. Some brother!"

Kelby laughed. "I guess as a client, he gave me full privileges and didn't spill a word to his sister."

"I'm glad he was able to help you wade through everything. Did you know he's walked away from his job as an ADA to move back to Hawthorne?"

"Yes, he mentioned it to me."

"Well, I hope he knows what he's doing. He is taking over Isaiah Smith's practice, so he won't have to start from scratch, thank goodness."

"I probably owe him a dinner," she said, pausing a beat. "I'm in Hawthorne. There's more I need to tell you."

The next few minutes, Kelby shared everything about her dad's stroke. How she'd been at the hospital night and day, meeting with doctors, and watching his rehab.

"Oh, Kel, I'm so sorry. You should have reached out sooner. I would've come. I can still come."

"No, don't do that. No need to now. Dad was transferred yesterday to a rehab facility. He'll be there several weeks. Maybe even longer. They don't want me hanging over their shoulders or his, so he'll do all his PT and OT sessions under their watchful eye and not mine. Chance and I can visit a couple of times a day, though, so I'll be doing that. At least for the foreseeable future."

"What about work?" Darby pressed. "I can't see you hanging around the ranch for weeks with nothing to do."

"Frankly, I'm not certain who's going to hire me after being associated with this Bax scandal. It doesn't seem to matter that we've been divorced for five years."

"Oh," Darby said quietly. "I guess you've been so busy with your dad that you haven't kept up with the news."

Her heartbeat quickened. "What's happened? I haven't looked at anything online. I've been wrapped up in caring for Dad."

"It's bad," her friend said. "Bax is dead."

Nausea swept through her. "Did he commit suicide?" she asked, thinking how much her former husband hated being told what to do. Jail would be nothing but people in authority ordering him about. Plus, he would have had a hard time without access to alcohol and drugs. Quitting both cold turkey while in lockup would have been a nightmare.

"No. He ... was stabbed yesterday. By another prisoner."

Kelby gripped the phone tightly. "Stabbed?" she echoed.

"Don't read anything about it," her friend cautioned. "The authorities aren't even sure if it was one inmate or more than one."

Tears welled in her eyes and began spilling down her cheeks. "I can't imagine dying in such an awful way."

"I know."

They sat on the line together, neither saying anything. Kelby could hear Darby's quiet breathing.

After a few minutes, she said, "Thanks for just being with me in this moment."

"You're my best friend," Darby said simply. "I'll always be here for you."

"I think I'll go now."

"Call me if you need anything. To talk. Or to tell me to come to Hawthorne. I've got some vacation time coming that I could use."

"I promise I'll stay in better touch. Don't come home now. But I may ask you to soon."

"I love you, Kel."

"I love you, too."

Kelby ended the call and sat, her mind a blank. Finally, she called up a few news stories about Bax's death, despite Darby's warning not to do so. After reading a few, she set her phone down.

Bax was dead. News of his death would linger for several news cycles, but she couldn't help but think that just maybe, she was finally free.

Chance wouldn't know about this since he never paid attention to the news. Most likely, Tammy wouldn't know about it either. She decided to go for a drive, needing some time alone.

After she had driven around for an hour, she returned to Hawthorne, feeling more grounded. As she approached the town square, she decided to rely on her comfort food.

Ice cream.

Her dad had always said everything bad could be cured with a bowl of ice cream. She smiled, thinking how many times he had brought Chance and her to Burger Heaven. It was located on the Hawthorne town square and only served burgers, crinkle fries, and ice cream. She decided to stop in and have a treat. It had been a rough two weeks, and Kelby couldn't think of anything she wanted more now.

She parked and entered. It was just after four, and she was the only customer. Miss Caroline, the owner, who had to be at least seventy-five now, beamed at her.

"Kelby Blackstone! It's so good to see you, honey." Miss Caroline came from behind the counter and hugged her. "I'm so sorry about your daddy. I heard he got moved to rehab."

For a moment, she wondered how Miss Caroline knew that, but Hawthorne was a small town. Everyone knew everyone else's business, both the good and the bad.

"He did. Yesterday," she confirmed. "But we're seeing improvement each day."

Miss Caroline took Kelby's hands in hers. "I would say I'm sorry about that no-good ex of yours, except I'd be lying. You were smart to leave him years ago, honey. I know some of what's happened recently has washed back on you, but don't let it get you down."

"I won't," she promised, her eyes misting over. She had missed being in a place where everyone knew who she was and rooted for her.

"I'll bet you came in for some ice cream. Big Jim always did bring you and Chance here when you were troubled. What can I get you, dear?"

She wandered over to where large tubs of ice cream sat behind glass. Butter pecan. Rocky road. Strawberry cheesecake. And then the top trio of chocolate, vanilla, and strawberry.

"I think I'll splurge," she told the owner. "I'll go with a banana split."

Before she could ask for them, Miss Caroline said, "Extra nuts, right?"

Kelby nodded. "You remembered."

"I may be eighty, but I remember more than most people have forgotten." Miss Caroline cackled. "One banana split coming right up. Go have a seat."

She went to a booth and sat so that she could look out on the square. Not much activity was taking place at the moment. She stared lazily at the view.

Then she saw a fancy sports car pull up. A Jaguar, if she wasn't mistaken. The driver got out and strode toward Burger Heaven. Kelby's heart began to race.

Because it was West Sutherland.

CHAPTER
Five

W est sat opposite his former high school football coach. The office where they sat was quiet. So was the hallway and locker room. Three o'clock was practice time, so no one was present to disturb their conversation.

After greeting Coach Markham, they had talked about the most recent run up to the Super Bowl and the game itself. Although West had always offered his former mentor tickets to the game, Coach Markham had never taken him up on it. He'd told West he didn't want any favors from a former student and that he was happy to sit in his La-Z-Boy recliner and watch the game in the comfort of his den.

The older man studied him now. West knew not to back down from the scrutiny.

"So, you really think retirement was the right move?"

"I do, sir. I accomplished everything I dreamed of doing. Last year's ACL scare was a bit rough. The work I put in, though, made me stronger. A better, more sympathetic player. I wanted to prove to myself and all my teammates and the league that I could come back and do my job at the same level I'd been playing at prior to the injury. I got things done this season, and now I'm ready to move on."

Markham pursed his lips in thought a moment and then said, "You could coach anywhere, West. The Cowboys would be happy to make a spot for you. The Aggies would do the same. You lifted their program at a time when they badly needed that done, and they've traded on their success during your years there, continuing to recruit and play well in the most competitive conference in college football. You'd be a natural to coach at either level."

His mentor leaned back in his chair. "I guess what I'm asking is why high school."

"For the same reason you coach high school, Coach," he replied. "You've had offers to move up to a larger district. I know for a fact SMU and U of H has come knocking at your door before. Yet you've stayed in small towns your entire coaching career. Here in Hawthorne for the last eighteen, twenty years. Why do *you* stay?"

"Touché," Markham said. "I'm in it for the kids. For the pure joy of seeing their faces light up when they get a play. To me, the bigger programs don't offer the same advantages as working with kids in a small town does. My Hawks have heart, every one of them."

"I feel the same. I have a lot to offer. I won't sell myself short. But I want to get back to my roots. Back to that unvarnished game. I love football, Coach. I have since I first picked up a pigskin. I want to spread that feeling to others. I think high school is the last place a coach can make a true difference. Not just about football. The higher up the food chain you go in football, the more specialized it gets. The more knowledge you gain. The coaches around you are experts in a tiny fraction of the game, and they pour that knowledge into you.

"But I'm talking about molding character. Not just teaching

young men about football and how to be a better player. I want them to learn how to be a better man. How to take lessons from football and apply those lesson to their lives. Very few kids on your practice field out there will go on to play at the college level, much less in the pros. Yet every single player moves on after graduation to live his life. I want to help prepare them for that life. Use the tools they learned by playing football to succeed. Leadership skills. Discipline. Teamwork. All those things carry on beyond the football field."

Coach Markham grinned. "Hell, you've convinced me—and I'm the one who counts."

"Exactly what does that mean?" he asked.

"Most applicants in the district interview with a department head or a committee. Then the principal. Your daddy allows me plenty of autonomy since I also double as the district's athletic director. If I want to make a hire, I can do so. I found out the very day you called me that I was losing one of my coaches."

"Did he land a higher position at a different school?" he asked, knowing public school coaches usually started in middle school, then worked their way up to high school. A defensive back coach would aim to move up to being a defensive coordinator. A coordinator looked to be a head coach.

"Nope. He decided to pursue a career in administration. Earned his master's degree in public school administration. Has plans of working on his doctorate now. He interned as an assistant principal at HHS this past year, and he told me his heart is in helping all the kids in a school, not just the ones who play football. He'll leave at the end of the year for a high school in Wichita Falls."

"Good for him. It's good to know what you want to do," West said. "And I would appreciate your consideration for his position."

Coach Markham laughed. "You don't even know what positions he coached, West."

"I'll learn," he promised.

"Fortunately for you, he was my quarterbacks and running backs coach. Also our offensive coordinator. That's a lot to be on your plate." He paused. "No, I'll shift things around. I can't waste your experience as a receiver. You'll handle QBs and wide receivers. I'll move running backs to someone else on the staff."

"I can do whatever you ask of me, Coach." He paused. "I want to be a team player."

"Hell, West, I'd be a fool *not* to put you in his slot. That includes being offensive coordinator."

"Will that cause some ill will with the other coaches who've been with the program? I don't want to step on anyone's toes."

"I always have to do a little shuffling each season," Markham told him. "When you've got a winning team as I do, your assistants get plucked left and right. I'm probably going to also lose my defensive line coach. Maybe one more. Coaches are used to being shuffled around, West. You should know that. And if you don't, then that's the first thing to consider. Now, do you want a job on my staff or not?"

"Absolutely," he declared.

"Then it'll be as my Number Two. Assistant head coach. You'll specialize in the QBs and receivers. For now. We'll see how things shake up by the end of the year."

"What would I teach? I've got my composite in Social Studies. I kept up with the certifications and paid my fees over the years, just in case, so I'm good to go."

"That'll be for Dex Danby to decide. He's head of the Social Studies Department. For now, I'll call central admin and let your daddy know you're my hire. Blanche Biggerstaff, too. She's the principal here at HHS. Been here three years now.

Blanche is a good leader, and her boy is on the team. Will be a junior next year. Second-string quarterback."

He raked a hand through his hair. "This is really happening."

Coach Markham rose and offered West his hand. "It is absolutely happening. And don't worry about nepotism. *I'm* the one hiring you. Not your daddy." He grinned. "Besides, I'm getting a Super Bowl champ on my staff. The town'll be thrilled."

They shook hands, and Markham told him he'd be in touch soon. West would have to sign his contract. Meet with the principal and his department chair. Learn his teaching assignment.

"In the meantime, I have something for you. You'll know to guard it with your life." Reaching for a notebook on the shelf behind him, he handed it to West. "This is our playbook. Revised from last fall. It's what we're going with in spring training this year. I can have you visit practice a time or two, but until you're officially onboard, you can't do any coaching."

"I understand. Once I've signed the contract, can I at least tell people I'll be coaching with you next year?"

"You can tell anyone now since I'll call Dr. Sutherland and make it official with him. I'd introduce you to Blanche, but she's at some conference for principals and won't be back until Monday. In the meantime, that loud whoop you'll hear will be your daddy hollering, happy to have you back in the Hawthorne fold."

"Dad will be pleased. And I plan to make him proud. You, too, Coach."

"I don't doubt that at all, West."

He left, the playbook secure under his arm. By the time he saw Coach Markham again, he would know it backward and forward.

In the car, he let out a whoop of his own, one which would

do any Aggie proud. West couldn't believe that he would be living in Hawthorne again, working at his former high school as one of the football coaches. He'd also have lesson plans to create. Kids to teach in the classroom. His life was changing radically.

As he pulled out of the parking lot by the field house, he decided to do a little celebrating. In the Sutherland household, that had meant burgers, fries, and a chocolate shake at Burger Heaven. He turned in the direction of the town square, elation filling him.

The square wasn't busy at this time of day, and he easily found a parking place across from Burger Heaven. Opening the door, he pulled off his sunglasses and looked around, seeing only one patron sitting in a booth. He swallowed, his heart slamming against his ribs. Sitting there was the girl he had never forgotten.

Kelby Blackstone ...

He would know her anywhere. They hadn't seen one another in over a decade, but she was a more mature, more beautiful version of the girl he'd briefly dated in high school. Well, not even dated. He'd broken up with his girlfriend. Kelby was his best friend's little sister. They'd just teamed up and gone to a bunch of senior activities together during those last couple of months of school.

And they'd kissed. Once. West had meant for it to be a friendly kiss, one to thank her for acting as his date and helping him celebrate the final events of their school years. Instead, it had turned hot and heady.

He'd never forgotten it. Or her.

Smiling, he made his way toward her. She slid from the booth. Her long, raven hair was swept back in a high ponytail. Those large, gray eyes drew him in. She still had a knockout figure, with curves in all the right places.

"Hey, West," she greeted, her voice low and musical.

"Hey, yourself, Kelby."

They moved toward one another, and he gave her a good hug. Warmth filled him. Kelby had been one of the friendliest, kindest girls in their senior class. She was smart and dependable.

And sexy as hell now.

Before, she'd had that small-town, girl-next-door glow to her. The years had been kind to her, though. Where she was once pretty, she was now beautiful. And single. He recalled Chance telling him a few years ago that Kelby had divorced her husband, a journeyman NFL player who never made it in the big leagues, thanks to both injuries and addiction. Chance hadn't mentioned Kelby in a long time. Then again, they hadn't been in touch with each other much, something West was ready to change now that he would be a fulltime resident of Hawthorne.

He released her. "You look good. Better than good."

She laughed, and it was like a chorus of angels. He laughed with her.

"Have a seat," she said, and he slid into the opposite side of the booth, drinking her in.

Miss Caroline appeared, setting down an enormous banana split. "Why, West Sutherland. What are you doing here?"

"Catching up with Kelby, Miss Caroline." He glanced at the ice cream. "And I'd like to get one of these."

"No, you don't," Kelby corrected. "This is ginormous. Miss Caroline, if you could bring another spoon, West can help me with this one. There's no way I could finish this by myself."

Quickly, another spoon was brought, and they both dug in. For a moment, they simply looked at the huge banana split and then sighed.

"Is there anything better on the planet than ice cream?" she asked.

"Sex. Sex is better," he quipped.

She laughed, deep from her belly. "You haven't changed a bit, West."

"Well, I hope I've grown up some. What are you doing in Hawthorne?"

"Dad had a stroke."

As they shared the banana split, Kelby told West about Big Jim's rehab and how Chance was assuming a lot more responsibility on the ranch.

"I'll definitely give him a call. It's been too long. And I'm back here permanently. I just accepted a job as a football coach and teacher at the high school for next August."

"Really? That's great, West. A hometown boy returns in triumph. It's not many small towns that can claim to have a Super Bowl winner on their staff. I can see good things coming your way."

He studied her a moment. "You don't think it's foolish for me to want to coach here?"

"Here is where you can make a difference," she said firmly. "The kids on the team have grown up on stories about you. They've cut their football teeth learning about your legend. Friday night football in Texas is magic. Besides, college football is a business these days, with NIL now. And the pros are so sterile." Her mouth turned down.

"I'm sorry about your marriage," he said quietly.

She sighed. "It's the only thing I ever really failed at. Bax was never a partner to me. I see now how self-centered he was. He was in everything for himself. And when his magical run dried up, I got all the blame."

West frowned. "Verbal? Or worse?"

"Lots of verbal, which I stupidly took. The drinking, which

I shouldn't have tolerated, but I did. When I found the drugs, though, I was done and washed my hands of him."

"Are you seeing anyone now, Kelby?"

She looked at him, tears welling in her eyes. "No. I decided I didn't have good judgment when it came to men. I've focused on my career these past five years, and now that's circled the drain."

"What do you mean?"

"I was let go. Because of the whole Bax thing."

Confused, he asked, "I'm not following."

Kelby shook her head. "You're worse than Chance. Do either of you ever turn on the TV news? Or read any online news?"

"Not if I can help it," he admitted. "The so-called news lies about every woman I've gone out with. They've made up stories about my contract negotiations and my injury last year. I don't trust the media. But what is it that I should have seen on the news?"

"Bax killed a guy over his gambling debts. And then yesterday, another prisoner in the jail stuck a shiv in Bax. He's dead," she said flatly.

Immediately, West left the booth and slid in beside her, wrapping an arm about her.

"I'm so sorry, Kelby. That had to hurt like hell. Even if you left the guy years ago, you loved him once."

She leaned into him, pressing her cheek against his chest. "It's pretty bad. It's messed with my head. I lost my job over Bax because my employer didn't want to be associated with any scandal. My picture with Bax was everywhere a couple of weeks ago. I had to stop looking, especially once I came and stayed by Dad's bedside day and night. I'm at loose ends today only because he's just been transferred to a rehab center, and they're evaluating him today. They don't want me lurking around."

He pulled her closer to him. "You've had it as rough as anyone can imagine. But you're such a positive person. Good is going to come out of this. Either you'll land a new job, or you'll start your own company."

"My own company?" She looked up at him. "I'll bet you don't even know what I do for a living."

West kept her close, feeling as if she fit perfectly, exactly where she was. Their gazes held.

"It doesn't matter. Because I think you can do anything you set your mind to, Kelby Blackstone."

CHAPTER
Six

K elby had put off thinking about what to do, career-wise, focusing on her father's road to recovery. It should be something she began to consider, however.

West's idea of her starting her own business intrigued her. She was a social media guru and tech expert and knew quite a bit about branding. Could she build a client base and handle social media accounts or build websites, working remotely? It was definitely something to investigate.

Suddenly, she realized West still had his arm around her—and how good it felt. He had a clean, masculine scent about him, and she had sorely missed a man's company since her divorce. She had put up impenetrable walls, so thick that no man had wanted to scale them. Kelby could count on one hand the number of dates she had gone on since her divorce. Work had become everything to her, that and seeing her friends.

But could there be more to life? Was she willing to open her heart?

Then again, West was a professional athlete. A football player, no less. Though she had never vocalized it, he was the exact type of man she needed to stay away from. She might lose her head—and her heart—over a man like West Sutherland.

And Kelby decided that simply was not going to happen.

West must have sensed the tension now flooding her body because he removed his arm and exited the booth, returning to the other side and sitting opposite her once again. He picked up his spoon and took another bite from the banana split.

Trying to lessen the sudden awareness between them, she said, "Watch how much of the chocolate ice cream you eat, Sutherland. I might just have to rethink this sharing idea unless you do."

He laughed easily. "I'll go for a bite of strawberry next." He sighed. "There's nothing like Burger Heaven. I can't recall the last time I ate a banana split, much less shared it with good company."

"Ice cream has always been my comfort food."

West smiled at her. "You don't have to remind me about that. Remember the time Tony Gonzales broke up with you in ninth grade? You went straight to the freezer for a tub of Bluebell. Back then, vanilla bean was your flavor of choice, with a healthy squeeze of Hershey's dark chocolate syrup covering it. I remember you used to beat the ice cream and syrup together until it turned into a smooth, chocolate mess."

She grinned at him. "And you used to tease me unmercifully for doing so," she remembered. "You used to ask why I didn't just go for the chocolate in the first place. I will have you know that my horizons have expanded. I still am a Bluebell girl, and I go for whatever seasonal offering they have before anything else. Bride's Cake. Peaches and Cream. Southern Blackberry Cobbler."

Kelby paused and took another bite, savoring the cold sweetness on her tongue.

Then she asked, "Since you won't start your job for a while, will you stay and visit family and friends for a bit? Or are you off to Rome or Hong Kong or Rio?"

He chuckled. "Someone's been keeping up with my Instagram."

She shrugged. "I handle social media. Or at least I did before my boss let me go. It was my job to see what was out there and how I could keep Wyndham & Warren relevant. Unique. Trending. Yours isn't the only account I follow."

He pulled out his cell. "What's your handle? I'll follow you."

Kelby looked at him for a moment, stunned. "West Sutherland wants to follow *me*? You don't follow anyone. You're the guy who has over a million followers and has never clicked to follow a single person."

His gaze met hers. "Maybe it's time I shook things up."

She gave him her handle, and he typed it into his phone.

"There. You're the first person I'm following." He grinned. "I had no idea I didn't follow anyone. To be honest, I don't think I've ever looked at my own account a single time."

"You had a social media manager who handled your account for you."

He nodded. "I left all that up to TTM. Touchdown Talent Management. Steve in their office posted to all my social media accounts. I would send him a little something every now and then. Pictures from practice or a few shots from my latest vacation. I don't know what he posted the rest of the time."

"Uh, you and whatever gorgeous gal you were squiring about that week. I think you changed girlfriends more often than your socks. You are quite the ladies' man, West. I don't know if there's a beautiful woman out there whom you haven't dated."

She'd almost said slept with but managed to correct herself

before it came out of her mouth. Why should she care who West Sutherland slept with? It was none of her business.

"Dated is a loose term," he replied. "I associate that with someone you like and are interested in. Someone you go out with multiple times and have a relationship with." He hesitated a moment, looking a bit sheepish. "If we go by my definition of dating, then I haven't dated anyone in a long, long time."

His words interested her. "It was all for show?"

"I wouldn't exactly say show. I just needed someone to accompany me to events. There were women who, if they were seen with me, it would raise their profile. Sometimes, they'd broken up with someone and wanted a brief fling with a revenge boyfriend."

West raked a hand through his hair, and Kelby recalled the familiar gesture from years past. It usually was when West was unsure about something or having a hard time expressing himself.

"I enjoyed my twenties, Kelby. I'm not going to apologize for that. I was playing a game I loved with a team I grew up worshiping. Going to all kinds of places, with or without a beautiful woman on my arm. That continued into my thirties, but I found I was ready to make a change, both professionally and personally."

He took a bite of banana as she watched him chew. The man oozed sensuality. His handsome face was simply perfection, with those high, cut cheekbones and sensual lips. West, like his two siblings, had a remarkable shade of turquoise eyes which stood out, something which drew people in. They were drawing her in now.

She knew he had grown reflective, and she was interested in what else he had to say.

"I left football before it could leave me," he revealed. "I always played the game with such abandon. I was fearless on and off the field. Things changed. Not just because of the injury I suffered last year." He met her gaze. "I hurt my ACL last year. A serious sprain. Thank goodness, it wasn't a tear that required surgery, but it still took a hell of a lot of rehab to get back both physically and mentally. To be able to play this year. It was important to me to return to the field, though. Not just to show the fans and my teammates. I wanted to show myself what I was capable of doing. That I could still be the great West Sutherland and play at an elite level that only a few receivers managed to do.

"That part was satisfying, but football had already begun to lose its sparkle for me. I couldn't see myself playing beyond this year. I'll be thirty-two in a week. I found there were no new mountains to climb. No records to break. The fun of the game seemed to have vanished. That's why I've come home to Hawthorne, Kelby."

Intrigued filled her. "You're sitting on a bazillion dollars. It's not as if you have to work for a living."

"But I want to do that, Kelby," West said earnestly. "I think I'd go out of my mind if I didn't have something worthwhile to do. I want my life to mean something beyond football. I want to be useful to other people."

He set down his spoon, looking at her. "That's why I wanted to be on Coach Markham's staff at HHS."

The idea of West as a high school coach still surprised her. "You know that with your background and name recognition, you could have done whatever you wanted. Earned millions as a broadcast analyst for a major network. Or if you truly wanted to coach, the Cowboys would have been onboard and hired you themselves."

He shook his head. "That's not what I wanted. I want to be at this level. I need to be here. I know how much Coach Markham touched my life. He—and my parents—are the people who molded my character and made me the man I am today. A man who, at times, forgot that upbringing, the values they instilled in me. I haven't always been proud of myself."

The look on his face, along with his words, hurt her heart, and Kelby reached out, covering his hand with hers.

"West, you reached the pinnacle of your sport. It's okay if you had some fun doing it. Seeing a lot of women while you were breaking records, left and right."

His free hand covered hers, and he squeezed it. "But don't you see? I want to be a better man. I want to get back to my small-town roots and the values which have carried me this far in life. In my core, I'm a good man. Yes, I've had a little fast living. Lost my way for a bit. Driven sports cars and taken lavish vacations. Had more than a few flings along the way. But I've got the chance now to live in Hawthorne. My hometown. Where I can make a difference in the lives of my players and students."

He searched her face. "And I want a family, Kelby. I'm tired of playing around. I want to settle down. Be the kind of parent my own parents were. And I wouldn't want to do it anywhere other than Hawthorne."

Their gazes held, and she saw the sincerity in his eyes. this was a man who had sown his wild oats, even as he made a name for himself professionally.

Slowly, she pulled her hand from his, placing it in her lap again. "I think that's really admirable, West. It must be a small percentage of professional football players who reached your level and choose to return to the coaching ranks, much less at such a small football program. I admire you for wanting to be there for teenagers. To make a difference in their lives."

She took a last bite of the banana split and placed her spoon on the table. "I respect you for what you're going to do, and I hope you'll find happiness in doing it."

"You sound like you're washing your hands of me, Kelby," he said astutely.

"I will always have a fondness for you West," she said sincerely. "You were so much a part of my years growing up in Hawthorne. You were like a second brother to me, always hanging around the ranch. I know Chance will be thrilled that you've come back to stay. He's never had as close a friend as he made in you."

Kelby looked him in the eyes. "I hope we'll become friends once again. I cherish the friendship we had long ago, and I'm happy to renew it again."

"But you're shutting the door to any idea of romance," he said flatly. "Of going down that road we chose not to travel because we were headed for different colleges at the time."

He had vocalized what she had yet to say. Kelby nodded, taking her time before she spoke again.

"You've got to understand how brutal things were with Bax. Everything was absolutely perfect between us in college. I cheered at his games. I celebrated his victories with him. I managed to pick him up from the dumps on the rare occasions the Longhorns lost. I married Bax, stars in my eyes, thinking that our storybook college romance would simply continue on as he went pro. That he would become this bright, shining light, breaking NFL records. Being named All-Pro. Wining Super Bowls. Making enough money to secure our future, especially when we had children."

She swallowed, looking away. "But not every fairy tale has a happy ending. There was no happily ever after for us. We eloped to Vegas after graduation. Bax started training camp soon after that. Then we trod along the long road to his downfall, with all its twists and turns. He hurt me, West. Not just physically. Emotionally. I lost any confidence I had because of Bax Porter. Once we divorced, it's been a long way back to finding me. I've poured a solid foundation for myself and began building a life I liked. One I enjoyed. Unfortunately, Bax had a hand in tearing that structure down. But my foundation is still rock-solid. Just like hurricane victims who lose everything, I'm going to start rebuilding my house again. I may even do what you suggested and consider creating a business of my own. I am not invincible, but I am strong. I will get through this and come out the other end a better person."

Kelby lifted her head, once more meeting his gaze. "But while I like you as a person, I liked you years ago, West. I don't really know the adult you've become. I've changed in my twenties. A lot. I know you've done the same. I simply don't think I can trust my heart again when it comes to giving it away to a handsome NFL legend. I will try to be your friend, but don't ask anything more of me—because I don't have it to give."

West pulled out his wallet and tossed a twenty on the table. "Thanks for sharing the banana split with me, Kelby. It was really good seeing you."

She tried not to be affected by the hurt she saw in his eyes. He had bared his soul to her. Told her that he was trying to be a better man and start a new life. Kelby just didn't have the bandwidth to start up something with him and then be disappointed. Or worse, brokenhearted. She told herself that she was glad she had let West know where she stood.

But Kelby couldn't help but wonder if she had made a mistake and kissed goodbye the opportunity to change her life.

And his.

CHAPTER
Seven

"What the hell were you thinking?" West muttered under his breath as he pushed open the door and left Burger Heaven.

He made certain not to glance over his shoulder as he strode to his car, cursing what had just gone down between Kelby Blackstone and himself. He reached his car and climbed behind the wheel, quickly leaving the town square and heading to the rental. Based upon the realtor's directions, he should be there in five to seven minutes.

Boy, he'd made a fool of himself. Seeing Kelby again had done that to him. The moment he walked into the burger joint and caught sight of her, a rush of unresolved feelings bubbled up to the surface. It was funny because he had not thought of Kelby in years. Well, that was a lie. He would think of her every now and then but tamp down the notion of ever seeing her again.

She had always been around his entire childhood, and he supposed he had taken her for granted. Chance had been his friend, and West had been perfectly at home anytime he went to Blackstone Ranch. Kelby was usually there, sometimes with one of her friends, including his cousin Darby, who was Kelby's best friend. As they'd reached middle school and then high school, Kelby had just been one of the group, hanging out together.

It was not until the spring of their senior year, when he had broken up with his girlfriend, that West really got to know Kelby one-on-one. Chance wasn't dating anyone either, and so Darby and Chance, along with West and Kelby, decided to enjoy attending all their senior activities together as a foursome. There had been the senior trip to Austin and San Antonio. The sports banquet and talent show. Prom. Graduation activities and parties. Throughout all of these, he and Kelby were thrown together, and he'd found himself liking her, more and more. She had a sweet nature, with a bit of a kick to her. He'd actually liked when the feistiness made an appearance.

When he kissed her, just to show his appreciation for her accompanying him and making the last couple of months of senior year so much fun, sparks had ignited between them. The kiss had taken on a life of its own, and they both were a bit stunned when it finally ended. They had behaved maturely and talked it through, however, pointing out that they were both going to different universities. He had been offered a sports scholarship to Texas A&M in College Station, while Kelby had made the cheer squad at UT in Austin. They wouldn't be like regular students, ones who could come home on a weekend and relax. Instead, they would be committed to nights, weekends, and even some vacation breaks because of what they had chosen to do, so they decided to step back and simply remain friends.

But West had never forgotten that kiss. Or Kelby.

He heard about her peripherally through the years. They saw one another two or three times while still in college. They were both involved in bowl games over Christmas and New Year's. He thought he might have seen her once or twice during a spring break, but summers he remained in College Station, taking classes in summer school, working out, as well as going to a part-time job. Hawthorne had been in West's rearview mirror. He was constantly looking ahead to a career in the NFL.

Chance had shared that Kelby was dating UT's talented quarterback, Baxley Porter. Bax had a terrific junior year and a phenomenal senior year, breaking a couple of NCAA passing records and winning the Heisman Trophy. He'd been drafted number one in their class, with West going at the end of the first round to the Cowboys, while Bax was anointed the savior and starter for the Cleveland Browns. He knew Kelby eloped with Bax to Vegas, and that was really all he'd heard until Chance had texted several years ago that Kelby had divorced her husband.

Bax had never lived up to his college potential in the pros, something all-too familiar with Heisman Trophy winners. He recalled Bax being hurt and out that entire first year, but West was concentrating on making the Cowboys roster. It helped that one of their star receivers retired just before training camp began and another one was traded when he demanded his contract be reworked. Suddenly, West found himself as a starting wide receiver with the best-known team in football, and he never looked back.

He couldn't ever recall playing against Bax in a game. Some gossip had circulated about how Bax had lost his touch and was prone to injuries. The fact that Bax had fallen so far and committed a murder shocked West.

It pissed him off that Kelby's company dumped her because of her past relationship with Bax. Then again, everything these days was all about image, one carefully curated on social media.

You could be the most miserable person on the planet, but if you posted pictures on Instagram of great meals in restaurants, trips you took, or selfies with smiling family and friends, no one ever knew you were hurting inside.

West turned on the street where the rental was located and easily found it, pulling to the curb and cutting the engine. He saw his cousin Sawyer's sensible sedan sitting in the driveway. West wasn't ready to talk to Sawyer just yet. Instead, he took out his cell and wanted to learn more about Kelby and Bax.

He Googled Bax first, and all the lurid headlines were splashed across the internet. It only took a few minutes to discover that Bax had a bad drug and alcohol addiction and had been in and out rehab numerous times. It was a bookie he owed money to that wound up dead, shot twice by Bax. The former pro athlete's booking photo startled West. He remembered the guy with the golden arm and soft touch on the ball, not the hollow-eyed, gaunt man staring back at him. West read how Bax had been shivved by one or more inmates, ones who gutted him and left him to bleed out. It had yet to be determined who was responsible for the former quarterback's murder.

Digging deeper, West found photographs of Kelby and Bax over the years. At first, Kelby had that sparkle in her eyes, the one which had drawn him in. She looked adoringly at her husband. Then things changed over time. Kelby looked grimly at the camera, a haunted look in her eyes. The final photographs before she filed for divorce on the grounds of irreconcilable differences had her looking like a shell of her usual, bubbly self.

He searched for her name now, seeing what would come up, and learned she had reclaimed her maiden name after the divorce. West found several flattering articles and pictures from the last five years. The photographs showed the old Kelby had reappeared. She looked happy and healthy. She had won a few industry awards and spoken at a couple of conferences. It seemed she was damn good at her job. That's what made all this so unfair. She was being judged for being in a relationship she had ended five years ago. It seemed she had done everything to help Bax beat his addictions, but her husband hadn't been interested in doing so. Because of that, she'd left him. Kelby had gone on to make a good life for herself, only that life had now shifted radically, sweeping her away as if she were debris.

He'd been an idiot to open up to her the way he had. Seeing Kelby unexpectedly had been like finding an oasis in a desert he'd wandered through for years. West had kissed his fair share of women in those college years and beyond, becoming very skilled at kissing, learning how to make a woman feel satisfied.

Then one night as he came home after a win over the Eagles, he'd flipped on the TV. An old Julia Roberts movie was on. She played a hooker and had a unique philosophy. She didn't seem to mind selling her body for money. She looked at sex strictly as a business transaction, but the one thing she refused to do was kiss a client on the mouth. Her character said that was too intimate. Too personal.

And West took that philosophy to heart.

From that moment on, he also gave up kissing anyone he went out with on the mouth. He did everything else—and thoroughly enjoyed it. He was a physical person. Sex was almost a recreational sport for him. But he never kissed another woman again, realizing deep down inside it was because he knew he would never connect with another woman the way he had with Kelby.

That was why he had opened up to her. Told her that he'd lost himself for a while but that he was ready to be a better man. He mentally kicked himself, thinking how he'd shared with her how he looked forward to having a family. Somehow, although he had never formed concrete thoughts about it, he wanted to do that with Kelby. Or someone like her. Someone who was raised a certain way and possessed the same values he did.

After his internet dive now, he knew how deeply she had been hurt in her relationship and marriage to Bax. She'd been kicked to the curb. Like a phoenix, however, she had risen from the ashes and made something of herself. She wouldn't stay in Hawthorne for long. She was only here because of her dad's stroke. Once Big Jim was on the mend, Kelby would be gone, looking for the next job opportunity in a big city.

Maybe she was right. Maybe they could try and be friends during her limited time in Hawthorne. He had a job here. West intended to sink his roots deeply into Hawthorne's soil. Kelby Blackstone would not be playing any role in his future.

He picked his cell and got out of the car, making sure to grab the playbook Coach Markham had given him. Now, he was in a better frame of mind now to talk with Sawyer. He definitely would have a lot to unpack in his FaceTime session with Dr. Linda tomorrow, though. West had never mentioned Kelby in any of his sessions. It was time he did so and resolved the conflict he now felt, having seen her today.

Opening the front door, he shouted, "Honey, I'm home," hearing Sawyer's laugh. He had seen his cousin every now and then since they both lived in Dallas. Curious about what a prosecutor did, West arranged to have dinner with Sawyer one night and asked if he could come to the trial that day. Sawyer had agreed, asking that West don one of his usual incognito outfits. West Sutherland showing up at a stranger's murder trial wouldn't just be distracting. It would turn the proceedings into a zoo.

So, he'd put on an old flannel shirt, jeans, and cowboy boots. Added dark sunglasses and a cowboy hat, as well as a surgical mask. People still wore them sometimes, especially during the winter months when viruses spread quickly.

West had sat in the back row and saw an entirely different side to Sawyer. Usually a kind, easygoing man, his cousin had been a barracuda during the courtroom's proceedings as he cross-examined defense witnesses. West had been fascinated by the change in his cousin, and his admiration for Sawyer grew exponentially as he listened to the closing summation. Though West had not attended the trial every day, he thought Sawyer would easily gain a conviction, based upon the little he had seen that day and Sawyer's irrefutable restatement of the facts in his closing. Late the next day, the jury had returned with a guilty verdict, and the defendant was sentenced to thirty years in prison, with no chance of parole.

That's what surprised him, Sawyer wanting to come back to Hawthorne. His cousin was a rising star in the Dallas District Attorney's office. Then again, it might be similar circumstances to his own. Sawyer may have achieved everything he wanted. Or perhaps he had burned out because of the heavy case load placed upon him. Maybe they would talk about it. Maybe they wouldn't. He was used to guys only conversing in surface talk. That's what Dr. Linda called it. West talked mostly football with his teammates and coaches. Sometimes, they even ventured into discussing another sports, but they never seemed to talk about the nitty-gritty. That was something Dr. Linda encouraged. Hopefully, West could take her lessons to heart and get to know Sawyer—and other people—on more than a surface level.

Sawyer entered the room, his hair damp, and West guessed he had recently showered.

"Hey, West. Your two guys were here. Brought in all your boxes. They even helped me bring some stuff in."

"Was it a productive day, Counselor?"

"I just got home a few minutes ago from my new office. That's where a bulk of my things went. All my law books. Copies of old case files for reference. Hung a few prints to cheer the place up. I'll use all of Isaiah's furniture for now. It's a little worn out but still serviceable. My next step is to start going through his case files and get up to speed on current ones so I can be informed as I take over the practice and hopefully drum up new business. I don't think he left a lot of loose ends. Frankly, I'm ready for a slower pace."

"You're looking at a new teacher and coach at Hawthorne High School," West shared, a tinge of pride evident in his voice. "Coach Markham offered me a position as his quarterbacks and receivers coach next year."

His cousin's face lit up. "Fantastic, West! I'm really happy for you. I know what Coach Markham meant to you."

He held up the thick playbook. "I need to start familiarizing myself with this. Coach said he'd be in touch, but I can come to a few practices. Probably the spring game next month, too. It's important to keep everything above board, though."

Sawyer nodded. "UIL rules. I know them well."

West set down the playbook on the coffee table, and the two cousins took a seat, catching up with one another. Sawyer told West about his final case as an ADA and then said, "I think we might be in the same position. We've both reached a certain age and were at the top of our game. But that wasn't enough, was it?"

"I agree. I had my health. I'm lucky I wasn't concussion prone. I came back from my knee injury, but that cloud was always hanging over me, thinking what if it happened again. And that next time it might be career-ending and physically life-altering." He hesitated. "Then again, you know about that."

Sawyer had been an outstanding basketball player in high

school and had won a scholarship to play at the University of North Texas. A knee injury ended his college career.

"Yes, I wasn't able to walk away from the game. The game left me behind. That's okay. I wasn't good enough to turn pro. UNT had to leave me on scholarship since I'd been injured on their watch, so at least my undergrad was paid for. I had some financial assistance at Baylor Law School, but I racked up my fair share of loans. I'll still be paying them off for a while."

West frowned. "You graduated from law school years ago, Sawyer."

His cousin shrugged. "If I would have gone into corporate law, they would easily be paid off by now, but public servants just don't earn enough, Cuz."

"Let me pay the balance," he said quietly.

Shock filled Sawyer's face. "Hell to the no. It's my debt to carry. Why should you do that?"

"Because I can. Because you're family. You need to start in Hawthorne with a clean slate, Sawyer. I can make that happen. I made great money during my playing days, and I've invested wisely. I don't have to work for a living. You've never asked anything of me. Please, let me do this for you. I want to."

"I'll have to think about it, West. That's a big ask. A big give, as well."

He grinned shamelessly. "Well, I *would* expect to have free legal advice and representation for the rest of my life. You know, defending me for my speeding tickets, for example."

"Are you still driving that fancy Jag? If so, it's a cop magnet."

"I thought on the drive up here that I needed to trade it in. For a truck."

"Now, you're talking. A small-town coach driving his Ford pickup truck." Sawyer paused. "Is this truly the life you envision for yourself, West? You've lived high on the hog for over a decade now."

Kelby had asked him the same question. Determination filled him as he responded, "It's exactly what I want. That life off the playing field wasn't truly me. I want what's real, Sawyer, and I can find that here in Hawthorne. I'll be in a position where I can make a difference in the lives of others. Hopefully, I can find someone who will put up with me and marry her. Raise a family together."

His cell rang, which was unique in itself. People only texted West, and very few had this number beyond his immediate family and Jace. He pulled the phone from his pocket and glanced at the screen.

Looking at Sawyer, he said, "It's Chance Blackstone."

CHAPTER
Eight

Kelby nodded encouragingly as her dad took the last bite of his chocolate pudding, saying, "You did a really good job, Dad."

For a moment, their gazes met, and she saw a glimpse of the father she had known her entire life. Then it was gone. She had experienced a few of these fleeting moments over the last several days, but it seemed to her as if her dad were slipping away. Despite numerous therapy sessions each day, Big Jim Blackstone had not made any improvement. He also had not spoken once since his stroke occurred.

As he set down the spoon, she smiled brightly at him. "It's just going to take some time, Dad. You know anything worth it never comes easy. You've told Chance and me that our entire lives."

He merely stared back at her. His eyes misted for a moment, and she took his hand.

Chance entered the room. "Okay, Dad. I got everything settled with your occupational therapist." He took a seat on the opposite side of where Kelby was and glanced at the tray. "Looks like you had a good dinner. Except for the peas."

"He enjoyed the pudding cup the best," she said. "As always, Dad is not a fan of English peas." She glanced back at him. "Even though you insisted the two of us finish every last one on our plates."

Her brother laughed. "I used to slip them into my hand and feed the dog," he admitted. "I don't know why Tammy insisted on serving them, knowing Dad didn't eat them."

"Tammy was always trying to get us to broaden our tastes. I was such a Daddy's girl. If he ate salad, so would I. If he gobbled up his carrots, I did, too." She smiled. "You never would eat any kind of fish, Dad, so neither did I. Then in college, I had a guy make dinner for me at his apartment my sophomore year. He served baked salmon and was so proud of the meal he'd prepared for us. I didn't know if I'd make it through the meal, much less the date. Then I took a bite—and fell in love with salmon. I eat a lot of seafood now." She smoothed her dad's hair. "You don't know what you're missing."

"So, your tastes for fish remained, but the guy was history?" Chance asked. "Because I can't see Bax ever cooking you anything."

The mention of her ex caused her stomach to go queasy. "We didn't start dating until the beginning of junior year," she said lightly. "And no, Bax never lifted a finger in the kitchen."

Chance gave her a sympathetic look. "Sorry I brought him up. Especially with what just happened to him."

Kelby had told her brother about Bax's murder, just to prepare him in case someone asked him about it. "I'd appreciate if you didn't mention him again."

"Got it." He looked at their dad. "Guess Kelby and I will

head home. I'll see you tomorrow night, Dad." Chance squeezed his father's hand and released it.

Kelby brushed a kiss on his brow. "I'll be back for lunch, Dad. See you then. Work hard at therapy tomorrow."

They left the rehab center and climbed into Chance's pickup. Kelby's thoughts turned to West, and she decided to tell her brother she had seen him.

"West Sutherland is back in Hawthorne," she said. "I saw him this afternoon. Told him about Dad's stroke."

"I hope we can get together and catch up. I sent him a text after his big retirement announcement. He thanked me and said he'd see me soon."

"You may be seeing a lot more of him than you think." She paused. "Coach Markham offered him a coaching position for next year, and West accepted."

"Wait. You're telling me that West will be moving back to Hawthorne?" Chance asked, excitement in his voice. "That's pretty crazy to think he'd come back and live here after all he's seen and done."

He reached for his cell, which was sitting in the cupholder. Handing it to her, he said, "Call him for me."

Kelby did as he asked, handing Chance the phone as it started to ring.

"Hey, buddy. Long time no see. Kelby just told me you were back in town. For good. Yeah. Uh-huh. She and I are driving back from seeing Dad. Hey, would you like to grab a bite? Maybe Sonny's Sports Bar? He's moved to a bigger place. It's about two blocks off the square. Yeah. Sure. It'll be good to see him. Okay. Be there in thirty. Bye."

Chance placed his phone in the cupholder again. "We're meeting West and Sawyer at Sonny's in half an hour."

"We? No, just drop me back at the ranch," she said quickly. "That way, you guys can reminisce as you always do."

"No, West specifically said to bring you. Besides, taking you to the ranch and then doubling back would be out of the way. Besides, you need to eat."

Knowing she wouldn't win this battle, she said, "I'd better text Tammy and let her know we won't be home for dinner."

"It was just leftover enchiladas tonight. Remember, she has book club tonight. That's why she made a big batch last night, so we could simply heat things up."

Kelby worried seeing West again would cause her to want to heat things up between the two of them. She couldn't allow that. It would be a mistake to get involved with him.

Even though she badly wanted to do so.

She had never forgotten the single kiss they'd shared. She'd kissed a handful of guys during college, finally settling into a relationship with Bax. While she had been physically attracted to her ex-husband and they had enjoyed a healthy sex life until his first serious football injury, his kisses had never stacked up to the one she had shared with West.

Was the universe telling her something, placing West and her in the same place again after fourteen years apart? She had never been a believer in fate or coincidence. People made choices on their own. Yet the fact both she and West were now in Hawthorne at the same time, neither involved in a relationship, gnawed at her.

Maybe one kiss. Just to prove it wasn't as big a deal as she remembered. Memory was a funny thing. It could play tricks on you. Kissing West once might free her from thinking how special he was. He was just another guy. Plus, she had no plans to stay in Hawthorne once her dad came back to the ranch and was settled into a routine with a caregiver. She needed to find a job. Dallas was home now. Not Hawthorne, where West would be settling down.

Kelby desperately wanted to pull down the visor and look

in the mirror. If she did, though, Chance might pick up on it. She had never told him that she and West had kissed, and her gut told her West had never shared that with his best friend. She took a deep breath, letting it out slowly. Her appearance was fine. She was just going to have a casual meal with an old friend. It would also be good to see Sawyer, her best friend's brother. In fact, she would pay for Sawyer's meal since he'd helped her with her negotiation with Wyndham & Warren. Sawyer had teased about sending her a bill, something he had yet to do. She would insist upon it tonight.

They reached the outskirts of Hawthorne, and a lump formed in her throat. Images of the past flooded her, the happy days of her childhood. Riding horses. Roasting marshmallows. Swimming at the lake. Leading cheers on Friday nights for the Hawks. Whether he realized it or not, West was woven into many of those childhood memories.

They pulled into the parking lot of Sonny's, which was about half-full. She spied the sleek Jaguar which West had gotten into after leaving Burger Heaven. Butterflies beat in her belly, causing nerves to ripple through her. She couldn't help it as anticipation filled her at seeing him again.

Chance held the door for her as they entered the sports bar. Sawyer spied them and waved. Her heart beating fast, she walked toward the booth. Should she sit next to West? Or Sawyer? Such little decisions like this reminded her of high school.

Sawyer slid from the booth, wrapping his arms about her. "Good to see you, Kelby." He released her. "I'm sorry to hear about Big Jim."

"Thanks. I've got a beef to pick with you, Montgomery. Where's that big bill you promised to send me?"

He laughed. "Must've gotten lost in the mail."

She frowned. "I mean it, Sawyer. You went to bat for me at

a critical time. And now that you're opening a practice here in Hawthorne, I expect an invoice. By snail mail or email. Please send it."

"Okay," he said reluctantly. "But no rush in paying it."

Kelby turned and saw that West had also climbed from the booth, greeting Chance. Her brother went to shake hands with Sawyer, and West looked at her.

Gesturing, he said, "Want to slide in first?"

Decision obviously made.

She sat on the bench and scooted over, West slipping in beside her. She caught his scent again and chastised herself for wanting to lean into him and sniff his neck.

"I'm glad you and Chance could meet us for dinner," he said quietly. "I'm open to being friends. If you are," he added, hesitation in his voice. "I acknowledge that I was a real jerk before, Kelby. I apologize for that. That isn't really who I am."

Smiling encouragingly, she said, "We've known one another forever. Being friends is part of that."

He relaxed visibly. "Good to know." Looking to Chance, he said, "Glad you could grab dinner with us."

"I'm starved," Chance declared. "We've been going to see Dad each evening around suppertime, making sure he's eating okay. Checking in with the nurses and therapists on staff."

"How is he doing?" West asked.

"Kelby knows more about that. She's been with him a lot during his therapy sessions at the hospital, and she goes to the rehab facility twice a day."

A server came and took the drink orders, and they opened their menus, looking over the options. Then she told them about the lack of progress she was seeing.

"Dr. Brock told us that Dad's personality may have changed with the stroke. It affects each patient differently. He's always been such a go-getter. The bigger the challenge, the harder he would push. This is different, though. I know everyday tasks are difficult for him now. I've watched him try to wrap his fingers around a pen and sign his name. I'll admit that it hurt to witness it, Dad slowly and painstakingly forming each letter. It took about three minutes for him to write his compete signature."

"That's a fine motor skill," West said. "Those may take longer for him to reclaim. How is he doing on other things, like combing his hair or getting dressed?"

She shook her head. "Not good. The right side of his body is paralyzed. Dr. Brock had thought he might regain feeling and motion, but that hasn't happened. And since it hasn't, it probably won't return this late in the game."

"That's rough," Sawyer said sympathetically. "Big Jim has always been bigger than life. He must really be down."

"Once he leaves rehab, we'll need to hire fulltime help," Chance said. "While Kelby has been doing so much for him, he is a big guy and hard to handle."

The thought of a nurse always being present the rest of her dad's life disheartened her, yet she couldn't see any other outcome. During his time in the hospital, Kelby had to ask for help from the nursing staff when she bathed or dressed him. With him in rehab now, they were handling those tasks. So much would need to be done at the ranch before he came home. She couldn't believe she hadn't thought of it until just now. A ramp leading up to the front steps would need to be erected so that they could push his wheelchair up it. Some doorways would need to be enlarged. The downstairs full bath would need to be totally reconfigured so that he could be rolled into the shower. His upstairs bedroom would need to shift to a room on the first floor.

All this seemed overwhelming, and Kelby couldn't believe she hadn't already begun planning for Dad's return home.

She'd always been so organized, but seeing her dad weak as a kitten had affected her, as well.

West's hand slipped around hers under the table, as if he sensed her distress. She looked at him, but he merely nodded, looking straight ahead. The server returned and took their orders, and Chance changed the subject, turning the conversation to West's new job. Still, his hand covered hers, bringing her warmth and reassurance that everything was going to be all right.

West detailed his interview with Coach Markham, speaking about his great respect for his former coach.

"Coach Markham knows X's and O's better than any other coach I've ever had," he explained. "I had some great coaches in both college and the NFL, and sometimes a suggestion I would make, they jumped all over. And you know what? It would usually be something I learned from Coach Markham. He's an offensive genius. He taught me the skills every quarterback needs to have. How to read a defense. Everything about throwing mechanics. The importance of studying game film. But beyond that, he taught me how to be a leader."

He grinned. "It also didn't hurt that he was my Sunday School teacher back in middle school. I got my share of life lessons on that front, too. I look at him as a second dad."

Their food arrived, typical sports bar fare, and she dug into her fajita nachos. West stole one, a typical move on his part, but she slipped a few fries off his plate in retaliation. She found herself relaxing in his presence.

And missing his hand holding hers.

Kelby listened as the three men began talking specifics about plays. Having grown up around them and loving sports, she was able to contribute to the conversation with ease. She recalled other cheerleaders wouldn't have a clue what was going on during a play. They would look to Darby or her for their reactions and take their cues accordingly.

Talk turned to Sawyer's move to Hawthorne when Sonny Smith stopped by their table to say hi. He had quarterbacked the Hawks a decade before West had played on the varsity and broke all the records Sonny had held, from number of touchdowns thrown to number of completions in a season.

"Dad told me you've taken over his office," Sonny said to Sawyer. "My advice to you? Don't let him back in the door."

Sawyer laughed. "He's already threatened to stop by once a week and give me his sage advice. I appreciate Isaiah selling the practice to me. The office space, as well. Of course, I don't own it outright just yet. I'll be paying Isaiah monthly until I own the space." He cut his eyes to West and said an emphatic, "No."

Kelby wondered what that was about when West merely chuckled.

"Your dad will find things to fill his time," Sawyer continued. "Fishing alone should keep him occupied."

Sonny nodded. "Dad has always loved to fish. He's going to volunteer at one of the elementary schools. Reading to kids. And he's working on some kind of mentoring program with a teacher at the high school. He's also got his weekly poker game. Says he wants to travel some. I'm hoping he'll be able to stay busy and active."

The owner wished them a good night and left. West handed the server his credit card, instructing him to use it to pay the entire bill.

"I was going to pay for Sawyer's dinner," Kelby protested. "As part of my payment due for him helping me with my separation from Wyndham & Warren."

"Another time," West said. "I'd like to go see Big Jim. Could I tag along tomorrow?"

"Go at lunch with Kelby," Chance suggested. "She's said

Dad is a little bit perkier than he is at the end of his day." He laughed. "Kind of like us after two-a-days. Wiped out."

West looked to her, and she saw the uncertainty in those turquoise blue eyes. "Would that be okay? I could pick you up."

"How can I resist riding in a sports car worth more than I make in a year?" she teased playfully.

Kelby told him what time to be at the ranch, and they left the sports bar. West passed along his address to Chance and her, telling them that he and Sawyer wanted to have a little party soon in order to let others know they were back in Hawthorne.

"We do?" Sawyer asked. "Oh, I guess we do."

They all laughed, and West asked Kelby for her number.

"I'll text you when I'm on my way tomorrow," he told her.

She and Chance returned to his truck, and her brother did not hide his enthusiasm.

"West is the same as always," he said. "I've only seen him a handful of times over the years, but he hasn't gotten the big head. He's just as down-to-earth as always. I hope he's going to be happy living in Hawthorne again. I know I'm glad to have my best friend here again."

"It's also nice to have Sawyer back in town," she said. "Now, if I could only talk his sister into coming here, that would be ideal."

Chance glanced at her. "Are you thinking about staying, Kel?"

She shrugged. "Maybe. Dad is going to need a lot of help, and I—"

He shook his head. "Don't think about Dad. Think about yourself. I don't want you tied to Dad and the ranch, trying to be his full-time caregiver. I don't want that for you, and neither would he. What I do want to know is what you're thinking about doing, work-wise."

"The settlement Sawyer negotiated allows me to take my time," she began. "But I've begun toying with the idea of maybe starting my own business."

"Doing what?"

"The same as I've been doing. Social branding. Handling social media accounts for others, be they individuals or businesses. In fact, it was West who gave me the idea that I should start my own business. If I do, I could work from anywhere. Including the ranch."

"Huh."

They rode in silence a few minutes, and then he asked, "Would you truly want to live in Hawthorne again? I mean, you've lived in a lot of big cities. I know you were happy in Dallas."

"I was happy there. The happiest I'd been since my college days. I enjoyed my job, and I got to see some good friends. I could still drive into Dallas and stay a couple of days each month. Maybe meet with clients, as well as friends. What I need to do is really think things through. Come up with a business plan and a way to attract people."

"Maybe West could help you with that," Chance said.

Her hackles went up. "I don't need West Sutherland drumming up business for me."

"I didn't mean that. It's just that he's got a lot of connections in a lot of different places. We've chatted briefly over the years, and West has invested in all kinds of things. He might be able to point you in the right direction."

"Then I might talk with him about it," she mused.

"I think it's nice he wants to go see Dad."

"West and Dad always got along. Dad treated West like another son."

They arrived at the ranch, and Kelby went to her room. She picked up her tablet and began jotting down random ideas, from the services she might offer to names she could use for her company. The more she thought about it, the more excited she became. So many people worked remotely these days. If she could build a clientele, working from the ranch while helping to care for Dad, that would be ideal. It would also allow her to stay in Hawthorne.

And see if anything still might be between West and her.

CHAPTER
Nine

"Hey, Doc," West said as Dr. Linda's image appeared on his phone's screen. "You get my T-shirt? You know, the one which reads *Dallas Cowboys, Super Bowl Champions*. I wanted to make sure you had something new added to your wardrobe besides a pathetic Packers shirt."

She pursed her lips, trying not to laugh. "I did indeed receive it in the mail. I bunched it up and placed it in my chihuahua's pet bed. Tiki loves it."

He roared with laughter. "Perfect way to start a session." Then he grew serious. "I have a lot to unpack today."

"Then let's get started. What do you want to talk about first?"

"Something that I don't want to talk about, so I'm going to tell you about other things before we get to that. First, I got the job at the high school. I interviewed yesterday with Coach Markham. He has an assistant coach moving on to an administration job, so a slot on his staff was already open. He texted me first thing this morning to go over to the admin building and sign my contract. Got that done, so the job is officially mine."

"Tell me about how it makes you feel, going back to work with a man you respect so much."

"I'm excited. A little nervous. I know how much Coach influenced my life, and I want to do the same thing with today's young men. I'll have to temper my expectations, though. Not every player is going to be all-in, like I was. I was a sponge, soaking up everything Coach said. Every suggestion, I acted on. Every criticism, I took to heart. But I get that to some of these kids, it's just a sport they play. Not the be-all, end-all in life."

"What about working under your mentor?" she prodded.

"I don't want to let him down. Again, I know the Hawks won't win every game, but I'll be in charge of quarterbacks and receivers. It'll be great to work with receivers and a challenge to manage quarterbacks. I'm up for it, though. And I plan to keep learning from Coach Markham. That's something I want to pass along to my players. You never stop learning. It's a lifelong process. A person can always pick up new things. I was at the top of the food chain in football, Doc. These kids will know that. So if I tell them that *I'm* still learning, from Coach Markham and others around me, that may be the biggest lesson I can impart."

Dr. Linda smiled. "I haven't heard you this excited in a long time, West. That's a really good thing."

"It's good to be back in Hawthorne. No one ever took the small-town out of me. I may have appeared to be city slick, but inside? I'm pure Hawthorne, through and through."

"Do you know what your duties will be beyond coaching?"

"I'll be teaching Social Studies. I have what's called a composite, which means I'm certified to teach any subject in that area. History. Government. Geography. I'll have to meet with the department chair closer to the end of the year before I'll know what my assignment will be. When creating the master schedule, they have to take into consideration who's left.

Retired or transferred to another school district. What class sizes are. I'll be prepared, whatever subject it is."

He reached for his water bottle and took a long swig.

"Okay, ready to talk about Kelby Blackstone." He paused. "Long story short is that she's my best friend's sister. I thought of her as another sister all those years growing up. Then we both wound up out of relationships the last couple of months during our senior year in high school. We went to things as friends. Prom. Parties. I kissed her once."

West shook his head. "It was ... magic."

Dr. Linda said, "What happened after the kiss?"

"We decided it would be foolish to do a long-distance relationship. We were headed to different universities. Football players don't get to come home on weekends. And she was a cheerleader, so same thing. You've got games. She also had tournaments to cheer at. We only saw one another a couple of times during college and none since we graduated."

When he paused, the therapist said, "Have you thought about Kelby over the years?"

"Yes and no. I never found the kind of connection I had with her with any other woman. She married. Divorced. I really didn't know where she was. Come to find out, she was in my backyard the past five years, working in Dallas. And I ran into her yesterday in Hawthorne."

He raked his hands through his hair. "Doc, all kinds of feelings flooded me when I saw her. She'd always been so easy to talk to, and I wound up opening up to her, just like I do you. I told her about my new job. How excited I was to come back to Hawthorne. How I'd sowed my wild oats but was ready to settle into marriage and start a family."

"Tell me what I'm hearing in your voice, West," she nudged.

"Hurt. A little anger. Basically, she told me we could try to be friends, but she didn't have anything to give me, as far as a relationship goes."

"You asked her out?"

"No. But I think she knew the conversation was heading that way." He shook his head. "She's a hot mess right now. Her dad just had a stroke, and she's worried sick about him. She also lost her job recently because the husband she divorced five years ago wound up in the news. He killed his bookie and then was shanked in jail."

"I read about that. Pretty awful. It seems he was troubled. An addict."

"Yes, that's why they divorced. I don't think Kelby harbored any feelings for him. They seemed to have ended on a pretty bitter note. But his murder spooked her very proper company, and they terminated her."

"I'm sure you can understand why Kelby would be reluctant to start up a relationship with you, West. The rug has been pulled out from under her. Her father is gravely ill. She's unemployed. And even if she didn't have feelings for her ex-husband, she did at one time. Hearing of him murdering someone and then being murdered himself has to cause her a great deal of conflict. She probably needs a good therapist now, not a former almost-flame trying to rekindle the spark with her."

"I know," he said, a little too harshly. "Sorry. I truly get why she wanted me to back off. But I saw her again last night. Chance, her brother, called. Had me meet them, along with my cousin, for dinner. I don't know, Doc. She gave off a different vibe. Like she might be receptive to at least seeing where things could go between us. In fact, I'm going with her in an hour to see her dad at the rehab center where he's recovering from his stroke."

"Read the cues we've discussed before, West. It's not only what a person says. It's what they do. Their demeanor. How they respond to you. Take it very, very slowly," she cautioned. "She might just need a friend and not a lover. Would you be willing to step up into that role?"

"Yes," he said firmly. "I do want to be her friend. I know things are tough for her now. They are for me, too, as I'm transitioning, but she's got a tougher row to hoe than I do. Then there's the fact that she won't stay in Hawthorne forever. Once Big Jim is better, she'll probably leave and look for another job."

"And you've told me you're tied to Hawthorne."

"For now and the future," he asserted. "It's where I want to be. With or without Kelby. So, what's your advice, Doc?"

"I think you've already laid out a good plan, West. You want to be her friend. You already know she has a lot on her plate and her emotional state is shaky. Be her friend. Don't push anything. You can't just think about yourself. You have to think about Kelby, too."

"Got it. Okay. I'm good." He glanced at his watch. "We're about out of time, so I'll sign off. Next week okay at this time?"

She reached for a pen and jotted something down. "Yes, that's perfect. In the meantime, if you need anything, you know you can contact my office."

"I do."

Dr. Linda smiled. "I'm proud of you, West. For taking a huge leap of faith by moving back to Hawthorne. For landing a job which I think will become more satisfying than your previous one, though it will pay a heck of a lot less. And for respecting Kelby's boundaries. You've come so far in the year we've been working together."

"I appreciate all you do for me," he said. "I mean that. It's not lip service."

"I know it's not. You've always been frank. You speak from your heart. You don't give false compliments."

"Okay. Give Tiki a pat and tell her to enjoy her new T-shirt."

"I'll do that. Bye, West."

He clicked out of FaceTime and set his phone down. Talking over things aloud with Dr. Linda always brought them into perspective for him. Yesterday, it had been all about him. How he was hurt that Kelby didn't leap into something with him. Telling his therapist all that Kelby was going through, however, let him see how fragile she was emotionally. That was not the way to start a relationship. He determined to keep things light and upbeat when in her company today.

An hour later, West texted Kelby that he was on his way. She texted back a thumbs up.

He was more nervous seeing her now than he'd ever been for any big game.

He reached the ranch in less than a quarter hour. His rental was on one side of Hawthorne, close to where the high school stood. The Blackstone Ranch was just north of town. Both cattle and horses were raised on the property, and he fondly recalled many days spent in the saddle or in what Big Jim called the Big House. The ranch had a large stable for horses, as well as several outbuildings for various use. A two-story bunkhouse housed all the ranch hands, though he recalled a few lived in town, maybe the ones who had families.

Once he reached the familiar turn, it seemed as if time had stopped. Everything looked exactly the same. West pulled up to the Big House, and Kelby came to her feet, leaving one of the rocking chairs sitting on the porch. She bounded down the stairs and opened the passenger's door.

As she got in, he said, "You moved so fast, I didn't even have a chance to get out and open the door for you."

"Not necessary," she told him, fastening her seat belt. "I

may not have West Sutherland's blazing speed running down a football field, but I do a little jogging to stay in shape."

"Which way?" he asked, taking the car back the way he'd come.

Kelby gave him directions and then reached to turn on the radio. He remembered she liked hearing music anytime she was in the car.

"Good, you have satellite radio. What I wouldn't have given to have that during our high school years."

She dialed around until she found a station she liked and then sat back.

"Thanks for wanting to go and see Dad. It will mean a lot to him. He was so proud of you, winning a scholarship and becoming an Aggie just like he was." She laughed. "Dad about disowned me when I told him I would be cheering for the Longhorns."

"You can't blame him. Bad blood between the Aggies and the Longhorns has existed since they first met on the football field in the 1890s."

"A game which UT won big," she retorted, flashing him a smile and a Hook 'em Horns sign."

"Fingers down, or you'll be walking home," he warned playfully.

They talked about Sawyer's new career in Hawthorne and what Darby was up to.

"I can't believe you girls have been friends for so long."

"Same as you and Chance."

West shrugged. "Chance will always be my closest friend, but I've been a lousy one to him for a long time. Guys don't stay in touch as much as girls do. I need to make things up to Chance."

"He's really happy you're home for good," she shared. "The

minute I told him that I'd seen you and that you would be living in Hawthorne, he couldn't call you fast enough."

That was a good feeling, one of the reasons West had wanted to come back to Hawthorne. Not just for football, but to be close to his parents and people like Chance.

"You going to see Darby anytime soon?" he asked.

"Being tied up with Dad right now, I don't feel right asking her to come to Hawthorne to visit me. But we stay in touch. We text all the time. I went to see her a couple of months ago, right after Thanksgiving."

They rode in companionable silence the rest of the way. West couldn't help but feel relaxed in Kelby's company. All the previous nerves had disappeared.

As he parked, she said, "It might be hard to do so, but try and watch your facial expression when you see Dad. He's already lost about twenty pounds or so. The right side of his face looks odd. His eye and mouth droop noticeably. And he hasn't spoken a word since Chance found him."

"Will he ever?"

"We don't know. Dr. Brock thought he would. There's still a lot we aren't sure of. Things we're learning every day. Just treat him normally if you can. Tell him what you've been up to."

"Will do."

They got out of the car and entered the facility, signing in at the reception desk in the visitor's log. Kelby took West to Big Jim's room, which was empty at the moment.

"He'll be here soon. He's got a therapy session that ends in a few minutes."

A worker came in with a tray and placed it on another table next to the bed. The meal itself was covered, but West saw a glass of iced tea, along with a plate containing a roll and pat of butter. Kelby thanked the worker and immediately dumped two packets of sugar into the glass, stirring thoroughly and placing a straw into it. She fluffed the pillows. Adjusted the blinds. Added fresh water to a vase of flowers sitting on a nightstand. By the time she finished tidying up the room, a nurse rolled Big Jim into the room.

"Hey, Dad. Look who came to see you. It's West Sutherland," she said brightly.

"Hey, Mr. Blackstone." He put a hand on Big Jim's shoulder and leaned close. "It's West. It's really good to see you."

"In the bed or chair, Miss Blackstone?" the worker asked.

"Let's do the chair since I brought company."

The worker wheeled Big Jim into the center of the room as Kelby moved the tray table in front of him. West brought two chairs over, placing one in front of Big Jim for himself and the other next to the wheelchair, expecting Kelby would help her father with his meal.

She lifted the cover from the food. "Hey, it's meatloaf. And mashed potatoes. Doesn't that look good, Dad?"

Big Jim had barely looked at West. He now stared down at the food. It was hard seeing such a powerful man brought down by illness.

West took a seat and talked through most of lunch, with Kelby encouraging her dad as he ate. He talked about the Cowboys' season since Big Jim had always been a football fan. Told him a few insider things that hadn't been reported in the press. Then he shared his news.

"I'm moving back to Hawthorne, Mr. Blackstone. Got a job coaching football and teaching at the high school. It just happened yesterday. I'm having dinner with my folks tonight. I know they're over the moon."

Big Jim grunted. Kelby's eyes widened. Then she smiled.

"I think Dad approves of that hiring."

After several more minutes, it looked as if Big Jim had finished, and Kelby asked, "Are you sure you don't want any more to eat, Dad?"

He glared at her, and she got the message.

"Okay then. Let me move the tray back. Do you need to use the restroom?"

Big Jim blinked once.

"That's a yes," she said. "Let me call for an aide."

"I can help," he offered.

"That's kind of you, West, but they know what they're doing."

She hit the call button, and a few minutes later, an aide appeared. He was taller than West and outweighed him by about thirty pounds. His jaw dropped as he spotted West.

"West Sutherland? My gosh, it *is* you!"

"Yes, I'm West." He shook hands with the aide. "Nice to meet you. I think Mr. Blackstone needs to go to the restroom."

The aide turned his attention to his patient. "Let's get you taken care of, Mr. B. Why, you didn't tell me you knew a famous football player. You should be ashamed of yourself, keeping secrets like that from me when I've told you all of mine."

He watched as the worker wheeled Big Jim to the bathroom and inside it, closing the door.

"It can take a bit of time," Kelby said, biting her lip.

"No worries. I'm in no rush. I have nowhere to be until six o'clock tonight. Coincidentally, Mom is making meatloaf and mashed potatoes."

"Both those are soft. Easier for Dad to eat. And I've told them no peas. That they'd just go to waste."

They waited in silence until the aide returned with Big Jim and said, "It's about time to get your daddy down to his next therapy session, Miss Blackstone."

"Right." She bent and kissed her father's brow. "Chance and I will be back to see you at dinner. Bye, Dad."

They waited until Big Jim had been rolled from the room before taking their leave. Kelby was quiet in the car. He could sense the tension rolling off her. He reached out and squeezed her shoulder.

"It's going to get better."

She sniffed. "It may not. It's so hard seeing him this way." She pulled a tissue from her purse and wiped her cheeks. "I keep wanting him to speak. Thinking the paralysis will magically be gone on the next day and that he'll be back to his usual self."

Blowing her nose, she slipped the tissue into her purse again. "And I know this sounds awful, but if he's not going to improve, I wish he'd just slip away."

She began to sob, and West could feel the pain radiating off her. He pulled off the road, onto the sparse grass, and cut the engine.

"It's okay to feel that way," he assured her. "Big Jim is the kind of guy who always took up all the air in the room when he entered it. He's a larger-than-life kind of guy. Seeing him like this has to be hard on you. You don't have to be strong all the time, Kelby."

West reached out, framing her face in his large hands. He swiped his thumbs across her damp cheeks, brushing away her tears, his own throat thickening with unshed ones.

Their gazes met, and she whispered, "Kiss me, West. Kiss me like you did before."

CHAPTER
Ten

Kelby found it hard to believe those words had just come out of her mouth.

But she didn't regret them one bit.

West seemed surprised for a moment, and then his head moved toward hers. She closed her eyes, waiting to see if what had been between them once before might ignite again.

The kiss was sweet. Tender. It was comforting, one meant to reassure her that everything was going to be all right in the long run. But it was not the kiss she had asked for. Not by a long shot. She gripped his wrists with her fingers and pulled his hands from her face, lowering them.

West looked at her, obviously confused. "I'm sorry. That was wrong of me to take advantage of you like that. You're really vulnerable now, Kelby. I should have never kissed you."

"I asked you to kiss me," she insisted. "It was a nice kiss, but I was expecting one to knock my socks off." She hesitated. "Like the one we shared before," she added softly.

"I don't think we need to go there."

"Let me be the judge of that," she told him, determination

filling her. "I tried not to think about you for almost fifteen years, West. For the most part, I succeeded. I buried all thoughts of that kiss between us." Her gaze met his. "Since I was eighteen years old, I've never had a kiss like the one we shared that day. I want to see if there's still anything between us."

Kelby licked her lips. "And pursue it if there is."

Her hand moved to his nape, pulling him down to her. Their lips touched, pressing against each other's. Every fiber of her being was aware of him. The feel of his sensual lips. The hint of mint on his breath. His clean, masculine scent. Her heart crashing against her ribs painfully.

West didn't rush things between them. He started slowly, just as he had that first time so long ago.

And just as before, the kiss caught fire.

Kelby opened to him, and he accepted her invitation, his tongue easing inside her mouth, stroking her own. Energy crackled in the air as their tongues began warring, things heating up fast. She felt her blood heat, feeling the fever sweep through her. *This* is what she had wondered about. Hoped for. She tried to move closer to him, but the console was in her way. She heard his own low growl of frustration as he broke the kiss. Her hand still cradled his nape as their foreheads rested against one another's.

"I guess a sports car isn't the best place to try and kiss you." He lifted his head, and she saw his turquoise eyes had gone an even deeper bluish green, desire changing them. "Would you like to come back to my rental?" he asked huskily. "Just to finish the kiss. Nothing else."

She sensed West would be a gentleman and keep his word, so she whispered, "Yes."

They broke apart. Immediately, he said, "Uh-oh. We have company."

Looking over her shoulder, Kelby saw a deputy's cruiser pulling in behind them.

"Let me handle it," he told her. "We'll be fine."

She grinned at him. "Something tells me that you've been in a situation with the law before, and it turned out in your favor."

"Well, there may have been a time or two where a speeding ticket was on the table. That is, until the issuing officer saw who I was, and I managed to get off with a warning."

West rolled down his window, placing both hands on the steering wheel in plain sight.

"Hello, Officer," he said pleasantly as the deputy reached them and looked inside the vehicle.

"Is there a ..." The law officer's voice trailed off, and then he exclaimed, "Oh, my gosh! You're West Sutherland. West Sutherland! Are you in trouble, Sir?"

"Not a bit, Deputy Jackson. I just got an important phone call and decided to pull off to the side of the road and take it. I thought it was better to do so instead of only half-concentrating on my driving."

West's answer, combined with him using the lawman's name, seemed to fluster the young deputy. "Well, all right. Good. Boy, West Sutherland. You were my idol growing up. I was in seventh grade when the Hawks went to the state championship game. You caught that forty-two-yard touchdown, and then in the last few seconds of the game, you pulled in that Hail, Mary from the quarterback. Ran sixty-seven yards for a touchdown. Man, I was crying in the stands. I was so proud to be from Hawthorne that day."

"Hey, the offense only got the chance to get the ball back that final time because Chance Blackstone intercepted a pass and gave our offense a last chance at victory."

Kelby had listened to this kind of talk her entire life. Her brother and West. Bax and his teammates. They loved to relive games in great detail. Where women filed away the names of shades of lipsticks and where to pick up bargains on shoes, men knew sports stats like the back of their hands and shared them with one another with ease.

"Did you play any ball for the Hawks?" West asked pleasantly.

"I did, Mr. Sutherland. I was a defensive tackle. We didn't quite have the glory days of your teams, but we made it to the quarter finals my sophomore year and the semifinals my senior year. Coach Markham is a good man and a great coach."

"I agree," West said easily. "In fact, I think so much of Coach that he's going to be my new boss."

The deputy's eyes widened. "What? You're going to coach the Hawks?"

"I'll be an assistant coach for next year's squad," West said proudly, and Kelby knew he would be just as happy doing that as he had been playing in Super Bowls for the Cowboys.

A part of the barrier she had erected to keep men out seemed to invisibly crumble.

"Well, if you're okay, it looks like your call has ended, Mr. Sutherland, so you might want to get on the road again."

"I'll do so, Deputy Jackson. Thanks for stopping to see if we needed any help." Then West asked, "Would you like a selfie together?"

The young deputy grinned from ear-to-ear. "If you don't mind, sir."

"Make it West in the future."

Jackson's smile grew even wider. "I'd be happy to, West."

"Let me take it for you," Kelby offered, getting out of the Jaguar.

"How about in front of your squad car?" West suggested.

The officer started to hand his cell phone to Kelby, but she waved him away, pulling out her own.

"I've got it. Move together now."

Deputy Jackson stood proudly next to West. She took several shots, both vertically and horizontally, and then zoomed in for a couple of closer shots.

Lowering her phone, she said, "I'll text these to West and you. He'll probably want to put them up on his Insta."

Jackson looked shocked. "You'd do that?"

"I'd be happy to, Deputy Jackson. I've always been a big supporter of law enforcement."

Kelby handed Deputy Jackson her cell, asking him to input his number so she could send him the pictures. As he typed, she asked, "What's your handle? He can tag you."

The deputy shared it, and West shook hands with him. "Good meeting you, Deputy."

"It was an honor meeting you, West," enthusiastically pumping his hand. "And it'll be great to have you on the side-lines come Friday nights this fall."

They returned to West's car, and he opened the door for Kelby before going around to the driver's side and climbing behind the wheel. He started the car and gave a wave, signaling to move back onto the two-lane road.

"Thank you for not accepting his phone for the pictures," West told her. "I hardly ever give out my number. Not that I think the good deputy would abuse it if he had it, but I appreciate you using your number to text him from."

"I figured as much. You realize now that everyone in Hawthorne and miles beyond will know about your coaching job after your encounter with Deputy Jackson."

"I don't mind a bit. I'm excited about it. I'll be proud to be a part of Coach Markham's staff."

"Is it going to be hard for you, West? Adjusting to civilian life in a small town?"

"I had wondered a little bit about that myself. Dallas Cowboys are treated like gods in the city. I've told you, though, that I'm looking for a different kind of life. Besides, I'm thrashing it all out with my therapist. She's helping me to lay a strong foundation for the future."

"You have a therapist?"

"You sound surprised. Therapy isn't just for people who have massive problems, Kelby. It's a great place to work out little things. To learn about yourself. Even about others."

"How long have you been in therapy?" she asked.

"I started last year after my ACL injury. I knew I had the tools and personnel to help my body to heal, but sports is a mind game. The smallest thing can psych you out. I needed someone to bounce ideas off of, and Dr. Linda fit the bill. My mental health is just as important to me as my physical health."

Kelby found it very interesting that West had a therapist and had been open about sharing that fact. "You played this entire season. Starred in the Super Bowl. I really haven't kept up with football much, but I know you reached the pinnacle again. Did therapy help?"

"Sometimes, I feel as if Dr. Linda saved my life."

His words moved her. "Was she the one who recommended that you retire?"

"No, she's not like that at all. It's hard to get her to express her own opinion or make any kind of suggestions to me. She wants all that to originate with me. Did I talk over retirement with her? You bet I did. But it was more how I was going to announce it and what I would do once I did retire."

He grinned. "And I can't believe it, but I just recently found out that she's a Green Bay Packers fan."

"That's sacrilege," Kelby said teasingly. Then she grew serious. "I also have seen a therapist. When I was at my lowest, just before I filed for divorce, I sought out help. I'd already joined Al-Anon, trying to understand Bax's addiction and how I should handle it, but I needed an extra bit of help to give me the strength and courage to walk away from my marriage. I credit that therapist with helping me to realize that I could be brave and strong and make it on my own.

"When I landed the job and moved to Dallas, she gave me the name of one of her colleagues she'd gone to school with, and I saw him for the first two years I lived there. I still go in a couple of times a year, like a tune-up."

"Have you been recently?"

"No. Things happened too fast. I found out about Bax's arrest and Dad's stroke within a couple of hours of each event. I raced to the hospital, and then I got the call from Reginald, my boss, early the next morning. Chance was the one who suggested I call Sawyer to help me. That severance package got taken care of, and I've devoted myself to Dad night and day. It's only in the last couple of days that I've had to back off since the live-in rehab place didn't want me around all the time. It's fine for me to visit, but they believe Dad will make more progress in his therapy sessions if he attends them alone."

By now, they had reached his house, and he pulled the car next to the front curb.

"Do you still want to go in?" he asked quietly. "No obligation."

Determination filled her. "I think we owe each other at least one more decent attempt at a kiss."

He bounded out of the car. Kelby waited, sensing it was important to him to be a gentleman and assist her from the car. They went to the front door, and he opened it.

"It wasn't locked?" she asked.

West shrugged. "It's Hawthorne. You think after Sawyer

and I lived in Dallas all those years that we'd be more safety conscious, but it kinda feels good being back in a place where people respect your privacy and crime is low."

"I shouldn't be one to talk. We never lock doors at the ranch. I don't even know if any of us even have a key to the Big House anymore. It's so deep into the property, I guess we figure we don't need to keep one."

"Let me show you around. It won't take long. There's not much to see, but it fits our needs right now. Living room and kitchen, as you can see from the front door here. The place came furnished, which was nice. The realtor told us that's rare these days."

She saw a small table in the kitchen as he led her down the hallway.

"Sawyer's bedroom is on the right. On the left, this room wasn't furnished. I had told Sawyer since he insisted I take the primary bedroom that he could use this as his home office. He told me that he had an office on the square. If he needed to work, he'd go there. He wants to keep a separation between work and his personal life. So, it's empty for now."

They moved up the hall, and he said, "Only bathroom is here." He stopped at the end of the hall, staying in the doorway. "And my bedroom."

Kelby noticed he remained on the threshold and didn't move further into the room.

"It's nice. It'll be adequate for your needs for now."

"I'll want something more permanent down the road, but I didn't want to rush into anything. Besides, we were pretty lucky to even find this available. With the new hospital being built, my realtor told me it's going to be increasingly harder to find housing in Hawthorne unless someone starts building it. She also mentioned that the hospital will bring a lot of jobs to Hawthorne."

West waited, and she realized that he wanted them to move back down the hallway to the living room. She did so, her pulse elevated now, knowing they would be sharing another kiss soon.

She liked that West had been open with her, sharing that he had seen a therapist. That gave them something in common. They had gone through different kinds of trauma, and both had been smart enough to seek professional help.

As they took a seat on the couch, Kelby asked, "Are you driving back to Dallas for your therapy sessions?"

"No, I usually FaceTime those. I saw Dr. Linda in person all last winter and spring. Then the team left for training camp, so we moved to FaceTime sessions. With me practicing and spending long hours watching film, as well as being on the road, in-person therapy wasn't going to happen, and I was definitely committed to continuing it. I still am. I had my weekly session with Dr. Linda this morning." He hesitated. "We even talked some about you."

"You did?"

Kelby knew that the fact that West had brought her up to Dr. Linda meant something. Having been in therapy herself, she knew patients didn't waste time on the trivial. If the relationship between patient and therapist was right, as it seemed in West's case, then talking about her to Dr. Linda was very significant.

West nodded. "I told her how we had been pretty darn mature for kids of eighteen and had decided not to act on the kiss we shared."

"Well, we both knew we were going different places, and there would be no time for a long-distance relationship." She smiled. "We did have our heads on pretty well back then. What else did you talk about with Dr. Linda? If you feel comfortable telling me," she added.

"How much I still like you. How vulnerable you are now, with all the stuff that's been dumped on you. That's why I think you were right to say we should just try to be friends, Kelby."

Disappointment flooded her, but through therapy, she had learned to speak up for herself.

"I may be fragile now, West, but my core is strong. I know I decided to push you away yesterday, but that's only because I was seeing West Sutherland, recent NFL player. The league left a bad taste in my mouth. I thought there was so much more they could've done to help Bax instead of letting him slip away. For a moment, I was associating you with Bax—and all the hurt I had gone through with him."

She reached for his hand, threading her fingers through his.

"I had gotten to where I didn't trust my gut because it had led me to Bax. Kept me with him far too long. I know now, though, that I *am* a strong person. I am in control of my future. No one else has the key to my destiny but me. I can also see that you're more than some ex-pro football player. You have more depth than Bax ever did."

Squeezing his hand, she added, "I want to kiss you, West. I want to see if there's anything still between us. One way or the other, I think this kiss will resolve a lot of things left unsaid. From the past—until now."

His free hand cupped her cheek, and Kelby leaned into it, feeling safe with this man. Then his mouth met hers.

The kiss started gentle, but the sizzle was there. This time, West wasn't trying to comfort her. Instead, he was giving them a chance, via the kiss.

Before she knew it, he had pulled her into his lap, his strong arms enveloping her. She wrapped her arms around his neck, pressing her body against his. His tongue glided back and forth across her bottom lip, teasing her, sending chills running along her spine. Then the tip of his tongue outlined the shape of her mouth, causing a fire to light within her.

She opened to him, and he greedily took from her. One arm anchored her, wrapped around her back, even as his hand pushed into her hair, finding her nape, holding her steady. Her heart began to speed up, racing like a galloping horse as he explored her mouth. She tasted mint and recalled how he loved to chew gum, often getting in trouble with teachers who made him spit it out every day.

The kiss was all fire now, and she fought him for control of it. She wanted to tear off her clothes—and his—but kept her head. Eventually, he gentled the kiss, then broke it. His lips grazed her cheek. She wanted more from him. Much, much more.

But this had been a wonderful start.

They both breathed heavily as their gazes met. His crooked smile tugged at her heartstrings.

"How was that, Kelby?" he asked, his voice low and rough.

"Really, really good," she replied. "Enough to make me want to set friendship aside and explore more with you."

He frowned slightly, and she asked, "What's wrong?"

"I don't know if I can do temporary with you," he admitted. "My heart is already asking more than it should." He brushed a soft kiss on her lips. "I told you that I'm ready for a new life. One with a woman I love. Kids. A dog and cat and guinea pig and whatever else we add to the mix. Once Big Jim has recovered, you'll be gone." He swallowed hard. "I don't think I could take that."

Regret filled his turquoise eyes. "Much as I want to start something with you and see where it goes, I think I'm going to have to pass."

She framed his face in her hands. "I'm feeling a bit Dorothy-ish myself, as in there's no place like home. I don't know how long Dad's recovery is going to be, but the idea of working remotely here in Hawthorne appeals to me. I'm not certain what I'll want to do. I toyed with some ideas last night, but my gut is telling me I need to stay in Hawthorne. To give myself the best chance at happiness."

Kelby kissed him tenderly. "And to take a chance with you, West." Tears misted her eyes, as she asked, "So, what do you think? Do you want to risk both our hearts—and see where this goes?"

West studied her a long moment before speaking. "If you can keep an open mind, Kelby, and really think about staying in Hawthorne, then I'm all in."

CHAPTER
Eleven

West had spent the day learning all he could about the Hawks' playbook. He recognized several plays he had run during his days as the high school team's quarterback, as well as new ones. It was good to see that Coach Markham had stuck with the tried and true and yet continued to stretch himself as a coach.

He took a break for lunch, making himself a quick sandwich, and called his mom.

"Hey, Mom."

"Hello, West. I can't wait to see you at dinner tonight."

"That's what I'm calling about. Would you mind if Kelby Blackstone joined us?"

"I sense a story here. I'd heard Kelby was back in town because of her father's stroke."

"Yes, she's been spending a lot of time with Big Jim. We connected, too."

"I always liked her, West. I was disappointed when nothing happened between the two of you in high school."

"We knew we were headed in different directions, Mom." He paused. "But we're both back in Hawthorne now and want to figure out if there's still something between us."

"I see."

Those two words seemed to speak volumes to him. "So, would it be okay for Kelby to come to dinner tonight with me?"

"Absolutely, honey."

"Now the big ask. Could we move dinner to six-thirty instead of six?"

Meg Sutherland chuckled. "My goodness. I'm happy to push it back half an hour."

"It's just that Kelby and Chance go visit Big Jim at five when he has his dinner at the rehab center," West explained. "I want to make sure she can see her dad and have time to drive back to Hawthorne. I know Dad likes supper on the table at six and *Jeopardy* on at six-thirty."

His dad recorded the game show every night and then watched it after dinner, being able to run through commercials since it aired while he ate dinner.

"*Jeopardy* can wait. It was going to anyway because I know we have a thousand questions to ask you about your new job."

"Thanks, Mom. I'll let you go. See you tonight."

West texted Kelby that dinner would be at six-thirty. She replied and said she would simply meet him at his parents' house to save time. He went back to the playbook for the next several hours and felt he had down everything. He'd always been a quick study when it came to analyzing football plays. Having played at both the college and pro levels, where schemes were highly complicated, it was much simpler to master a high school playbook. He was supposed to go to practice tomorrow afternoon, meeting the coaching staff first and then the players. Now, he felt prepared. No matter what Coach

Markham said, West believed there would be some resentment from a few coaches, with him stepping in and moving up to be number two on the coaching staff.

He went for a run, wanting to clear his head. He would need to get into a workout schedule. Everything he had done in the offseason had always been geared to making certain he was in the best condition possible before leaving for training camp. That would be a thing of the past. West wanted to stay in shape, not only because it was important to him to keep up with his physical and mental health, but he also wanted to be a good example to his players and students.

After a quick shower, he dressed and found Sawyer had arrived home. He told his cousin where he was going and then left, driving to his childhood home. Joe Sutherland had kept the same house he'd bought when he was a teacher and coach at Hawthorne High School. He'd worked his way up to principal and was now the school district's superintendent, thanks to earning his doctorate and years of experience in the district. The pay bump had helped, but Joe Sutherland was an unpretentious man. Both his parents had always stressed to their children to live within their means and save as much of their salaries as possible. West had taken that advice to heart. He knew Autumn was struggling financially, having put her slacker husband through med school. She was always picking up extra shifts. Summer seemed to be doing well at her publishing house although she said that the cost of living in New York was sky-high.

Though he knew they would never ask, he would be happy to help either twin financially, the same as he had offered to do so with Sawyer. He was sitting on a pile of money from a lucrative career and was more than happy to share with his siblings and cousin.

It took ten minutes to reach his parents' house, and his dad greeted him at the door, enveloping West in a bear hug.

"Son, I'm so proud of you. Not just what you accomplished as a Dallas Cowboy, but the fact you want to come back to Hawthorne and influence the lives of young people."

"Thanks, Dad. That means a lot to me."

"I know a few people will think nepotism, with you landing a job on the football staff, but Coach Markham assured me that you were the best candidate for the position." Dad grinned. "And that you'd be working longer hours for a whole lot less cash."

They stepped into the den, and West said, "I know the hours will be long. I'm not concerned about that. I know what I'm getting myself into."

His dad cocked an eyebrow. "And do you know what you're getting into with Kelby Blackstone?"

He laughed. "I guess Mom told you she'd be at dinner tonight."

"Kelby was a good girl. An excellent student and a true student leader. I'm sure she's matured into a fine woman." Dad frowned. "Despite that jerk of a husband."

"Ex-husband," he corrected quickly. "They've been divorced five years, Dad. I don't think we need to bring up Bax Porter."

"I agree," Mom said, coming into the den. "Poor Kelby. I can't imagine how rough things have been for her, what with Big Jim's stroke and the lurid headlines about her ex."

West cleared his throat. "Before she gets here, I want both of you to know that it looks as if Kelby is going to be staying in Hawthorne. We're going to see where things go."

Mom lit up. "That's wonderful, West. But what will she do? She can't let her life revolve around caring for Big Jim."

"She's working on that."

The doorbell rang, and he said, "I'll get it."

Heading to the door, he took a deep breath and then opened it. Kelby stood there, her long, raven hair shiny, her gray eyes bright.

"Come on in," he said, pulling her inside and kissing her lightly. "How's Big Jim?"

"Pretty much the same." She hesitated. "Did you explain to your parents why you wanted to invite me to dinner?"

"They know we're together. They both think it's a great idea. So, two cheerleaders in our corner."

"I told Dad about us at dinner tonight. Naturally, Chance was there and heard. I thought he would pump me for more details on the way home, but he just gave me a knowing smile. I'll also tell Darby."

"And I'll tell Sawyer." He paused. "It's going to be weird. Finding a place to be together. Almost like being teenagers again. I've got my cousin as a roommate in a small house with thin walls. You're living at home again."

"I hadn't thought about that," Kelby admitted.

"Let's go eat. We'll work things out," he assured her.

His parents welcomed Kelby. They ate in the kitchen, the dining room being reserved for holiday meals and a bigger crowd. Mom had made meatloaf and mashed potatoes, as promised, along with corn on the cob and a Caesar salad. Dessert was a chocolate lava cake, and West only had a small slice of it.

"You should take more," his mom urged. "You're not in training now."

"I also don't want to balloon up," he said. "I've seen too many pros let themselves go after their playing days. I don't feel good when I carry too much excess weight. I also want to be a good example to my players. That means sweets are a treat, not a regular menu item."

Kelby chuckled. "I'm happy to take any sweets West won't, Mrs. Sutherland. I still jog almost daily so I can enjoy chocolate whenever I want. And ice cream."

"You still look like you did in high school when you were cheering on the sidelines," Mom told Kelby. "Except you're even prettier now."

"Thank you. High school seems a long time ago. A lot has happened since then."

"West tells us you're planning to stay in Hawthorne."

Leave it to Mom to go straight to the heart of the matter.

"Yes, ma'am. I handled social media and branding for my last company. I'm hoping I can pick up a few clients and do the same on my own. I also am skilled at creating graphics and can design websites, things I've done in previous jobs. All of that can be done remotely."

"Summer has mentioned to me that a lot of authors are moving away from traditional publishing," his dad said. "That they want more control over their work. If you could tap into that market of indie authors, Kelby, that might be a goldmine. Authors need websites. Graphics for ads. And they must do stuff on the TikTok."

West loved how his dad always called it the TikTok. "I agree with Dad. That would be a lucrative market. Let me put you in touch with Summer. She might be able to steer you in the right direction," he offered. "Tell you what authors need and suggest a few prospective clients to you."

His thoughts began swirling, thinking of a few of his teammates. Maybe they, too, needed social media help. TTM had handled everything for him, but he didn't know if that applied to some of the other big names on the Cowboys roster, much less players who didn't have the big marquee recognition but still had a solid fan base. West knew that Van Foster was due a new contract. He didn't know if the quarterback was happy with his agent or if he would be seeking a new one for the contract negotiations. He decided to reach out to Van. Maybe he might have something Kelby could work on. Other Cowboys players might, as well.

They spent a few minutes lingering over dessert, with West talking about the playbook Coach Markham had given him. Dad said he liked the chances of next year's team, saying the linebackers were solid, and that the Hawks had a talented quarterback and receiver duo.

"The spring game is in about a month," West said, recalling how the entire town seemed to turn out to watch it. "I think watching the players during it will give me an idea of what I'll have to work with next year."

He offered for Kelby and him to do the dishes, but his mom wouldn't hear of it.

"You two go and enjoy yourselves. I'll handle the dishes while your dad heads for the remote and *Jeopardy*."

They said their goodnights and left the house, with West asking, "Where's your car?"

"Chance dropped me off here on his way back to the ranch. I told him you could give me a ride home."

"Let's go for a drive," he suggested.

They drove around town, pointing out places they used to go when they lived in Hawthorne, and seeing new businesses.

"Hawthorne is really growing," Kelby said. "I know with this new hospital coming, it'll bring more jobs. It's about time we had a facility like that and not have to drive so far for surgeries or to have a baby."

"When does it open?" he asked as they passed it, thinking it looked close to finished on the outside but knowing the inside would take a lot of work, especially with various equipment arriving and needing setup.

"I think another three months, but I'm not sure. I'd ask

Chance, but he never pays attention to things like that. I'll ask Tammy. She'll know."

West found himself driving toward the lake, which was just outside of town, past the Blackstone Ranch.

When he flew by the entrance to the ranch, Kelby said, "You missed your turn."

"I thought we'd go to the lake." He glanced over, grinning. "Maybe make out a little."

"Why, Mr. Sutherland," she said coyly, batting her eyelashes at him. "Do you think I'm that kind of girl?"

"I'm hoping you're exactly that kind of woman." He reached and took her hand, threading his fingers through hers. "Am I crazy to think how right this feels?"

She smiled shyly at him. "I was thinking the same thing. I haven't held anyone's hand in a long time, West."

"Neither have I. I also stopped kissing women."

He explained how seeing *Pretty Woman* had changed the idea of kissing for him and added, "You are the first woman in years whom I've kissed on the mouth." He squeezed her hand. "And I really liked it."

They reached the entrance to the lake, and West turned in, winding his sports car along the road. He made the choice to go high and turned to the right when he came to a fork. Minutes later, they parked at the top of a bluff which overlooked the lake. It had been a favorite spot of couples in high school. He'd brought his fair share of girls up here and assumed Kelby had visited the spot a few times herself.

They sat in contented silence for several minutes. He caught the scent of her perfume, which admittedly revved his engine a bit. Kissing Kelby had been good. Really good. He wanted more but didn't want to rush her. West told himself neither of them was going anywhere. That they needed to learn who the other had become in the years they'd been apart before they committed to a more physical relationship.

Instead, he asked, "Have you thought of any names for the business you'll establish?"

"I've played around with a few. I don't think I'll be able to make enough by sticking to social media and branding alone. I'll need to add in other services. Website design and maintenance. Creating graphics for logos and ads. Maybe even teach myself about cover design so I can take advantage of the indie author market. That's why I need a name that acts as an umbrella for all my services."

"How about Blackstone Digital Agency?" he suggested. "Or Blackstone Digital Solutions?"

She nodded. "I like those. I'm not certain if I want to use my name, though."

"You could go more personal. Kelby Connections. Connections covers a lot of ground. Or Kelby Digital Connection."

Her nose wrinkled. "No. Kelby is too informal. I want to be taken seriously. Kelby sounds a bit too playful."

They brainstormed together, tossing out different names. West liked Blackstone Creative Hub, while she preferred Crafted Media Solutions.

"I like alliteration," she said. "I wanted to work that into the name if I could." She paused, mulling it over. "Wait. I think I've got it. Social Synergy Creations."

"What the hell is synergy?" he asked. "I've heard that word tossed around but never really knew what it was all about."

"Synergy is being compatible with something that's mutually advantageous. It's like a combined force. I like the thought of action in the word, plus it adds in the social aspect. Could be social media or the social feature of forming a cooperative business relationship between myself and someone else, be it an individual or corporation. You know, that idea of community between client and me."

He caught her excitement. "I can see that. I liked Crafted Media Solutions, but solutions makes it sounds as if there are problems you're trying to solve. With using creations in your business name, that runs the gamut of what you do."

She beamed at him. "Oh, I really like this idea, West. I never thought about starting my own business, but it makes total sense. It would allow me to be more creative and stretch myself professionally. It's also something where I would have flexible hours, so I could go and see Dad or handle something on the ranch. Hmm. I think I might start with the ranch. I haven't looked at the website in years, and I doubt Dad or Chance has updated it much. Maybe Blackstone Ranch could be the first makeover I do. Have a side-by-side comparison as an example of what I'm capable of doing."

West reached out and smoothed her hair. "You're beautiful when you're enthusiastic. It's like how you lit up the sidelines when you were cheering. Even though Coach ordered us to keep our eyes off the cheerleaders and drill team when we were on the field, I would sneak a look at you every now and then. You had this boundless enthusiasm and belief in our team, every single play. That was contagious, both on the field and in the stands. Your smile always spurred me on."

Her eyes grew large. "I never knew that."

"I never told you. Hell, Kelby, I think I was half in love with you during high school and never really knew it. I was caught up in playing sports and whatever girl I was dating." He rubbed a lock of her silky hair between his fingers. "You were right in front of me the entire time, and I was too stupid to notice it."

Her fingers encircled his wrist, her thumb rubbing back and forth, causing his mouth to go dry. "Maybe we weren't ready for one another back then. Fate had us going in different directions." She paused. "But it's brought us back together now."

West leaned over and kissed her. He took his time, nibbling on her lips before sweeping his tongue into her mouth, leisurely exploring her. He could taste the chocolate of the cake she had as dessert and a sweetness that was all Kelby. His heart began to beat faster, caught up in the idea that this second chance with her was meant to be.

When he finally broke the kiss, he rested his forehead against hers, one hand cupping her cheek.

"Do you believe in second chances?" he asked softly.

"I do now," Kelby replied, taking the initiative and kissing him.

They kissed several more minutes, limited by the seats of his sports car.

He broke the kiss and announced, "I need to buy a truck."

Her laughter was pure and sweet and touched a part of his soul that had been locked away from the world for what seemed like forever.

"It would be more comfortable," she agreed. "But a flashy sports car isn't who you are anymore, West. Besides, you don't want your players to think that's what football is about."

"You're right," he agreed. "It's about relationships. Teamwork. Discipline. Setting goals and striving to meet them. My Jag sends the wrong message. I think I'll drive down to Dallas early tomorrow morning and sell it at my dealership and then make it back in time to go to practice."

"Want some company on the way?" she asked.

He smiled. "That sounds like a perfect day to me."

West kissed her a final time and started the car, driving Kelby back to the ranch. They made plans to get an early start tomorrow. She mentioned working on the Blackstone Ranch's website and toying with a new logo for it. He planned to text a few football friends and see if he could help her land a few clients.

As he left the ranch and turned on the highway to head home, a feeling of satisfaction washed over him. West felt he was settling into the place he was meant to be, doing something he loved.

And hopefully finding love with Kelby Blackstone.

CHAPTER
Twelve

K elby packed up her toiletries and threw them into her purse. She and West were headed to Dallas this morning, and she wasn't taking any clothes with her. They would be staying at her apartment for a couple of days before she terminated the lease and moved all her possessions to Hawthorne permanently.

The last three weeks had been some of the best of her life. She had spent hours in West's company, getting to know him all over again. He still had parts of him which were familiar to her from years ago, but it was fun discovering things about him now that he was an adult. His taste in movies and music. His politics. The charity work he did and never took credit for.

In addition, she had spent hours working on Social Synergy Creations, designing a website for her new business, making certain she paid for her domain, as well as starting up an LLC. Kelby had spent hours polishing her new business' website and then creating examples for it, regarding the various services she would offer. She had completely redesigned the Blackstone Ranch website, as well, using different colors and creating a compelling new logo, completely rebranding everything about her family's business. Chance had turned over a portion of the business to her, as well as taking on more responsibilities himself. It was obvious to both of them now that their father would never recover enough to run Blackstone Ranch the way he had for the past forty years. They wanted Big Jim's legacy to continue, and so they each now handled various parts of Blackstone Ranch.

She went down to the kitchen, bringing her purse and laptop bag with her, finding Tammy sitting at the table, drinking a cup of coffee.

"You have everything you need?" Tammy asked.

"I do. I hate that I'm having to leave Dad for a couple of days, but I do have a few clients I'm meeting with, as well as packing up everything to move back to Hawthorne permanently."

Tammy stood and embraced Kelby. "I know this is hard, baby girl, but I think this is the right decision." She grinned mischievously. "Especially with that handsome West Sutherland in the picture again. I always did like that boy. He was here so much, I thought of him as one of my own."

Tammy moved to the coffee maker and asked, "Do you want coffees for the road for the both of you?"

"That would be terrific," she replied.

While Tammy prepared the hot beverages, Kelby downed a quick bowl of cereal, wanting something in her belly before leaving the house. West arrived soon after, and Tammy handed the coffees to them, wishing Kelby good luck on her presentations.

They got into the truck West had purchased, and he asked, "You have everything you need for today?"

She patted her laptop bag. "As ready as I'll ever be. And if I don't land these clients, I'll just keep going. I know I can't bat a thousand all the time. I'll have more turn me down than sign with me, but I'm confident I'll pull in my fair share of business."

As they cruised through the gates to the ranch, he asked, "Why don't you run through one of your presentations with me? It would give me a better idea what your business is all about."

"You don't mind?"

"Mind?" He took her hand, bringing it to his lips and pressing a tender kiss against her knuckles. "I'm eager to see what you're up to."

"I'll do the one for the athleisurewear company first," she said, pulling out her laptop and running through her notes.

The company was small but beginning to grow, and the two owners, close friends in their mid-thirties, were eager to get their brand out there and raise their social media profile.

As she spoke, she felt her confidence growing. West asked a few questions, and Kelby easily answered them.

When she finished, she said, "I think I'll work the answers to your questions into my pitch. I know they'll still have some of their own, but I feel really prepared now. Thanks for letting me practice on you."

"I found it fascinating, honey," he said, and she melted at the sweet endearment. "Would you like to do the other one for me?"

"No, I'm good. I want to save my voice and not be all talked out by the time we get to Dallas."

"Tell me how your writer clients are going," he urged.

"Better than I'd ever hoped. Summer has proved to be a great resource. I'm glad you connected us."

West had helped Kelby get in touch with his younger sister, who had worked her way up to being an editor at a traditional publishing house in New York. They had FaceTimed for a couple of hours, with Kelby sharing all the services her new company would offer clients. On the flip side, Summer had told her what authors needed, explaining how traditional publishing would always exist, but it was becoming the province of an elite few. More authors were going the indie route, either learning how to do their own formatting and creating websites and book covers or farming out those kinds of tasks to others.

Summer had shared with Kelby that she knew of three of her publishing house's former authors who had gone indie or were about to, and she got Kelby's contact information to pass along to the trio. All three authors had been in touch with her within a few days. She offered each a free, one-hour consultation, and two of them signed with her right away, with the other one coming back a day later and asking to become a client of Social Synergy Creations.

Kelby had totally revamped one author's website and created brand-new websites for the other two writers. She had taken over all their social media accounts, reading a book by each of them so she could get a flavor for what they wrote and their style. Already, she had received two more referrals from these three authors and signed them, realizing clients from the indie publishing world might very well turn out to be her bread and butter. She had created TikToks for all of them and had taken over everything from their Instagram to Threads accounts and was already posting daily. She was now working on teaching herself how to design book covers, and she was pleasantly surprised by how much she enjoyed it.

They hit Dallas and the subsequent traffic, Thankfully, she had built in enough time for them to reach her first appointment, scheduled for eight-thirty. She stopped by the restroom and even brushed her teeth to get rid of the coffee aftertaste in her mouth, quickly applying new lipstick.

Kelby entered the small office of Motion Mates athleisurewear, where Carol Cummings greeted her.

"Hi, Kelby. I'm Carol. Elaine is on the phone with a client right now. Come into the conference room. We've just signed a lease on this space. It's got the reception area, two small offices, and a conference room. It's nice to not be working out of Elaine's dining room."

They entered the conference room, which had a table and six chairs around it, and Kelby opened her laptop, setting up for her presentation.

"Would you like anything to drink?" Carol asked.

"A water if you have it," she replied. "Thank you."

"Be right back," Carol said. "Hopefully, I'll have Elaine in tow with me."

Two minutes later, both women returned. Elaine introduced herself, and Kelby said, "I like how you're both wearing items from your line. The fit is flattering, and I love the color palette for each."

"With so many people working from home, we believe athleisurewear is the way to go," Elaine said. "It's comfortable. Not sloppy like a sweatshirt or sweatpants. It's more fitted. You can wear our clothing to work out in, as well as work from home or run errands."

"Keep talking," Kelby encouraged, and she wound up learning the backstory of these two housewives and how they'd landed upon a way to stay at home with their kids and still have a part-time income, which was now growing.

After she finished asking a few more questions, Kelby said, "You're both walking advertisements for your clothing. I hope you're wearing it to everything from soccer games to casual lunches with friends."

She then launched into her presentation, seeing them nod in agreement with various points she made, and then watched the excitement light both their faces. She showed examples of what other athleisurewear companies were doing and how she wanted to distinguish Motion Mates from other lines available.

Concluding her pitch, she said, "I believe I can help raise your social media profile considerably. I also want to revamp your website entirely. The font and colors are all wrong, for your product, and it's too difficult to navigate. I'd like to use both of you as models on the site, as well as your family and friends. I don't want a high, glossy look. I'm going for the every-day. How your clothing can take people from their morning gym routine through their various activities during the day."

Not wanting to press too hard, she finished with, "I know you'll need time to discuss things with one another. I would appreciate if you would get back to me in the next week or so, however."

The two women exchange glances, and Carol said, "There's nothing to discuss, Kelby. You're exactly who we've been looking for. We don't have any experience in what you do, but we believe you're a perfect fit for us, and your pricing is so affordable. With Elaine handling the accounting and all the business aspects of Motion Mates and me working on designs, fabrics, and the manufacturing, we haven't had time—much less the know-how—of how to truly market us. That's where you come in."

"If that's the case, can we do a photo shoot tomorrow?" she asked. "I would love to take pictures of the two of you, along with other friends and family members wearing your lines."

"Can you hire a photographer on such short notice?" asked Elaine worriedly.

"No, I've done enough photography in the past for other social media accounts. I do want you to brainstorm some ideas for a tagline and mission statement for your company, though. I'll email you some examples of ones that I think are particularly good. I'll write it for you, but you know your product better than anyone else. If you can come up with a few phrases for me that capture the essence, I'll be able to massage and refine it. Try to work in something about that all-day aspect we mentioned before. How you can do most any activity in Motion Mates."

"From your morning workout to the end-of-day kind of thing?" Carol asked.

"Yes. I want customers to see your clothing not merely as workout wear but something that can be worn during everyday activities. Pushing a cart at Target. Picking up library books. Do either of you volunteer at your kids' schools?"

"I do," Carol said.

"Would you wear what you have on now when you do your volunteer activities?"

Carol smiled sheepishly. "I do all the time. I don't take time to dress up to go to school, but I never want to appear like a slob in T-shirt and shorts."

"That's what I like about your athleisurewear. It's not only good for workouts, but it can take you to different places throughout the day. Even volunteering at school. I'd love to get a shot of a group of kids around you and you reading to them."

Kelby typed up a quick list on her cell of different activities she wanted to photograph tomorrow and the types of people she'd like to use during the shoot wearing Elaine and Carol's clothing, sending it to the two partners.

"I know this is fast," she said, "but I really want to hit this quickly. Can you have people in Motion Mates clothing in some of these situations?"

"I guarantee we can do all of this," Elaine said. "We'll drop anything else we have going on and focus on this all day and go from there. Would you be interested in trying some of our clothing?"

"It's exactly what I would wear," Kelby said enthusiastically. "I also think the pieces are classic. Timeless. That any age woman could wear them and feel comfortable in them."

"Let me go grab a couple of things for you," Carol said.

Kelby tried on what Carol brought back. Everything fit perfectly.

"I can get behind any product and find some good in it," she told the pair. "Wearing this now makes me a true believer, though. I know you've been concentrating on women's wear and have a few items for men, but have you ever thought about expanding into a children's line?"

The two entrepreneurs looked at one another, slightly startled.

"No. The thought of children never entered our minds," Elaine admitted. "But I like it. I don't know of anyone else doing it. It would be a great new market to open up."

"I like it, too," Carol said. "Between us, we have five children of varying ages. We can have some samples pulled together and outfit our kids. Not by tomorrow. But soon."

"No rush on that," Kelby assured the two. "It's just an idea. Right now, I want to focus on our Motion Mates campaign, taking you from sunrise to sunset." She smiled. "Your company is going to take off. And when it does, you need to be ready. Not just in manufacturing your current lines but thinking about adding to those lines, as well as incorporating more clothing for men and possibly including children."

They arranged a time and place to meet tomorrow morning and a quick list of activities Kelby would capture through pictures.

When it came time to leave, she said, "I'll have the contracts drawn up and sent to you to sign electronically."

She was grateful Sawyer had agreed to work with her. He had designed a basic template for her contract and could include all her services or an a la carte rendering of them. His prices were quite reasonable, and she was glad to be partnering with him for her new business venture.

Carol hugged her enthusiastically, and Elaine did the same, with Elaine saying, "You really get us. That means everything in the world to us, Kelby. We're so happy to be working with you."

She returned their smiles. "And I'm very happy to be able to help brand you and get the word out about your clothing line."

She took time to change back into her own clothing and practically floated from the building, returning to West's truck. He saw her coming and got out, meeting her and giving her a kiss.

"How did it go? You were in there longer than you anticipated."

"It couldn't have gone better, West. Let's head to the bistro."

On the way to her next potential client's restaurant, Kelby recapped her meeting with Carol and Elaine and some of the ideas they had talked about. They also discussed the different places she intended to photograph them and their friends tomorrow.

"You said they also do menswear?"

"Some. It's a small part of their current operation. Just a few items, but I'm hoping if Motion Mates catches on, they'll expand to offering more for men and even children."

"If you're looking for models tomorrow, I'd be happy to put something on and pose for you."

Her jaw dropped. "You would do that for them? West, you still endorse products for millions of dollars. Watches. Liquor. Cars. There's no way they could pay you much of anything."

"You believe in them and their product—and I believe in

you, Kelby." Their gazes met. "I'm happy to appear in a few shots. Besides, you're wanting to raise their profile, aren't you? What better way than having a Super Bowl champion appear in a few Instagram photos?"

She squealed as he pulled up to a stoplight, grabbing his nape and pulling him to her for a quick, hard kiss.

"This is fantastic. Let me call so they'll have something in your size ready tomorrow."

Kelby quickly made the call, saying, "I have a proposition for you."

"We've got you on speakerphone," Carol said. "What's going on, Kelby?"

"I have a friend who is happy to appear in some of tomorrow's pictures, wearing your athleisurewear." She glanced at West. "He's *very* photogenic."

"Send us his measurements. We'll be able to outfit him," Elaine said.

She turned to West and looking at him, said, "He's six-two. One hundred and eighty pounds."

He nodded, quickly spouting his measurements, and she passed those along, realizing that his casual knowledge of size meant that he had worked with a tailor, which was why he had always looked so good in the pictures she had come across of him on social media.

"That sounds great," Carol said. "We look forward to seeing you both tomorrow."

"Bye," Kelby said, ending the call.

"I notice you didn't tell them who your friend was," West said.

"I decided it would be better as a surprise. I don't want word leaking out. While these two housewives are serious about their business, I'm afraid they'd spill the beans to their families, and it would mushroom. I want the photographs we take tomorrow to not have an entire army of groupies present in the background. Yes, word will get out, but hopefully, we can move from location to location and save a crowd from gathering."

She took his hand. "Thank you, West. This means a lot to me."

"I want to help you get Social Synergy Creations off the ground and noticed. I have a high enough profile to make that happen. From what you say, Elaine and Carol seem like really nice ladies with a quality product in Motion Mates. They just need a break, and I can give it to them."

They parked and entered the bistro shortly after eleven, and the owner greeted them enthusiastically, especially after he saw West accompanied Kelby.

She introduced herself and West and said, "I hope you don't mind if West came along to sample your food, Chef."

"Sample away," he said. "To have West Sutherland eat at my establishment? This is the highlight of my cooking career. I'm a huge Cowboys fan. I myself played football, but not the American kind. I was a goalie."

Kelby had requested having a simple meal before she did her pitch, wanting to taste the food and photograph some of it. They were led to a private dining room, where several courses came out. The food was all fresh and tasty, seasoned to perfection. She took pictures of everything on the table, from the grilled salmon to the chicken Caesar salad to the mini-muffins and onion soup. She even had a few of the chef's employees strip off their aprons and sit at the table so that she could get candid shots of them eating and drinking a crisp Moscato.

The staff cleared the dishes, and West said he would wait outside.

"No, stay," Kelby urged. "I want you to see what I do and contribute any ideas you might have."

Once more, she called up the pitch on her laptop and walked through it, elaborating on each point, explaining what she could do for the chef's social media sites and how she could refine his website to appear more elegant. She displayed different fonts, explaining why they were more appealing than the ones his current website displayed, and discussed using some of the colors from the bistro itself on the website.

By the time she finished, Chef Marceau was eager to become her client. He studied the mock-up of a few web pages she had done and chose the one he liked best. She even changed his Instagram handle and posted a few of the pictures from the lunch, telling him to keep an eye on his profile and number of follows. Kelby tagged West in one of the pictures she took and knew that alone would bring in new followers and more customers.

They talked about the contract, and she told him it would be emailed to him so that he could sign virtually, which he liked.

"Thank you for what you will do for Bistro Beauvais, Kelby," Chef Marceau said. "I look forward to working with you." He turned to West. "I am only sorry I will not see you play again, Monsieur Sutherland. Please, come to my humble restaurant anytime you wish. A table will always be waiting for you."

"I appreciate that, Chef," West said easily, shaking hands with the man and even posing for a few selfies with the owner before they left.

He took Kelby's hand as they returned to the truck. "You were amazing. So organized. So creative. People will love working with you."

"It's hard to believe I've landed two clients today."

As they got into the truck, she texted Sawyer the details of each so he could draw up the contracts.

"Where to now?" West asked.

"Those were the only people I needed to see today," she told him. "We have the rest of the day. Tomorrow will be taken up with the photo shoot."

"What would you like to do then?" he asked. "We could go for a walk in the park since the weather is so nice today. Or you might want to go shopping. I know women plus Dallas equals shopping."

"No, I have something else in mind." Kelby worked up her courage. "I'd like to go to my apartment now."

"Oh, that's right. We've got packing to do."

"I don't have packing in mind, West," she said flirtatiously. "I was hoping now that we finally had a place we could be alone, we might do a little exploring."

"Oh, it's called *exploring*?" he asked, chuckling softly.

"All I can think about is getting you out of your clothes and touching you everywhere."

His radiant smile caused her heartbeat to speed up. "Then you better give me directions fast, honey. Because I want to kiss ever naked inch of you."

Kelby couldn't help but laugh. "Okay. But no speeding tickets."

"Scout's honor," he promised, crossing his heart.

She had wanted to make love with West from the first moment he kissed her. The thought excited her, but it terrified her at the same time. She hadn't been with any man since Bax, and their days of lovemaking were far in the past. Kelby only hoped she would be enough for a man like West.

They arrived at her apartment. Before she could open her door, he caught her chin, turning her face up so that their gazes met.

"I don't want us to rush," he said huskily. "I want to savor every second with you."

"I'm rusty," she admitted.

"Me, too," he replied. "But we aren't going to think about any past experiences with anyone else. This is something new. Something between just the two of us. We know we have chemistry. We're going to take our time. Be thorough. And enjoy being together—with no interruptions."

His words caused the tension to leave her body. All thoughts of any other man fled. She only wanted to be with West.

"Are you ready to take a leap of faith with me?" he asked.

Kelby gazed at him a long moment before answering. "I think I've been waiting for this moment my entire life."

CHAPTER
Thirteen

They left the car and went upstairs to her apartment. Opening the door, Kelby sensed the air being stale. It had been weeks since she had been home.

Only this was no longer home now. Home was in Hawthorne.

With West.

She definitely saw a future with this man. She hadn't told him that she loved him yet, but her heart sang out that she did. Kelby only hoped that their time together now would be as perfect as she had imagined.

Going to a candle, she lit it. "I hope this will help," she said.

When she turned back, she started to speak again, but words wouldn't form. West was looking at her ravenously.

"Come here, Kelby," he said in a low rumble, causing her pulse to leap.

She did as he asked, stopping just before him. He ran his fingers through her long strands of hair.

"Do you know how often I've thought about doing this?" he asked, his head cocked to one side.

His fingers continued to sift through her hair, their tips brushing her scalp and then trailing through her locks. It caused her heart to quicken. Her mouth to grow dry. Heat pooled in her belly.

"Maybe once or twice?" she asked, a smile playing on her lips.

His fingers stopped, and he cupped her cheeks. "You were all I could think about those last few weeks of high school. I failed an economics test because I was daydreaming about you. The bell rang and jolted me. I hadn't written a single thing on the pages. I waited until everyone left and handed in my paper. Miss Alexander asked if I hadn't studied for the test, seeing the blank pages. I admitted to her that while I had studied, I couldn't concentrate on anything. Because of you."

Kelby's heart skipped a beat. "Seriously?"

"Seriously. She told me that she'd been in love once, so she knew exactly how I felt. Asked if I could stay after school that same day and take the test. I had to miss baseball practice to do it, but the coach cleared me. Miss A put me on the clock. Told me she wouldn't remind me of the time if she saw I was wool-gathering. I buckled down and forced myself to think about monetary policy and the Fed. Net exports and international finance."

West grinned. "When we got our tests back the next day, I had an A+."

"Well, you always were a top student." Kelby hesitated. "I thought about you, too. It's funny how we had known each other since we were in diapers, but I suddenly saw you in a different light those last couple of months of school. I even thought about giving up going to UT so I could be near you, but I knew you wouldn't have a lot of time for me. Plus, Mom would have been so disappointed since she had cheered for the

Longhorns. Darby, too. We'd made the squad together and were slated to be roommates."

His hands framed her face. "I still think we made the right decision back then. But that was then. This is now. And I still have all those unresolved feelings, Kelby."

"Then you better do something about them."

West's mouth moved to hers, hovering over it slightly for a moment as her heart slammed against her ribs. Then his lips were on hers, moving, nibbling, teasing her mouth open. He kissed her deeply, leisurely exploring, playfully moving his tongue against hers.

Each kiss was more drugging than the one before. His hands slid down her back, cupping her buttocks and squeezing, bringing new sensations. She leaned into him. Into his heat. His scent. Wrapping her arms about him and moving so close that their bodies were pressed together, molded against one another as if they were two halves of a whole finally coming together after being separated.

The hunger grew inside her as their kisses became more frantic. She felt West branding her as his, and she reveled in that idea. His fingers matched hers as they both unbuttoned each other's shirts, parting them. Her hands moved up and down his sleek chest, her fingers brushing against abs hard and flat.

He pulled her blouse over her shoulders and down, kissing her neck as he did. It fluttered to the floor, his lips traveling along her collarbones, heat trailing as he did. She managed to get his shirt off him as he slid her bra's clasp apart, ridding her of it. His arms wrapped around her, pulling her close. Her breasts pressed against the hard wall of his chest, her core beginning to pound violently, wanting his touch.

They kissed again for a long time, his hands stroking her back. Then he broke the kiss.

"These have got to come off," he insisted, undoing her tailored trousers. His mouth followed the pants, his tongue gliding along her thigh to her calf. She slipped off her shoes and stepped from the black slacks, only wearing her panties now.

He peeled them away and she stepped out of them as he stood, his hands firmly gripping her buttocks. He walked her backward, all the way to her bedroom, kneading her bottom as he did so. The back of her legs bumped against the bed, and he lifted her onto it, leaning her back against the mattress. Then he kissed her, hard and possessive, causing the fire within her to turn into a blaze. His tongue worked its way down her body again as he nudged her legs apart. It plunged inside her.

Instantly, she arched, need pouring through her. His tongue stroked her deeply, and she found herself whimpering, meeting each thrust of it. He teased her with tongue, teeth, and fingers, causing a sudden, violent orgasm to erupt. She bucked against his mouth, crying out, tears escaping her eyes as he gave and gave and she continued to take. Then she grew limp, not thinking she could lift a finger.

West stepped away, stripping away the rest of his clothing as she looked at him through slitted eyes. He had a magnificent physique, the body of a professional athlete in his prime.

And that body was hers for the taking.

Energized now, she was ready when he lifted her from the bed, pulling back the covers, and placing her against the pillows. He climbed up, hovering over her, but she shook her head.

"My turn for fun," she told him, pushing him to his back and having her wicked way with him.

Kelby touched him everywhere, stroking him with hands and tongue, learning every bit of his incredible, muscled body. He seemed to do the same, as if he memorized her every curve.

They became frantic, their hands searching, seeking, their kisses almost desperate now.

"My wallet," he croaked. "Need a condom."

"I'm on the pill," she told him. "My periods were always erratic. It helps even them out."

"But I—"

"When was the last time you were with someone?" she asked, almost hating to hear his answer.

"It's been a while. Months."

"Then I think we're fine."

His crooked grin tugged at her heart. "Then I think it's time you rode this Cowboy."

West lifted her by the waist, settling her atop his cock. He lowered her onto it, and it sank deeply into her. Filling her. Satisfying her as never before.

She began moving sensually, finding a rhythm that pleased them both, starting slowly and then building, the pace becoming more frenetic. Desire poured through her as she moved. Stroked. Caressed. Kissed.

And then exploded.

Her orgasm rocked her, and she felt him tensing, his voice calling her name, even as she called his. They climaxed together, in a rush of heat and need. She collapsed atop him, her cheek resting against his heart, its erratic pounding in her ear.

His hand stroked her hair, and he kissed the top of her head. No words were necessary. They lay against one another, their hearts calming, their bodies cooling.

Then West lifted her chin, causing their gazes to meet.

"That was mind-blowing sex, Blackstone. You almost killed me."

"Ditto, Sutherland."

They grinned at one another.

Then he grew serious. "I need to tell you something. Something important."

He was still inside her, their bodies connected, and she didn't want to move from him. Pillowing her hands atop one another, she rested her chin on them and asked, "What?"

Raking a hand through his hair, he said, "I know this is probably the wrong time to voice this. People would think I was crazy if they knew I was saying this to you now." He hesitated, his gaze searching hers. "I love you, Kelby. I always have. I forced it deep inside me because I couldn't do anything about it years ago. I've never found any woman who comes close to holding a candle to you. You're smart. Beautiful. Caring. I don't expect to hear you echo anything, but I had to tell you."

Hearing these words from West caused a ball of happiness to form in her belly, a ball of sunshine which quickly spread through her. She brushed the back of her fingers against his cheek.

"I love you, too, West. I can't believe I'm saying that. That we've found one another again. That we're finally in the same place at the same time and free to be together."

He pushed his fingers into her hair, massaging her scalp. She closed her eyes and almost purred because it felt so good. So right.

"I'm yours if you'll have me, Kelby," he said softly.

She opened her eyes, meeting his turquoise ones. "I want all of you, West. Now. And always."

They made love again. Tenderly. Slowly. When they came again and pure pleasure washed through her, she felt as if making love with West was the beginning of a new life. A new her. A new them. Together.

Finally, after all these years, Kelby knew that she had found her soulmate. The One.

And the fact that it was West Sutherland made the dream a solid reality.

They snuggled together, their limbs entwined. It was as if they couldn't bear not to be touching one another. They talked for a long time, about everything and nothing, and then they fell asleep.

When she woke, the sun was setting. West stirred, and they kissed deeply.

Breaking the kiss, he said, "Hey, Kelby?"

"Yes?" she said sleepily.

"I think we should get married."

Her body stiffened. She was now wide awake. "What did you say?"

"I want to marry you," West said. "I've never come close to wanting to marry anyone."

His thumb caressed her bottom lip, and then he kissed her, long and slow.

She pulled away. "Does it bother you that I was already married once?"

"Vaguely," he replied. "I'm a little jealous that Bax got to spend years with you."

"They weren't good ones, West. I think we were too young to get married. When his first serious injury occurred, he didn't have the maturity to know how to handle it, and I didn't know how to handle him. He turned into someone I never knew existed. Things went downhill fast."

He kissed her softly. "I'm sorry you went through all that pain. I'm not saying our life together will be perfect. We're both strong personalities. We'll clash every now and then. But I think we have the maturity to talk through things when a problem crops up. We won't hide anything from one another. We won't ignore if a problem arises. We'll deal with it, head on.

And we love one another, Kelby. The love has always been there. It'll guide us and keep us true."

A peace settled over her, a calmness she had never known. And she liked it.

"So, we're really going to do this."

He grinned. "Yup. We're really going to do this."

"Don't tell me you want to get married now. In Dallas."

"Why not?"

"First, your mom would kill you. And then me. It would be the shortest widowhood in history. Seriously, West. I think you owe it to your parents to have at least a small wedding." She kissed him. "And then we could have plenty of time for a honeymoon before you start your new coaching job."

"I guess you'll always be my voice of reason. Okay. A small wedding in Hawthorne. Just family. I'll want Summer and Autumn there. And it would be nice if both Sawyer and Darby could come."

"Darby definitely. She'll be my maid of honor. And Chance." She paused. "I want Dad there, too. That might be a problem."

"We'll figure it out when we get back to Hawthorne," West promised. "Right now, I'm starving. For food first. Then you."

"Campisi's?" she asked, knowing how much he loved pizza. "It's the best in town."

"I agree. But let's call in the order and bring it back here." A shadow crossed his face. "It's hard for me to be out in public, Kelby. I know we won't be in Dallas often, and my fame will fade quickly. I just don't want people coming up, interrupting our dinner, asking for selfies. I selfishly want you all to myself tonight. And after pizza?"

He waggled his eyebrows, which made her laugh.

"After pizza, we'll get to know one another better," she promised. "In every single way we can imagine."

CHAPTER
Fourteen

Kelby awoke, enveloped in West's warmth cocooned around her. For a moment, she still thought she might be dreaming, the most wonderful dream she'd ever had. Then she realized everything that had happened was no dream. It had been a reality.

And West was all hers.

She wanted to chastise herself for having ever dated Bax, much less marrying his sorry ass, but she knew that the years away from West had taught her much about herself. She had gone through experiences which she wouldn't wish upon anyone else, but they had made her into the strong, confident woman she was today. She might not be West's financial equal, but Kelby felt assured in who she was and the business she was building from scratch.

His hand began to move, his palm slowly rubbing circles against her belly. Need immediately sprang within her. Yes, everything was new and shiny between them now. She knew that newness would eventually fade, but she couldn't see her desire for this man ever ebbing.

They made love quickly, frenzied in their need for one another. When her orgasm tore through her, she wondered how she had ever lived without West's touch.

They got ready quickly, Kelby dressing in the athleisurewear which Carol and Elaine had gifted to her. Thankfully, she still had coffee pods and brewed coffee for them, giving them each an energy bar as she collected her camera and lists. They headed for West's truck.

"Sorry I had to throw out the sour milk," she apologized. "It had been sitting in the fridge ever since I left in a hurry to go to the hospital in Decatur. At least the creamer was still good."

"You don't have to apologize for a thing, Kelby." West laced his fingers through hers as he pulled out of the parking lot. "And you look mighty fine in what you have on."

"Thank you. This is from the line I'll be helping Elaine and Carol to sell. I thought what better way to get to know it than to wear it today during this photo shoot."

They arrived at a locally owned coffee shop, their designated meetup. She went inside and had the two owners of Motion Mates and their spouses come back outside, not wanting to cause a commotion with West's appearance in the establishment. Although it was just after seven on a Saturday morning, the coffee shop was already about a third full, with a long line waiting to order.

Fortunately, Kelby had checked her email before they left her apartment and had seen the list of people available today to use as models. It included Elaine's two sisters and cousin, along with Carol's mahjongg partner and her next-door neighbor.

They reached West's truck. He leaned against it, and Carol let out some garbled noise, clearly recognizing him. Elaine simply stood there mute, looking starstruck. Their two husbands, however, had no problem moving toward West for quick handshakes and introductions.

When Kelby introduced the two entrepreneurs to West, Carol blurted out, "We can't afford you, Mr. Sutherland."

"I don't know what you're talking about, Carol," he said easily. "I'm just doing a favor for a friend of a friend by being here today."

They had talked it over on the way to the coffee shop, and Kelby had asked West not to mention anything about their upcoming wedding plans. She wanted that to stay private for as long as possible. It would be hurtful if their family and friends heard about it from social media before they had a chance to sit down and talk with everyone.

West smiled affably and asked, "What am I supposed to wear today?"

"I'll get it," said Elaine's husband, hurrying over to a truck parked three places away.

He returned and handed over a couple of shirts and pairs of pants, and West ducked into his truck, peeling off the T-shirt and cargo shorts he wore, and replacing them with Motion Mates apparel.

Kelby consulted the list she had printed out and said, "I don't want to stay in any location too long. I want your campaign to be a surprise. Having West along will make that a little more difficult, which is why we need to keep on the move. Let's start with you four in the coffee shop. I'll do a few individual photos, a couple of you as husband and wife, and a few of your group seated at a table together. Then a few more bringing out your coffees."

She then told Elaine, who was in charge of the list of models, to text everyone else to meet at the next location in half an hour so that Kelby could see who she had to work with, their ages, and what they wore.

West emerged from his truck, and Kelby couldn't help but

see Elaine and Carol almost drool over him, wearing their apparel.

"This really fits like a snug glove, which I like," he commented. "I've never liked baggy workout clothes. This set feels comfortable, too. I think I'm going to have to recommend your line to a few of my friends."

Carol made another squawking noise, and West merely took it in stride.

"Stay in the truck, Sutherland," Kelby told him. "When we're ready to leave the coffee shop, I'll snap a few pictures of you then."

She brought the two couples inside again, putting them in line and taking a couple of pictures. She asked to see the manager, and a tall, capable-looking brunette came to speak with her. Quickly, Kelby explained why they were there and asked if the manager wanted the store's named blurred in the background and whether they wanted to be tagged on social media. The manager, who turned out to also be the owner, readily agreed to having her shop visible in the photos and was ecstatic to be tagged on social media.

"Being an independent coffee shop pitted against the big dogs as my competition can be hard," the owner admitted. "Any leg up I can get would be nice."

Kelby handed the woman one of her new cards. "If you'd like to consider using me, I'm a social media consultant and can handle all that for you, including your branding, ads, and website needs."

The woman bit her lip as she studied the card. "I'm pretty small potatoes. I'm not certain I could afford your services, Miss Blackstone, but I'll keep you in mind."

"Check out my website. I think you'll find my prices reasonable. There's an a la carte menu and then several packages that bundle various services. If you have any questions, give me a call, and we can talk."

By then, the two couples had their ordered coffees in hand, so she placed the women at one table and the men at another, photographing both separately. Then she got several shots of all four together, and they left the coffeehouse.

"One of you give West your coffee as a prop," she said.

West accepted it and followed Kelby inside the coffee shop. He took a seat and pretended to scroll through his phone while he sipped his coffee.

They quickly left as the buzz rippled across the coffeehouse, getting out before anyone approached West for a selfie. She went out the door first and made certain she photographed him with the name of the coffee shop in the background as he exited it.

They met the other models for the day in the parking lot of a grocery store. Kelby made mental notes of who wore what colors and was pleased that all the women had different hair and skin coloring. It was a nice surprise to see Carol's neighbor looked to be in her late fifties or early sixties because Kelby wanted to market the Motion Mates line to women of any age or lifestyle. Elaine opened the tailgate of the SUV she was driving and showed Kelby some of the other pieces the women and men could change into, as well as what was in her husband's truck. Quickly, Kelby formulated a plan, distributing different outfits to certain people. She created a schedule and over the next several hours, captured photos with this group participating in different activities. Grocery shopping. At a hardware store. Checking out library books. Picking up dry cleaning. At an ATM.

At each location, she only took a handful of pictures of West, not certain how much she truly wanted to use him. She didn't want this campaign to be all about him, especially since the menswear line was limited at this time.

Close to noon, the entire group had been told to rendezvous at a local park, bringing their children along. Carol and Elaine's husbands had gone and picked up their own children, and now Kelby did group shots of the parents playing with their kids. Pushing them on swings. Watching them as they went down slides. Standing nearby as one boy skillfully climbed a small rock wall and another traipsed back and forth across a moveable bridge.

"I think I have everything I need," she said.

"I can think of one more thing," Elaine's husband said. "If you look over there, it looks like a Little League game will start soon. So many parents go to their children's activities, from sports to ballet to gymnastics competitions. We should try to snag a few photos over there, maybe as a group."

Kelby agreed, and everyone but West made their way over to the bleachers. She sent Carol's neighbor to buy a few boxes of popcorn and soft drinks, giving her a twenty to do so. The food and drink made for excellent props as she got several shots of a larger group pretending to watch a game which had yet to start, cheering an imaginary home run being scored.

They returned to the parking lot, where Kelby thanked everyone for participating. West, who had been waiting in his truck so he wouldn't be a distraction in the bleachers, got out and joined her.

"I know you were all unpaid for this gig and are doing it because you love Elaine and Carol and want to support them. I really think you've contributed to the success of Motion Mates today. Thank you for spending part of your Saturday with me."

She heard someone's stomach grumble and glanced at her watch. "It's almost one. I better let everyone go so you can eat lunch."

Timidly, Elaine's sister asked, "Do you think we could get our picture made with West before we go?"

"Absolutely," he said, smiling graciously. "I'd be happy to take a few pictures. Kelby, would you do the honors?"

For the next several minutes, various people passed their phones to her, and she captured the joy on their faces, having their pictures taken with a living NFL legend.

Returning the last phone, she told West to get in the truck before anyone else asked for pictures outside their group of models. She pulled Elaine and Carol aside and told them that she would begin rolling out their campaign on Monday.

"I saw you've already signed the contract virtually. Thanks for being so prompt. I'll get on this campaign first thing Monday morning. I'm in the process of moving this weekend and better get some packing done, else I'd start on it today."

"We don't expect you to work weekends, Kelby," Carol said. "The fact that you took out time on a Saturday today shows us how hard you're willing to work for us and Motion Mates. Take your time. We need to get together ourselves and figure out how to expand our menswear line, as well as think about adding some children's pieces along the way."

"I'll roll out everything from today's shoot gradually," she shared. "I promise I'll never do a photo dump. I want to space them out, so you'll see different pictures from different activities and places on various social media sites. I know your friends will want to post their pictures with West immediately, though. If you would, ask them to please tag Motion Mates in their posts."

"Will do," Carol said. "Thank you again."

She smiled brightly at the pair. "Thank you for becoming clients of Social Synergy Creations."

Kelby returned to the truck, satisfaction filling her. West

leaned over, his hands going around her nape, pulling her close for a lingering kiss.

"I'm so proud of you," he told her. "You're organized. Talented. You have an easy charm about you. People trust you. When these pictures hit social media, I think Elaine and Carol's athleisurewear company will really take off."

She brushed her fingers against his cheek. "Thank you for being such a good sport and coming along today."

"Hey, I like what I have on. Elaine told me to keep everything from today's shoot. Their clothing is very comfortable, and I can see the fabric is durable and the pieces are well made. I'm happy to do whatever I can to help a small company go from struggling to successful."

"I appreciate you doing that. Right now, though, I'm starving. How about getting some Chinese takeout and going back to my place?"

Giving her a wicked smile, West said, "After we eat, I have a few things we might like to try."

Kelby laughed. "I'm sure you do, Sutherland. And I can't think of a better partner to try them out with than you."

They stopped by a mom-and-pop place near her apartment and ordered moo goo gai pan and General Tso's chicken, along with a few eggrolls and chow mein. Back at her apartment, they ate quickly and then made love slowly. West was an inventive lover, thoughtful of her needs. She had never been very adventurous in the bedroom, sticking to a few tried and true positions, but he was expanding her horizons.

And Kelby liked that. Quite a bit.

He stretched lazily on the bed, saying, "I think I'm ready for a nap."

"Take one. I'm going to start packing. I also need to go down and give the manager my notice."

West climbed from the bed. "I can't leave you to do all the work, Blackstone. I came along to help you."

She pulled out the few boxes she had and gave him instructions on what to box up while she went to speak to her apartment manager. He was sorry to see her go because she had been a quiet tenant who always paid on time.

"I'm actually leaving Dallas. Moving back to my hometown," she shared.

He wished her the best of luck, and Kelby returned to her apartment. They spent a couple of hours packing, with West going to a storage facility to buy more boxes. She had arranged for movers to come for her boxes and furniture first thing Monday morning, where her things would be taken to the ranch and stored in a couple of empty stalls until she decided what to do with everything. Since she and West had decided to marry, they would need to find somewhere to live. She didn't know if he liked any of her furniture. It was cheap and practical, and she knew he could afford top of the line for anything he wanted.

"Let's take a break," West said. "We need to grab some dinner. If you don't mind, I'd like to take you to meet a few of my friends."

"Okay," she said slowly, surprised by the idea. "What friends will I be meeting? And are we still agreed that we aren't sharing anything about our relationship?"

"They'll know we're dating. I'll leave it at that," he replied.

"Let me jump in the shower then," she said. "And don't follow me, or we might never make dinner."

He chuckled as she left the room.

An hour later, they were both ready and headed out to his truck.

"Are you going to tell me which friends? Or where we're going?"

"We're having dinner at Van's house. I told you that going out is hard."

Her eyebrows shot up. "Van. As in Van Foster, starting quarterback for the Dallas Cowboys?"

West nodded. "It'll be Van, Darius Johnson, and Boo Finnster."

He had named the Cowboys star running back and another wide receiver.

"Any women at this dinner?"

"No. Just you. I wanted you to meet a couple of guys without any pressure."

"Do I need to change?" Kelby asked, glancing down at the casual shirt and jeans she wore.

He came and slipped his arms around her. "You look perfect just the way you are." He kissed the tip of her nose. "Ready?"

"To meet three starters from the current Super Bowl championship team? Oh, piece of cake. I do this kind of thing all the time."

He grinned. "Well, you *are* sleeping with a former starter from that team."

She punched his arm playfully. "Let's go, Sutherland."

Kelby couldn't have been more at home once she met the superstar players. Van's house was large and tastefully furnished, not pretentious at all. He was easygoing, getting her a glass of wine and setting out a cheese and fruit platter.

"My personal chef prepared this. She also cooked dinner for us," Van told them.

Boo said he was looking into getting his own chef during the season, saying, "Our hours can be really irregular when we're playing. I'm so tired when I get home, I don't have the energy to eat healthy. I wind up snacking at home. At least the Cowboys provide healthy and tasty breakfasts and lunches for us when we're training. Are you a good cook, Kelby?"

"I have a few recipes I can trot out for guests. I hate to admit that I'm a snacker, too. When I was working in Dallas, I usually ate out for lunch and ate pretty healthy, but dinner at home could be anything from tossing a salad to a bowl of cereal to stopping for fast food."

Van took a sip of his light beer. "West says you've moved back to Hawthorne, same as he has."

"Yes. I'm in the process of doing so. My dad suffered a stroke a few weeks ago. I'm helping out some at our family's ranch, but I've also started my own business. Social Synergy Creations. I'm pulling from my previous jobs and offering everything from posting social media, branding, graphics, and website designs. I've already picked up a few clients. It's something I can do remotely and help look after my dad once he comes home from live-in rehab."

"I'm sorry to hear about your dad. I hope he makes a full recovery. Mind if we talk a little business?" Van asked.

"Sure, go ahead."

"I have a charity that I sponsor. Van's Kids. It helps provide school supplies for kids in need, as well as clothing, shoes, and coats."

"I've heard of it. Haven't seen a lot of press about it, though," she told him. "You definitely need a higher profile."

"That's the problem. I've hired a director to manage the foundation, but I need to get the word out to help with fundraising. So many kids in Dallas live below the poverty level. Kids can't learn if they come to school on an empty belly or go home and there's nothing to eat in the pantry. They can't think about how to add if they're wearing shoes so small that they pinch their feet. Or they walk home when it's thirty degrees and they don't have a coat."

Van held her gaze. "I need ideas on how to draw attention to Van's Kids."

"I can work up a proposal for you. Share it with you and your new director," Kelby offered, excited about the opportunity to work for such a good cause. "A social media blitz would be the place to start, but I'd also like to see your website."

"Anything you can do, I would appreciate. And it's a blank check, whatever you come up with. I'm paid well, and these kids have nothing. I want to give them more than material things, such as clothes. I want to give them hope."

"Can you give me a few days? I'm in the process of packing and moving my things from Dallas to Hawthorne, but I'm very eager to work on this project."

"Not a problem. How about two weeks? Could you come back to Dallas and present your ideas then? I'll have the director sit in on our meeting."

"That would be perfect."

They pulled out their phones and added the meeting to their calendars.

"I'll email you a few things, just to give you a preview of the direction I'm going in."

Van smiled, a smile Dallas Cowboys fans were very familiar with. "Thank you."

They went into dinner, with Van serving what his chef called summer roll bowls. Van explained they were like a Vietnamese summer roll without the wrappers. They contained rice noodles, shrimp, avocado, and lots of thinly sliced vegetables, mixed together with greens and coated in a tangy nướ́c chấm dressing.

"Now, this is what I'm talking about," Darius said. "This is bursting with flavor, but it's got to be healthy." He turned to Kelby. "Van doesn't eat anything that's not good for him."

"You must be really disciplined," she told Van.

"I do whatever I can to extend my shelf life," he said.

Talk turned to other things. Van had just returned from a trip to Thailand with Darius. Boo had visited family in Louisiana, doing lots of fishing.

"How did you get your nickname, Boo?" Kelby asked.

The receiver laughed. "My mama's favorite book is *To Kill a Mockingbird*. She reads it once a year. She loves that Boo Radley character. Always thought it was a cool name. So, Boo isn't my nickname. It's my actual name."

For dessert, they had a watermelon fruit pizza. The crust was actually a slice of watermelon, topped with yogurt sauce, berries, and mint.

"I'm stealing your chef," Boo declared, with Darius arguing that he wanted to hire her.

"You can share her. Not steal her," Van told his teammates.

They talked for an hour after dinner, and she found herself really enjoying being with West's friends.

As they left, she gave Van her card. Boo and Darius asked for one, as well.

"I was just a rookie this past year, but I want to really get to know my community here," Boo shared. "Maybe you could point me in the right direction. Help me with social media and stuff."

"I'd be happy to do that, Boo." Kelby gave him her card. "Your homework is to think about how you'd liked to help the Dallas community. And why. Van has a heart for kids in need. You need to find out what would make you invest yourself in. Once you have, give me a call. We can FaceTime."

"How about we meet after you have your meeting with Van and his charity director?" Boo suggested. "I like face-to-face."

"I can do that. My number is on my card. Email, too. Text me your number. I'll be in touch." She turned to Darius. "Let me know if you need help with anything, as well."

"Will do," the running back replied.

She and West left, and in the truck, Kelby said, "You were pretty quiet tonight."

"I liked hearing you interact with my former teammates. Talking about business. To be honest, I wasn't that close to many people on the team. I always kinda kept to myself, but I do like those three. Hopefully, you can connect with them for some business opportunities."

"You are helping me get established in so many ways."

A mischievous gleam entered his eyes. "I'd like to think I'm helping you in other ways, too."

"Oh, really?" she asked coyly. "Maybe you can walk me through some of those ways once we get home."

The car immediately picked up speed, as West told her, "If I get a speeding ticket, I'm blaming you."

CHAPTER
Fifteen

After West took a quick shower, Kelby continued her cleaning spree, scrubbing the tub, toilet, and sink until everything sparkled. She had already swept and mopped the floors, telling him that she wanted the place to be in perfect shape for the next tenant. She was also eager to get back her two-hundred-dollar deposit. He couldn't help but think that she was marrying a man sitting on millions of dollars, and yet Kelby was thinking of others, as well as excited to reclaim her deposit in full.

He loved her all the more for it.

The movers arrived at eight on the dot, and Kelby surprised West when she said, "If you would take all the boxes down to the truck first, I've decided not to take my furniture with me to Hawthorne." She flashed a shy smile at him. "My circumstances have changed, and I'm not going to be needing any of it. I'd like you to drop it off at a donation center in Dallas before we hit the road. Do you know of a good one?"

One of the movers spoke up. "Miss Blackstone, my sister is going through a rough time. She just left her husband and took her kids to a homeless shelter. They pretty much have just the clothes on their backs and two backpacks of their possessions. That's it. The rest of my family is trying to pool money to help her rent an apartment. She's got a decent job as an assistant manager at a grocery store, but she left with no money to her name and doesn't have much hope."

Kelby smiled gently at the man, whose eyes had grown watery as he spoke. "Then I would be happy to give her everything here, from the sofa to the dinette to the bed. I've got other things that she could have, too. The bedding. Linens. Frankly, all I need now are my clothes and the boxes marked personal."

West interjected, "Does your sister already have an apartment in mind to go to?"

"No, sir," the mover said. "Close to here would be convenient, though, since her store is only about two miles from this location. They had a joint account, and Mary Alice's check always went into it. Her husband pretty much cleans out the account every month. She had to beg him for grocery money or school supplies for her girls." His jaw tightened. "He's been abusive. We didn't know that until she left with the kids two nights ago."

He thought a moment. "What if your sister moved into this apartment?"

The mover looked startled, as did his co-worker. "Mary Alice doesn't have money for a deposit. That's why we're trying to help her, but things are tight for all of us."

"I'll pay the deposit," West said. "Along with some money to help her get back on her feet." He looked to Kelby. "Let's go and see if this apartment has been rented. If it hasn't, I'll make sure it's reserved for Mary Alice," he told the mover. "If it has been, we'll find somewhere else for her to go. Today. And you can take the furniture there before heading to Hawthorne."

The mover's tears began flowing freely. "I've heard about

the kindness of strangers before, but this is more than I could ever have expected. It's an answered prayer."

"Come along with us to see the manager," Kelby told him. "Let's see what we can work out."

The manager told them the apartment had yet to be rented, and West handed over his credit card, saying, "I'll cover the deposit and one year's rent."

"That's too generous," the mover protested.

West shook his head, telling the man, "Your sister and her daughters need a fresh start. This will help get them on their feet."

The man provided his sister's name and that of his nieces, and the manager said he would handle the paperwork and have it ready once she arrived. He charged everything to West's credit card, and they returned upstairs. Kelby began going through the boxes she had meticulously labeled, pointing out the ones containing her clothing and personal items, and those were the ones the movers took down to the van while West helped her unpack boxes. They placed dishes back in the cupboards. Towels were returned to the linen closet. Even cleaning items were stored under the sink again. By the time her items had been placed in the van, the apartment looked ready to greet its new tenants.

West slipped Mary Alice's brother some cash, telling him to give it to his sister so that she could stock the pantry and fridge. The mover profusely thanked them both.

"Your sister needs a clean slate. We're happy to give that to her," he said.

"You are both angels," the mover said. "Today is a happy day."

"We'll see you in Hawthorne," Kelby said. "Instead of going to the stables, please stop at the main house. The boxes can be taken up to my room and the bedroom across from it. I'll be there by the time you arrive."

"Now, go call your sister and tell her she has a place to live," West said as he and Kelby went down to his truck.

Once inside, she said, "That felt really good. Thank you, West, for being so generous. You've made a real difference in the lives of Mary Alice and her girls."

"It feels good to do good with the money I have. When my agent would negotiate my contract, the numbers never really seemed real to me. I would've played football for free, but Jace certainly made certain I was taken care of on the financial end. I've made some great investments over the years and am set for life. I want to do something with my life, though, and that includes the money. While I've done some charity work in the past with various organizations, it may be time to set up a foundation, similar to the one Van has created."

He slipped his hand around hers. "I'd like that to be something we do together, as a married couple."

"I do want to marry you, West. I'm just afraid what people are going to say. That it's too soon. Let's face it. We've barely been dating."

Immediately, he whipped into a parking lot and guided his vehicle into a parking spot, cutting the engine.

Facing her, he said, "Do you really care about what others think? Sure, there's going to be gossip, simply because I'm West Sutherland. I'm used to that. I don't pay any attention to it, and you shouldn't either, Kelby. No one but us is in this relationship. There are people who've dated one week and gotten married. Others who stay seven years in a relationship before they take the plunge. I don't judge either way. All I know is that I love you and I'm happy with you. That I'm ready to build a life with you."

He paused. "If you think I've moved too fast, that's one

thing. I'll bide my time, and we can wait as long as you wish for us to get married. What I don't want influencing you is how others view you. Or us. You have to live for yourself, honey. Not for others. The only opinion that counts is yours. And mine. I know you've gone through rough times and been judged for staying in a marriage with Bax. But I'm not Bax. We are who we are. It doesn't matter how long we wait. Gossip will happen about us. That's just a part of you being married to me. There'll be the judgers. The haters. We can't let them touch what we have, though."

Her eyes welled with tears. "You're right. I don't doubt us. I suppose there's still a part inside of me who's that good girl, wanting to please others. I need to let go of her for good and learn to please myself."

She leaned toward him, and West's lips met hers. The kiss was tender, one filled with the promises they would fulfill over the years to come.

Kelby was the one who broke the kiss. "Thank you for talking me off the ledge. I still think I'm going to wake up from the fairy tale. Everything between us has happened so fast. I guess I'm afraid I'll blink, and it will all have vanished."

He cupped her cheek. "We're in this for the long haul. Together. And think about it. It's not as if we were strangers and only met three weeks ago. Hell, we were practically in diapers together. I know exactly what I'm getting with you, Kelby Blackstone. A beautiful, intelligent woman who's a hard worker. You're creative and passionate. You're the one I've been waiting for my entire life. I'm going to be proud to call you my wife."

She smiled. "You're the one I'll always want, West. Even if you didn't have a dime to your name, I would love you just as much."

"We'll work together to find a way for all that money to go

to good causes," he promised. "To help others in need, like Mary Alice and her children."

"I think I'm going to enjoy spending your money to help others."

His thumb caressed her check. "It's not my money, honey. It's ours."

They drove to Hawthorne, stopping at the main house and going inside. Tammy greeted him enthusiastically.

"It's good to see you again, West. Did you help get our girl all packed up?"

"She has plenty of boxes coming, Tammy," he replied easily. "She'll be able to tell the movers where to put everything." He turned to Kelby. "Go ahead and set up the zoom we talked about for nine tonight. I've got a few things to do now."

On the way to Hawthorne, they had decided they would do a zoom call with those closest to them. They would tell their parents in person about their upcoming marriage and zoom with her brother, his sisters, and Sawyer and Darby. They would check and see what might be a convenient time for everyone to come to Hawthorne for their wedding.

West left Blackstone Ranch now with a purpose in mind. Call him old-fashioned, but he wanted to get Big Jim Blackstone's permission to wed Kelby. She had spoken with Chance every day while they were in Dallas, checking on her dad's progress. Nothing had seemed to change. West didn't think Big Jim would be able to talk with him now, but he knew the older man could nod a yes or no.

He arrived at the rehab facility and checked in at the reception desk, taking a selfie with the starstruck receptionist. She told him that lunch was now being served, and he could go straight to Mr. Blackstone's room.

When West arrived, he saw Big Jim sitting in his wheelchair, a tray in front of him. He held a spoon in his left hand, gazing vacantly into space.

Entering the room, he brightly said, "Good morning, Mr. Blackstone. It's West Sutherland again, here to see you."

He glanced down at the unappetizing meal. "Hey, why don't you let me help feed you? I know you're having to relearn doing everything with your left hand. I can give you a break. You just have to sit back and enjoy."

West pulled up a chair and took the spoon from the older man's hand.

"Let's start with the Jello, my personal favorite."

As he spooned bites of the red gelatin chunks into Big Jim's mouth, West talked about the past. Times he had been at the ranch. Football and baseball games he and Chance had played in. Big Jim hadn't missed a single game over the years, usually sitting with his parents.

He moved on to what looked like some kind of casserole, feeding Big Jim small bites as he spoke. The older man accepted each bite, and West made certain to pause and let him sip iced tea from the straw every now and then.

"Wow, you finished your lunch in record time. Good job, Mr. Blackstone. I know Kelby and Chance are so proud of you. You've been through a lot, but you'll come out on the other side and be just fine."

Big Jim shook his head sadly. He uttered one word. "No."

West didn't think the man had spoken since his stroke and thought it a good sign. Still, he knew Big Jim had to be depressed, knowing the life he had once led, running a large-scale ranch, was now over.

Putting down the spoon, he said, "I didn't come just to talk sports with you, Mr. Blackstone. I came here for a very special reason."

Clearing his throat, he said, "I'm in love with your daughter, sir. I think I have been all these years. We had feelings for one another back in high school, but college was taking us in two different directions. We decided to part as friends. My life has taken me to places I never dreamed of, including winning Super Bowls, but it's led me back to Hawthorne now. Kelby has also grown and changed over the years. But we've discovered those feelings from long ago are still with us. We'd like to get married. Live and work in Hawthorne. Raise a family.

"I'm here to ask if that's okay with you."

For the first time since West had visited him, Big Jim smiled. His eyes grew watery as he managed to say one sweet syllable.

"Yes."

West hugged him gently. "I'm going to take care of your girl, Mr. Blackstone. Not that she needs taking care of. Kelby is a pistol and always has been. I know she's told you all about starting her own business, but I've seen her in action, pitching to a prospective client. That girl has got ambition and creativity, along with the work ethic you imparted to her, and those are a great combination. Her business is going to take off, and you and I will both be proud of her."

An aide appeared in the doorway. "It's time for Mr. Sutherland to head to a therapy session."

West looked at the old man, who was but a shell of his former self. "Thank you, sir, for welcoming me into your family," he said quietly.

He took Big Jim's left hand and squeezed it, knowing he had no feeling in his right one. The aide rolled his patient away, chattering all the while to Big Jim.

West left the facility, happy to have received Big Jim's permission to marry Kelby, but thinking his new father-in-law would most likely never leave this place. If he did come to Blackstone Ranch, West would pay for round-the-clock nursing care for him. It was the least he could do for the man who had been like a second father to him during his years growing up in Hawthorne.

He called his mom after he turned onto the highway, telling her that he and Kelby were back in town. Mom invited them to dinner tonight. He accepted, reminding her that Kelby would need to spend the dinner hour with her dad since they had been gone several days. Mom happily agreed to push back dinner, telling West that she had already made up a chicken fettuccine.

After he ended that call, he decided to call Kelby instead of texting her, already missing her and wanting to hear her voice.

"Have the movers come and gone?" he asked.

"They're just wrapping up and should be on their way soon. Part of me doesn't want to unpack anything, West, especially since we'll be moving in together soon. That's why I let my furniture go. It was all cheap pieces, along with some hand-me-downs, and I wanted us to start fresh, picking out furniture we both like together."

"I'm hoping we'll be able to find somewhere to move. It took a while for the realtor to manage to find a place for Sawyer and me. I think what we'll wind up doing is finding a patch of land and building what we want. A house we can stay in the rest of our lives. I don't want ostentatious, but I sure want elbow room. We might as well put some of my contract money to good use and build something we can grow into and then keep."

"Then I guess we need to work out where we'll live until then. We can always move to the ranch. There's plenty of space here. I know it wouldn't offer us much privacy, but at least we wouldn't be homeless."

"We can talk about that when we see one another later. Mom asked us to dinner, and I think that would be the perfect time to share our news with them. We can do the zoom after."

"I've already sent the email invitation for nine o'clock tonight," she told him. "I texted everyone to give them a heads up, and I've heard back from everyone except Chance, which doesn't' surprise me. He's probably knee and elbow high in work in the fields, but I'll make certain he participates."

"Then it's all coming together," he said. "Once we talk with everyone tonight, all we need to do is decide on a wedding date."

"And buy a license," she said, laughing.

"That, too. You want to meet me at Mom and Dad's for dinner then?"

"Yes. I'm going to see Dad for dinner. I want to tell him about our plans in person."

West smiled to himself. "You do that, honey. I'll see you later. Love you."

He ended the call, a feeling of wonder filling him. Everything seemed perfect now. He would be marrying the woman who was perfect for him. Starting a new career in coaching and helping Kelby with her new business. They would build a house—and life—in Hawthorne.

Life didn't get better than this.

CHAPTER
Sixteen

K elby anxiously waited for Chance, who had yet to show up. They would need to leave in the next ten minutes in order to make it to Dad's rehab center for his dinner. Usually, her brother ended his physical workday by coming to the main house and showering before they left. He wouldn't have time to tonight.

Her cell dinged with a text, and she checked her screen, seeing the message came from Chance. He said there was trouble with a horse and that she should go ahead without him. Kelby texted back that she hoped things would work out and reminded him about the zoom call at nine this evening. She got back a thumbs up, so she trusted Chance would be on the call.

She did worry about him. Not only did he work all day outside, but he closeted himself for several hours in Dad's office after dinner, dealing with paperwork. Even though he had given her a few responsibilities, it might be time for a better division of tasks. They might even need to hire someone part-time. Since Dad was now incapacitated and would no longer be managing any aspect of Blackstone Ranch, it was probably time for Chance and her to sit down and figure things out.

Driving to the rehab facility, she found herself growing nervous. She wasn't worried about sharing her good news with Dad. What bothered her was how she would find him. Chance had been taciturn, as usual, but he had admitted to Kelby in their last phone call that he wasn't seeing any improvement. She suggested they might look for a new place to transfer Dad, but Chance didn't think a new place was the problem. He shared with her that he thought Dad had given up.

She could understand why. Big Jim Blackstone had always been larger than life. He never met a stranger. He could outwork anyone and knew more about horses and cattle than anyone in Texas. While it had been hard for her to see the man she had worshipped since childhood reduced to a shadow of his former self, it must have been ten times more difficult for Big Jim to see himself this way. Kelby tried to remain optimistic when she was with him, but she agreed with Chance that no improvement would likely take place. It was time for Chance and her to meet with his doctors and decide where he needed to be. At home, with round-the-clock nursing care and therapists coming in to work with him or having him moved to assisted living and continuing therapy from there. Both choices broke her heart.

Once she arrived at the check-in desk, she signed her name and time of arrival into the log and hurried down the hall to his room. Dad wasn't back from his last therapy session yet, and she went about the room, tidying up. She threw away an arrangement of flowers which was wilting and made a mental note to bring more tomorrow when she visited at lunchtime. Flowers always made a room cheery, and she wanted to do whatever small things she could to make Dad feel better.

An aide rolled her father in, and Kelby gave him a big

smile. "There you are. I've missed you, Dad." She brought an arm about him and kissed his cheek. "I hope you've been working hard at therapy while I was in Dallas."

He grunted, which was more than she had gotten before. The aide said, "The doctor is making rounds now, Miss Blackstone. I know he wants to talk with you."

"I'll be here," she said, her stomach tightening at what sounded like bad news.

Kelby brought a chair to place next to her father as his dinner tray was delivered. She sweetened his tea for him and unwrapped the napkin, removing the silverware. The chicken breast looked unappealing, though the zucchini and tomatoes both were colorful. She buttered a roll for him and cut up the chicken breast into bite-size pieces.

Handing over the fork, she said, "Let's get a good meal in you, Dad."

Unfortunately, he only picked at his food as she told him about her new clients and the photo shoot they had done on Saturday.

"I think I'll buy some of their pieces for you," she said. "Both West and I have worn some of their Motion Mates line, and it's really comfortable. I think you'd like wearing it more than your pajamas every day. Getting dressed in athleisurewear might not be your boots and jeans, but I guarantee you're going to like it."

He placed his fork on the tray, his gaze meeting hers.

"Oh, Dad, I wish you could talk to me," she told him. "I do have some more news that I want to share with you, something I hope you'll be happy about."

"West."

Kelby's jaw dropped. "You said West. That's great, Dad! Yes, I want to talk about West. Oh, I'm so glad you said a word. This is exciting."

"Marry ... him."

Again, surprise filled her. "Yes, that's exactly what I intend to do. Oh, I know it sounds too soon. We've only been back in each other's lives a short time, but you're the one who has always told me to trust my gut. And my gut is telling me I'd be a fool to let this man go."

"Here."

She frowned. "Here? Do you want something here? What can I get you, Dad?"

He shook his head, looking as if he struggled to say more. Then he got out. "West. Here."

"West came here?" she guessed.

He nodded.

"Today?"

The thought made her smile. "Did he come to ask your permission for us to marry?"

Dad gave the closest thing to a smile and nodded.

"I didn't know he was going to do that. He's a sweet, thoughtful guy. Just one of the many reasons I love him."

"Don't ... wait. Do. Soon."

"Oh, we want to marry pretty soon. It will be a small wedding, just our close family. Why, we could even have it here."

He shook his head, his disapproval obvious.

"Well, it would be convenient, Dad. We wouldn't have to get permission to check you out of here for several hours."

"Not here," he said, his voice steadier than before. "Tired," he told her, and she saw the weariness which blanketed him.

"I know you must be. I'll be excited to share with your doctor that you're speaking some now."

A nurse came and helped Dad into the bed. Kelby perched on the mattress, holding his hand. By the time the doctor arrived, Dad had fallen asleep. She went to greet the doctor, and they stepped outside into the corridor.

"Good to see you again, Miss Blackstone." The physician hesitated. "I wish I had better news for you."

"Dad was talking before you came in," she revealed, wanting to put off whatever the physician was about to tell her for as long as possible.

"Really? Well, that's good to know."

"Just a few words. But at least it's something."

"Miss Blackstone, I hate to say this, but your father isn't going to improve. In fact, he's gone downhill since he arrived here. I believe it's time to place him on hospice."

Her throat grew thick with unshed tears. "Really?"

"Yes, I would advise it. His vital signs are weakening considerably, as is his body. I really don't see any point to putting him through therapy anymore. He's too weak for it. Therapy is for those recovering. I'm sorry to say Mr. Blackstone won't see any more improvement. That he will go downhill fast."

"Should we take him home to die?" she asked quietly.

"You can. He would need someone with him twenty-four/seven, so I would advise you hire professional help if that's the route you decide to take. Of course, on hospice, he'll be off all meds. Only morphine is allowed. He might be more comfortable at home. Then again, moving him would be a very stressful process. I can arrange for you to meet with someone from hospice. They can go over everything with you in greater detail."

"Can I talk this over with my brother? It's a decision we'll need to make together."

"Of course. I just wanted you to know that I strongly advise that your father be switched to hospice care. He already had a

DNR. We will make him as comfortable as possible, but there will be no life-saving measures taken."

"I understand," she whispered.

She excused herself and went back into the room, seeing that her father slept peacefully. It was hard to think of the world without Big Jim Blackstone in it. She had always been a daddy's girl, and he had been her first and strongest cheerleader, supporting everything she did.

Kelby leaned over and kissed his brow. "'Night, Dad."

Returning to her car, she shed numerous tears. Everything was out of her control now. She wondered if Dad knew he was at the end of his road.

She drove to the Sutherlands' house, stopping a few blocks away to repair her makeup and collect herself. Mrs. Sutherland greeted her warmly, leading her into the kitchen.

"What can I do?" Kelby asked, pushing aside her sorrow and concentrating on being with others, knowing West and she would be sharing their plans to marry tonight, not only with his parents but other family members.

"I just set the fettuccine on the table. I'm tossing the salad now. You can pull the bread from the oven. French, though we're eating Italian. Dr. S is a fiend for French bread. And you can pour the iced tea, too. Pitcher's on the counter. Glasses of ice are already in the freezer."

"You're a woman after my own heart, Mrs. Sutherland. There's nothing like a frosty glass of iced tea."

They quickly got everything on the table, and Dr. Sutherland appeared with West, who kissed her cheek.

"Sorry. I was on a phone call. I'm glad you're here."

Dinner passed quickly, and Kelby was thrilled she would be a part of this family in the near future. She also looked forward to getting to know Summer and Autumn better. Since they had been two grades behind West and her in school, she knew them but didn't know a lot about them.

"Dessert?"

"No, Mom," West said firmly, patting his gut. "The fettuccine is already sticking to my ribs. Besides, we have something to talk to you about."

He reached for Kelby's hand under the table and squeezed her fingers reassuringly. She looked at his parents. Dr. Sutherland looked interested, but his wife had a knowing look in her eyes.

"I'm just going to blurt it out," West said. "We're getting married."

His mother gave a squeal of delight, pushing back her chair and coming to hug Kelby as she came to her feet.

"Oh, Kelby, this is just wonderful. I'm so happy for you and West." She turned and kissed her son. "It's about time you two figured things out."

Dr. Sutherland beamed proudly at them both. "This is a match I can get behind," he declared, first hugging his son and then embracing her. "When's the big day?"

"Soon," they both said in unison.

"How soon?" Mrs. Sutherland asked worriedly. "There's just so much to do. I'll need to get with Tammy."

"We don't want fancy, Mom," West warned. "It's going to be a very small affair. Just family."

"I've been married before," Kelby said, feeling embarrassed. "I know West hasn't, but we decided to opt for small and quiet."

"We've got a zoom set up with the twins," West revealed. "Sawyer, Darby, and Chance are also going to be on it. We'll chat with them and figure out when is a good weekend for the out-of-towners to come to Hawthorne."

"Whatever you decide, we're happy for you," Dr. Sutherland said. "Your mother and I eloped, and we don't regret that a bit. Instead of spending money on a fancy wedding and a single day in our lives, we put a down payment on this house and built a life together in it."

"Where are you going to live?" fretted Mrs. Sutherland. "Housing is really stretched in Hawthorne these days, what with the hospital opening soon. I know West and Sawyer had a tough time finding a place to live."

"We're going to meet with an architect," West informed them. "I've already spoken to one just before dinner. The house we build here will be the one we stay in and raise our family in." He grinned. "And I look forward to the day each of our kids comes to us and tells us that they're getting married." He slipped an arm about Kelby's waist. "Of course, we haven't negotiated the number of those kids yet. That's to come."

Both Sutherlands laughed, and Mrs. Sutherland said, "Watch out for twins. I didn't know that they ran in Joe's family. He'd neglected to mention that. Summer and Autumn were a bit of a surprise to me. Not to him."

"I think twins would be wonderful," Kelby said. "And I know exactly who to come to for help and advice."

"We need to leave to get on our zoom call," West told his parents. "Let's get this cleaned up."

Everyone took their dishes into the kitchen, where Mrs. Sutherland had them stack everything in the sink, saying she could handle cleanup. They received more hugs and kisses before being allowed out the door.

"Where to?" she asked.

"I thought we could go to the ranch. It would be weird, zooming with Sawyer right there. Besides, we need to share things with Tammy."

"She already thinks the world of you. And I know you went to see Dad today. He told me."

"He did?" West said, opening her car door for her.

"He only could say a few words, but I learned you had been there. He encouraged us to marry soon."

West grinned shamelessly. "I knew Big Jim would be on my side. See you at the ranch."

She got into her car, and he closed the door, following her the entire way to Blackstone Ranch. They both parked in front of the house. Inside, they found Tammy reading in the den, a basketball game muted on the TV.

"Got a minute?" Kelby asked.

Tammy set aside her Kindle. "What's up?"

"My mom is going to be calling you soon," West said. "To talk about the wedding."

It took a moment, and then joy spread across Tammy's face. She leaped to her feet, crushing Kelby to her.

"Oh, baby girl, I'm so happy for you." Tammy looked over her shoulder. "And for you, too, West. You're the one who's getting the best end of the deal."

"I agree," he said. "There's no one quite like Kelby."

Tammy released Kelby, smoothing her hair. "When? Where?"

"We don't know yet," she replied. "We're about to zoom with siblings and cousins. See when they might be able to make it to Hawthorne. But it's going to be small."

"If that's the case, we should hold it at the ranch," Tammy said. "It would be the perfect backdrop." She paused. "What about your daddy?"

She swallowed the lump which quickly formed in her throat. She decided not to bring up hospice until she'd been able to discuss things with Chance.

"We'll have to decide about that. I told him tonight. He doesn't want the ceremony at the rehab center."

Tammy cupped her cheek. "Then we'll find a way to get him here. He'll want to see you on your special day, Kelby."

"I know," she said softly, afraid that her father might not live long enough to witness the ceremony. "Okay, we need to get on our zoom call."

Tammy smiled. "Well, I'm going to go and call Meg Sutherland. We have plenty to talk about. Even a small wedding takes a lot of planning."

They went up to her bedroom, and West said, "This looks different now. No more concert posters on the walls or mums. That's a new comforter, too."

"Tammy turned it into a more adult-looking room after I graduated from college." She glanced around at all the boxes covering the floor. "I may need to move a few of these into the other bedroom across the hall in order to get around. I didn't realize I had so many clothes and shoes. Or books."

They slipped off their shoes and climbed onto her bed, bracing their backs against the headboard. She grabbed her tablet and clicked to join the webinar. Darby, Summer, and Autumn were already there and greeted them. Then Sawyer appeared and said hello.

"We're missing Chance," Kelby said. "Let me text him."

She did so, and within fifteen seconds, her brother had also signed in.

"What's this meeting you called?" Chance asked. "Are you even back from Dallas?"

"Yes, we're back," she said. "In my bedroom."

"Ooh," Darby said. "So, what's going on with you two?"

"We're getting married," West said matter-of-factly.

As everyone began talking at once, she glanced to him. "You didn't even prepare them. You just blurted it out."

He slipped his arm around her shoulders. "It's all good."

She turned her attention back to the screen. "One at a time," she pleaded.

Summer was the loudest, saying, "Quiet, everyone. Okay. Give us the deets, and don't leave anything out."

"Do you want my compact version or Kelby's long, drawn-out one?" West teased.

"Both," the twins said together.

"Me first," West said. "I figured out I loved Kelby back in high school. We kissed once, and I just knew. But with me having a scholarship to play at A&M and her scheduled to cheer for those despicable Longhorns, long distance would never have worked out. We decided to stay friends. Went our separate ways. I saw a lot of women over the years, but I never felt anything for any of them. Then I came back to Hawthorne. Kelby wound up here, too. Big Jim had a stroke recently, and she came back to help care for him."

West glanced to her, and she saw his love for her in his eyes. "The moment I saw her, the years melted away. I knew I had to convince her to be mine."

"It didn't take much convincing," she admitted. "Those old feelings caught fire pretty fast. West will be coaching at the high school starting in July. I'm in the process of starting my own business. We decided why wait? He just turned thirty-two. I'll hit that age come August. We don't want to waste any more time. We've been apart too long."

"*This* would make for a great romance novel," Summer declared. "Way better than what I've been editing lately. Maybe I'll write the story of the two of you. Changing the names, of course. And I'll make West a hockey player. They're hot in romance right now. And being the little sister of the hero's best friend is always a tried-and-true trope. I think I'll have a bestseller on my hands."

They answered a few more questions, and then asked when

ALEXA ASTON

everyone could make it to Hawthorne. Of course, Chance and Sawyer were already in town. The three women said they'd look at their calendars and text some dates. Autumn said she would most likely need to get a few of her shifts covered, but she was game for having a new sister-in-law soon. Kelby said she'd set up a group chat for the girls to communicate and another one for all of them.

"I don't want the guys to be bored by all the girly things we want to talk about," she explained.

"We want you all in Hawthorne at the ceremony, if that works out," West told the group. "But we're not going to wait around forever. I'd like to put a ring on this woman's finger in the next month or so."

"That is fast," Sawyer said. "I like your style."

"I know what I want, and I'm not letting Kelby go," West told his cousin. "We're going to end this chat now because we've got things to do."

"I can just imagine what those things are," Darby said, laughing.

"I'm in the same damn house," Chance growled. "Just keep it quiet. I don't want to think about what you two are up to."

They said goodbye, and Kelby set aside her tablet. "I'm glad we've told those closest to us."

West kissed her, so hard and demanding that her toes curled and her bones melted. Just like in one of the romances Summer edited for a living.

Only better.

She wrapped her arms around him, eager to see what would come next. Then her cell phone rang.

"Better not be one of my sisters," he said against her mouth. "There'll be hell to pay if it's one of them interrupting us, wanting to talk wedding stuff."

Kelby reached for her phone. The moment she saw the display, she tensed.

"What is it?" West asked.

"It's the rehab facility," she said, biting her lip. "I need to get this."

West threaded his fingers through hers as she shakily said, "Hello?"

She listened, her insides growing icy. "Yes. Yes. I understand. I'll tell my brother. Thank you. We'll be there first thing tomorrow morning."

Ending the call, she looked up at West, tears swimming in her eyes.

"Dad's gone."

CHAPTER
Seventeen

K elby sat inside the crowded downtown church, listening to the preacher in the pulpit extol her father's many virtues. She had grown up in this church, singing in the youth choir and playing on its coed softball team, but the clergyman from her youth had retired a few years ago. The man speaking of her father now was a stranger to her.

West sat to her left, his arm about her, holding her hand. Darby sat on her other side, tightly holding Kelby's right hand. Chance and Tammy were on the other side of Darby.

She felt numb inside and had ever since receiving the phone call notifying her of her father's death. It was hard to believe that Big Jim Blackstone had left this earth, but it was nice to see how loved he had been by the huge turnout today. Every pew was filled, and many stood along the aisles and back of the church.

West's father, seated in the pew behind them, stood now and moved to the podium, ready to eulogize his good friend. Both Kelby and Chance had passed on the offer to do so. Chance was a man of few words, while Kelby would have been a blubbering mess if she had tried to speak in front of such a large crowd.

Dr. Sutherland looked out over those gathered. "Everyone here had his or her life touched by Big Jim Blackstone," he began. "I have never met a kinder, gentler man. One willing to stand up to any injustice he witnessed and help neighbor and stranger alike." He paused. "Of course, Big Jim could also be the most stubborn, hardheaded, ornery guy in the room, too."

His words caused chuckles to ripple through the sanctuary.

Dr. Sutherland was a terrific speaker, mixing folksy humor with personal anecdotes about her father, bringing him back to life for the few minutes he spoke. He talked of their shared lives. How they'd become pals in kindergarten and remained close over the decades. Played ball and double dated. Gone away to college and come home to live and work in Hawthorne. How they'd both married and had children, the cycle repeating itself as their own sons became the closest of friends. He spoke of Big Jim's work ethic and how he had always given back to his Hawthorne community, from donating money to serving as mayor to actual sweat labor, helping to build a new wing onto the very church they now gathered inside.

By the time Dr. Sutherland finished, there wasn't a dry eye in the house, and yet everyone present basked in the warmth Jim Blackstone had brought anytime he entered a room.

A closing prayer was offered by the preacher, and then West left the pew, heading to the front to act as one of the pall-bearers who carried the casket to the waiting hearse. Other pallbearers were the movers and shakers of Hawthorne, and she saw on each of their faces just how moved they were by the legend's death, one which had come far too early.

No graveside services would take place now. Instead, her father would be cremated, his ashes scattered around Blackstone Ranch, the same as had been done for her mother all those years ago.

She, Darby, Chance, and Tammy left the church before anyone else, heading to Blackstone Ranch, where the citizens of Hawthorne would gather to complete their mourning of one of their leaders.

In the car, Tammy said, "Dr. Sutherland did right by Big Jim in his eulogy. He had just the right mix of humor and anecdotes as he reminisced about the good things your daddy stood for. I'm glad you chose him to speak on the family's behalf."

They reached the ranch and went inside. Though her father had been gone for many weeks due to his medical condition, this was the first time the house truly seemed empty. Kelby and Darby joined Tammy in the kitchen. Numerous families had dropped off everything from casseroles to cakes, and Tammy now brewed coffee while Darby and she set out gallon jugs of iced tea and bottled waters. Soon, they were joined by several ladies from the church, who shooed them from the kitchen, freeing them to speak to those who came to pay their respects to the family.

West found her and continued to stay by her side throughout the next few hours. Everyone who stopped by wanted to share with Kelby a story about Big Jim Blackstone and his influence in their lives. It was satisfying to hear these tales, but she felt drained at the same time.

The final visitor said his goodbyes, and West accompanied the mourner to the door. Darby led her to a sofa, where they both sat and kicked off their heels.

Her best friend looked at her questioningly. "How are you really, Kel?"

She shrugged. "It still doesn't quite seem real to me, if I'm being honest. I keep thinking I'll see Dad walk through that door any minute now. The dad I've always known, not the one from the last few weeks."

She swallowed. "I know his death was a blessing in disguise. He wouldn't have wanted to live such a restricted life the stroke had brought, his body useless and his speech severely limited. He had been adamant about not having visitors, either at the hospital or the rehab facility. I think he didn't want all his friends to see him in such reduced circumstances. I plan to keep him alive in my heart and remember him the way he was before the stroke occurred."

Kelby smiled wistfully. "I think Dad loved Chance and me twice as much as any father loved his child, trying to make up for the fact that we didn't have a mother. He imparted the values I live by today. To always be kind to others. To work longer and harder than anyone else. To give something my all, no matter how daunting the task which lay ahead."

Reaching for Darby's hand, she squeezed it. "Thank you for coming. This hasn't been easy, but it's helped so much having you by my side the last couple of days."

"You are more than a friend to me, Kel. You're my sister. I'm always ready to stand by you. To celebrate the good times and comfort you during the bad." Darby paused. "What does Big Jim's death mean in regard to your wedding?"

"Honestly, I haven't even given it any thought," she admitted. "Chance and I have had so much to do. West did go visit Dad and ask for my hand in marriage. I also talked to Dad about marrying West, and he encouraged me not to pussyfoot around. I don't know quite how I feel about it now, though. It's such an odd feeling, Darb. On one hand, I've lost the man I've admired my entire life, and there's a huge hole in my heart. On the other hand, I love West so very much, and my heart is overflowing with that love. I've got to decide how to reconcile the two."

West and Chance joined them, and her brother said, "The last of the church ladies finished the cleanup in the kitchen. They're gone. Tammy went upstairs to lie down. Dad's death has taken the wind out of her sails."

The two men took seats, and West asked, "Is there anything you need, Kelby?"

She knew exactly what she wanted to do. "I'd like to go for a ride. Dad taught me everything from how to sit a horse to how to throw a softball. I've always been most comfortable in the saddle. I draw comfort from the land. It's what I need now. To feel close to him."

Chance said, "I'll go with you."

West nodded. "I'll stay and keep Darby company. You two go."

She went upstairs and changed into jeans and boots. In the stables, she and Chance saddled their horses and rode out, no destination in mind. The many ranch hands who had attended their employer's funeral earlier in the day were back at work. A ranch never totally stopped, needing its workers to care for the herds.

They rode for over an hour and stopped at a creek, dismounting and allowing their horses to drink from it. Kelby decided to broach things with Chance regarding the running of the ranch.

"You've given me a few things to do regarding the ranch, but I can see you're burning the candle at both ends. What can I take off your plate, Chance? Better yet, do we need to hire someone to help with the workload? I know Dad seemed to do the job of ten men. With him gone, we'll need to make adjustments."

They tethered their horses to a tree and sat under it, Chance talking about things which needed to be done around the ranch. He assured Kelby that he could handle everything for now.

"I promise to be better at delegating tasks to others," he told her. "For now, though, I don't want to bring anyone else in. I may hire another hand or two eventually so I can devote myself more to the business end. That's what I've mostly done ever since I returned to the ranch. Dad was always the one out in the fields."

That had been a point of contention between Chance and their dad. When her brother graduated from SMU with his business degree, he was ready to come back to Blackstone Ranch and work. Dad had forbidden him from doing so, saying that his son needed to gain experience out in the world, doing other jobs before he came back to Hawthorne. It had only been in the last three years that Chance had returned to Blackstone Ranch and taken over various business aspects of running the ranch, while Big Jim devoted most of his time to the physical running of their operation.

"Were things settled between you and Dad?" she asked softly. "I know things were dicey for a while. I just hope you don't have any regrets."

Her brother chuckled. "Contentious would be the right word for how things were after I graduated from college. I thought I would tuck my degree in my back pocket and come back to Hawthorne and put to use all I'd learned the moment I earned it. That wasn't what Dad wanted for me. It was hard to see at the time, but I now appreciate the fact that he gave me the gift of time. To be on my own. To become more seasoned and learn about myself. I think I'll be better at running the ranch now because of those life experiences."

He paused. "Isaiah wants to meet with us regarding the will he drew up for Dad. I think it's all pretty straightforward. Sawyer will also be there, too, in case we have any questions. I told them ten tomorrow morning would be good if that's fine with you."

"Sure."

"Are you comfortable with the tasks I've given you to do? I know you're trying to get SSC off the ground. You have so much to do, not to mention planning a wedding with West."

"I've always found that I do better when I'm juggling a lot of balls," she admitted. "It's the Type A in me. As far as marrying West goes? I think I need to put that on the back burner. At least for a little while."

"Don't put it off too long, Kelby," Chance cautioned. "Not that West wouldn't wait for you. Of course, he would. He's crazy about you. I just think the sooner you start a new life with West, the quicker you will heal."

"What about you? You've been back in Hawthorne three years now. Are you seeing anyone? You're always so closed-mouth about your personal life. It's like pulling teeth to get you to share anything."

He shrugged. "I've gone out, here and there. No one's tickled my fancy, however. Do I want to get married someday and raise a family here at the ranch? Absolutely. But it's going to take a very special woman, and I haven't come close to finding her yet."

They sat in contented silence for a long time, both lost in their memories.

Something changed in the air, and Kelby noticed clouds blowing in, saying, "It looks like rain is headed our way. Let's ride back."

They mounted their horses and rode quickly to the stables. One of the hands said he would rub down the horses for them, and they returned to the house just as the bottom let out. She was glad they had gone for the ride. It had been exactly the medicine she had needed, plus it had given her a chance to see where her brother's head was.

Kelby hadn't eaten anything all day and found her stomach grumbling loudly as they entered the house. The four of them headed to the kitchen, putting together a quick meal they could share. West opened a bottle of wine and poured a glass for each of them. They began reminiscing, not only about her dad but their years growing up in Hawthorne. It was nice to have a shared history with these three. Despite not having a mother, Kelby realized her childhood and those of her companions had been idyllic. She hoped her own children would enjoy growing up in Hawthorne.

"How's work going, Darby?" West asked his cousin. "Not that I know exactly what you do."

Darby explained her role at the national cheerleading organization she had worked for since graduating from UT. Both Darby and Kelby had worked summers for the organization while attending college, touring the country and teaching cheer clinics from coast to coast. Her friend had continued doing much of the same with the group for several years, climbing through the ranks of the company. She now choreographed dances and created new cheers and motions which were taught at camps across the country, traveling to and supervising the other cheer coaches and campers.

"Sounds like you're really busy," Chance said.

Darby's nose crinkled. "Too busy, I'm beginning to think. I'm toying with a career change."

"That surprises me," Kelby said. "You haven't mentioned that before."

"It's been in the back of my mind for about a year now. I still have my teaching certification. Like West, I never let it lapse. It's my ace in the hole."

"You really are thinking about teaching?" she asked.

"I'm not certain exactly what I want to do," Darby shared. "Being back in Hawthorne, however, is helping the picture to clear." She smiled. "You know you'll be the first person I tell if I do decide to make a change."

They cleared the table and placed the dishes in the dishwasher. Darby and Chance both went upstairs. Her friend had an early flight out of DFW Airport tomorrow morning, and she would be leaving before the crack of dawn to turn in her rental and fly back to Kansas City.

That left Kelby with West. They snuggled together on the couch, talking about the different mourners who had attended the funeral and come by the ranch.

"Despite being gone for so many years, I really knew a lot of the people who came today," she said.

"Same," West agreed. "It's nice, coming from a place which is such a close-knit community." His gaze searched hers. "You haven't mentioned anything about the wedding. Have you changed your mind about us, Kelby?"

"No," she said quietly. "More than anything, I need you now, West. I'm just not sure when I want the wedding to occur."

"We can put it on hold for now," he assured her, kissing her. "The spring game is in two weeks. Coach Markham wants me to come to it and be on the sidelines with the rest of his coaching staff. After that, we can talk and see how we feel and if we can come up with a date."

He cradled her face with his palm, and she leaned into it, feeling safe in its warmth.

"Thank you for giving me time," she told him. "Just know that my future is with you."

Kelby came to her feet and took his hand, pulling him to his feet.

"Come upstairs with me. Stay the night. I don't want to be alone."

He accompanied her upstairs, making love to her slowly. She needed unrushed. She needed to feel cherished.

And West instinctively knew this.

He took her to the heavens and back down to earth, a gentle landing, cradling her in his arms. As she drifted off to sleep, Kelby realized one thing. West was a man who would never let her down. He would never let her go. Her dad had approved of her marrying this man.

That was exactly what she was going to do.

Soon.

CHAPTER
Eighteen

Wtest met for the third time with Coach Markham's football staff. Fortunately, he hadn't picked up on any negative vibes from any of them. They all seemed genuinely pleased to have him coaching alongside them next year. Rand Jones, the assistant leaving for an administrative job, had already invited him to the coaches' weekly poker game, telling West he would take his place.

"Hopefully, you'll win more than I ever did. Most nights, I felt lucky if I broke even."

He had made a few suggestions regarding the playbook, and most had been received well. Coach Markham had implemented some of the suggested plays, along with a few others on staff as the offense was tweaked. West could see the playbook gelling with the staff and hoped it would do the same with the players.

The meeting ended with Coach reminding him to be at the spring scrimmage tomorrow. This was an annual game, open to the public, so they could catch their first glimpse of the coming year's team and see which JV players had been moved up to varsity.

"I'll be there, Coach," he promised. "And I'll even bring donuts for the staff."

He accompanied his mentor and the rest of the other coaches to the playing field, where the team was gathering. This would be West's introduction to the players. Word had spread around Hawthorne about him coming to teach and coach at the high school, so he didn't see surprise on any of the players' faces.

What he did see was awe.

He'd asked Coach if he could address the team and was given that opportunity to now.

"Thank you, Coach Markham," he said, gazing out over the field, next year's Hawks seated on the turf, hanging on his every word. He smiled at the group of young men he would have a hand in helping to mature.

"For those of you who don't know me, I'm West Sutherland."

A few boys chuckled, and he nodded. "Yes, that West Sutherland. The receiver who still holds several records here at HHS. The one who earned a scholarship to Texas A&M and will be a Fighting Texas Aggie to the grave and beyond. The West Sutherland who was drafted by the Dallas Cowboys and played in the Super Bowl."

He paused, searching the faces of these teenagers. "And I sat right where you're sitting. Not that long ago. I'm here to tell you today that you are receiving the equivalent of a bachelor's degree in football education from this man right here. Coach Markham. I've had my share of coaches, and Coach taught me more than I learned from any of them."

West let that sink in. "Coach educated me in the rules of football, starting with the basics. Sometimes, knowledge of those rules is critical, especially in the heat of the moment, with everything on the line. He taught me about my position, giving me the instruction I needed to become a premier receiver.

"More importantly, he taught me lessons I've used throughout my life. How to be a good team member. How to care for your fellow players. How to compete without arrogance. How to win graciously and lose gracefully. I expect you to always listen to everything he says and take it to heart. Yes, I may wear a championship ring on my finger and have a fat bank account because of my time in the NFL, but everything boils down to one thing. Did I do my best today? That's what I'll expect from all of you. So don't let my past glories turn your head. Don't get caught up in the idea of playing professional football for a living. Those who do are a miniscule number of the athletes who take to the gridiron each year in high schools and colleges around America."

He paused. "Learn everything you can about the sport of football and play for the love of the game, but also take your academics seriously. You'll get a good education at HHS, and it will be something you use as you move on to the next phase of your life. I'll be checking on each and every one of you come progress report and report card time. You want to do more than pass. You want to succeed, both in the classroom and on the playing field."

West looked to Coach Markham. "Thank you for giving me the opportunity to return to HHS, Coach, and work beside you. I know I'll learn something new from you every day, as will these players. Thank you."

He stepped to the side as Markham made a few remarks of his own regarding tomorrow's scrimmage. Then they broke into position groups. West went with the receivers first, watching the routes they ran, giving a few tips. After half an hour, he moved to the quarterbacks. The roster only carried two at the moment. David Jordan would be a senior next year and serve as the starter. Fred Biggerstaff, the principal's son, was currently a sophomore and would play back-up.

Personally, he thought they needed a third-string quarterback. Injuries occurred all the time in football, with quarterbacks being targeted by the defense on every play. He would keep his eye out and see if anyone on the current squad might have potential. They could also move up the JV starter if necessary.

He put the two players through their paces, seeing that David was a good passer who read defenses well and could scramble from the pocket if necessary. Fred was a pure passer, his spirals a thing of beauty to behold. He seemed to think fast on his feet and knew to keep those feet moving as he did so. West knew he would enjoy working with both teenagers.

Coach Markham called an end to practice, telling the team to report at nine the next morning. The scrimmage would begin at ten. Coaches were to arrive at eight-thirty. Even though West wasn't officially one of them yet, he would be proud to attend and stand on the sidelines.

As he walked back to the fieldhouse, Fred and David accompanied him, both asking questions about playing at the collegiate level. Neither had had any nibbles regarding scholarship offers, and West hoped he would be able to change that.

He bid them and a few other players goodbye and went into Markham's office.

"Take a seat, West."

Doing so, he said, "They look to be in good condition. As far as the receivers and quarterbacks go, they have a great handle on the playbook."

"I appreciate what you said today. About me and education. These are small-town farm boys. Some will get a chance to go to college, a couple of them on an athletic scholarship. They need to know that education is important. It's the key to every-thing in life."

"You emphasized that to me." He chuckled. "Along with my parents. Having a teacher and a librarian in the family, the need to do well in school was in my DNA from the start."

"I think you're going to do a fine job at the high school, West. Dex Danby told me the two of you met earlier this week."

"Yes. I still don't know what my teaching assignment will be. I should find out by mid-May. Of course, that's if no one goes anywhere after the master schedule is created. Dex seemed to think I'd be teaching either World or US History. Either would be fine with me. I enjoyed studying both."

"I know I don't need to say this, but just as you'll lean on your fellow coaches, don't be afraid to ask for help from the teachers in those subjects. While a few might be a little selfish with their lesson plans, plenty of teachers will be willing to share with you. They want to see all kids succeed, not only their own particular students."

"I'll keep that in mind. Thanks, Coach. I'll see you at tomorrow's spring game."

West texted Kelby on the way to his truck. Sawyer had gone to Dallas for the weekend, so she was preparing dinner for them at his house.

When he got there, two tapers were lit and sitting on the table of the small dinette, and the house smelled incredible.

Kelby was pouring wine, and he went up behind her, slip-ping his arms about her waist. Nuzzling her neck, he asked, "What are you making that smells so divine?"

"Tortellini with sausage and mascarpone. I hope you like mushrooms. Mostly because I do, but they're also in the tortellini."

"I adore mushrooms," he assured her, turning her so that they faced one another. "Almost as much as I do you."

West gave her a slow, delicious kiss. "Mmm. You taste like wine."

"I may have sipped on a glass while I was making dinner," she purred, wrapping her arms about his neck and kissing him.

After a minute, he broke the kiss. "I want to kiss you all night, honey, but I'm starving."

"Dinner first. Then dessert after," she said, a gleam in her eyes.

Deciding to tease her, he said, "I told you I try not to eat dessert too much."

"Oh, this dessert has zero calories and is *very* satisfying."

West pulled Kelby to him, burying his face in her hair. "Oh, then it's right up my alley."

He finished pouring the wine and took it to the table, seeing the pasta dish already sitting there. Kelby retrieved piping hot Italian bread from the oven, buttering a slice and handing it to him. He took a bite and sighed.

"This is almost better than any dessert," he said.

"Wait until you try mine," she said, smiling flirtatiously.

They talked about their day, with West telling her about the players he had worked with and the potential he saw in them. Kelby had refined her own website, deciding to add executive summaries, mission statements, and taglines to her offerings.

"I have no idea what the difference is between that kind of summary and a mission statement. Taglines I get. I like the one you did for Motion Mates—Elevate your every move. That resonates."

"An executive summary defines the business. Here, let me read you the one I wrote for Motion Mates. Elaine and Carol really liked it, so I placed it on their website today."

She retrieved her tablet and when she came back to the table, West pulled her into his lap.

"Read it to me."

"Motion Mates is a cutting-edge athleisurewear brand focused on blending performance and style for any age individual. We provide high-quality, innovative, fashionable apparel which empowers our customers to lead active, healthy lifestyles while feeling confident and stylish wherever they are, from the gym to running errands to socializing with friends."

"That's pretty powerful. Now, give me the mission statement," he instructed.

"The mission of Motion Mates is to inspire and empower individuals of all ages to live happy, active lives. We create premium athleisurewear which combines durable materials with contemporary designs, ensuring our clients feel confident and stylish in all they do. We are committed to creating apparel that supports both physical pursuits while resonating with your lifestyle."

He thought a moment. "So, the summary hits key points regarding the business, while the mission statement is more about the customer."

"In a sense, yes. I always was good with writing essays. Word choice is critical with both of these statements. You need to select powerful verbs that resonate with people."

"I think you're smart to include working those up as part of a company's business plan."

Kelby slipped from his lap and took her seat again. "It's another service to offer. Not everyone will take me up on it, but I wanted to make it available, all the same. I figure most clients will strictly want me handling their social media. A few more will need websites or website help, plus a chunk will need me to design ads for them. What I just read to you will be a small fraction of my work, but it's an important part."

"I agree." He grinned. "You could also offer cooking services. Menus and meal prep." He reached and took her hand. "Then again, that would take you away from me too much, and I like you right here in Hawthorne with me."

"Speaking of that. I talked with the twins and Darby today. If you're up for a wedding next Saturday, they can all make it in for the weekend."

Pure joy filled West. "You're sure?"

She nodded. "Way past sure. I'm ready to start my life with you, West."

"Then give everyone the thumbs up that it's a go. We can apply for the license at the courthouse on Monday."

"I was hoping you'd say yes. I've already told Tammy and your mom that's the date we're looking at."

"Then let them do their magic. You still want it held on the ranch?"

"Yes. I don't want to worry about weather, though. Spring storms can appear suddenly. I'd rather just hold the ceremony in the great room. Just a few flowers. Maybe someone playing the piano in the room."

"No, Summer volunteered to play the violin. I think that sounds perfect."

He caught her nape with his hand and pulled her to him. "Dinner was great and all, but I'm hankering for some dessert. In fact, I see myself having an obscene amount of dessert tonight."

"You do?" she asked coyly.

"I most certainly do," he confirmed, coming to his feet and taking her hand.

"What about—"

"Leave it."

"Yes, sir."

West led her to his bedroom. Knowing that Sawyer was

gone and they wouldn't be interrupted was liberating. Not that his cousin had been a terrible roommate. If anything, Sawyer stayed out of their way entirely. It was just nice to know that if he wanted to chase a naked Kelby through the house, he could do so without consequences.

They came together, kissing passionately. It never took long for things to heat up between them. He found it pleasurable to undress her, kissing her after each item of clothing was removed. Once they had shed everything, they fell onto the bed, laughing, the need for one another building. He caressed her curves lovingly, in wonder, still amazed that this special woman saw something in him and wanted a life together.

He dragged his tongue to the pulse point in her throat, circling it, before journeying lower. Stopping at the swell of her breast, he outlined it with his tongue, his cock growing hard at her quick intake of breath as he did so. For her part, she reached down, encircling him, stroking him. Sometimes, firmly. Sometimes, more gently. The change drove his desire to spiral out of control.

West climbed atop her, spreading her legs wide, his fingers finding her. Stroking her. Pushing inside her and moving, even as his mouth took from her. His hand came to rest on her hips as she thrust them upward, meeting his fingers, whimpering. Then she tightened around them, the orgasm racing through her. She cried out his name, and it was the sweetest sound he had ever heard.

All he wanted was to love Kelby and experience her love, in return.

Quickly, West sank into her, pumping away. Their cries of ecstasy grew louder as each thrust brought more intense feelings of pleasure. Then a ripple of sensuality poured through him, and he roared, claiming her as his.

Collapsing atop her, he kissed her again, hard, wanting to

possess all of her. It seemed he would never be able to fill his desire for her.

Finally, he rolled to his side, his limbs wrapped around her, his need for her fulfilled.

For now.

"You said no calories, right?"

He felt her smile against his shoulder. "Absolutely none. Guaranteed."

"Then I'm going to need a second helping in a few minutes. When I recover."

"Second helpings are on the house," she said pertly. "And only provided to very special customers."

West laughed, running his fingers through the strands of her long, dark hair. They lay together, reveling in the feel of their bodies against one another's. After several minutes, he thought he might be up for round two.

"You ready for seconds yet?" he asked, lazily circling her nipple with the pad of his thumb.

"You have to earn seconds, Sutherland," Kelby said, leaping from the bed and taking off.

It didn't take long to catch her. The house was small, and he was pretty darn fast.

Then again, he was certain Kelby didn't mind being caught.

CHAPTER
Nineteen

West slipped out of bed, not wanting to wake Kelby. He needed his focus on this morning's spring scrimmage and not making love to his beautiful fiancée. He was glad they had finally settled on a date. One week from today, he would become a married man.

As he showered and then shaved, he thought how his life wouldn't be his own anymore. As a single adult, he hadn't needed to answer to anyone. He had made all his own decisions, be they on the playing field to the world of finance. From now on, he would always be thinking about himself as one-half of a couple. He and Kelby would be Team Sutherland for life. They would make decisions together which would affect both small and large outcomes. They would discuss trivial things, such as what to have for dinner. That would lead to bigger things, such as where to go on vacation. Finally, they would stand as a couple when making decisions about building their forever home and figuring out how many children to produce.

While West had liked being on his own for this long, he saw the definite advantages of being a united pair, standing with the woman he loved. He decided this would be the next topic he took up with Dr. Linda during their next weekly session. He'd already spoken to his therapist at length about marrying Kelby, and now he could share they had a date and were ready to move forward.

He dressed in the bathroom and then slipped quietly through the house. Coffee would be waiting in the coaching offices. Not the best brew in town, but the caffeine would give him the proper zing. As for eating, he didn't want anything heavy sitting on his stomach, though he would stop for a box of donuts so the other coaches would have a treat to eat. He grabbed an energy bar as he left, eating it in the truck on the way to the donut shop. Once he had a dozen glazed donuts in a box, he headed to the high school's fieldhouse, where the coaching offices were located. Only one other car sat in the parking lot at a quarter till seven, and he bid Coach Markham good morning as the two men entered the fieldhouse together.

"You always were an early bird, West," his old coach said, chuckling. "First in the mornings to practice and last to leave when things were done."

"Well, someone had to turn out the lights," he quipped.

They went to the conference room, where Coach Markham put on a pot of coffee to brew and West placed the donuts on the table. Somehow, his mentor seemed off to West. He moved a little slower this morning, and his coloring was ruddier than usual.

"You feeling all right, Coach?" he asked, trying to keep the worry from his voice.

"Didn't sleep well last night. The older I get, the less I sleep," Markham complained. "And don't give me that look. You'll be in my shoes before you know it. It's funny. Life seems to move slowly, and then it picks up the tempo when you aren't paying attention. Suddenly, you have kids. Then they're gone from the house. You notice more gray in your hair. You grunt when you sit and again when you stand. The missus calls those my grumpy old man noises."

"You aren't that old," he protested.

"I'm sixty-eight, West. Many in the profession call it quits before now. I'm hoping to make it to seventy before I start collecting my retirement check."

He couldn't help but think about Big Jim Blackstone being felled by a stroke and passing when he was only sixty-two.

Other coaches began drifting in. Rand Jones appeared with a second box of glazed donuts, and all the donuts quickly disappeared. West avoided them, still feeling the nerves.

Rand pulled him aside. "Thanks for being here today. Coach Markham appreciates that."

"It was good of you to turn out," West said. "I know you're still second-in-command, but you've got one foot out the door, headed to a new district and that cushy administrative job."

Rand chuckled. "Yeah, right. Cushy doesn't quite describe it. I interned here at HHS, and it's amazing the number of problems administrators deal with. It's not just kids acting up in class. It's everything from petty theft to domestic violence to sexual abuse. Even here in a little town like Hawthorne. My advice? Keep your eyes open, West, as well as your heart. I know you have a love of the game and kids, but don't let any of them pull the wool over your eyes. Be ready. Be open. Don't judge. Listen when they need an ear. You'll be fine."

His teacher training had been long ago. It had been over a decade since he'd done his student teaching and earned his certification and his bachelor's degree. He hoped he would get plenty of new teacher training before he set foot inside his classroom.

"Don't worry," Rand said, reading West's mind. "You'll put in a good forty hours of new hire training before you meet the rest of the staff and do the usual staff development. The actual teaching seems like a small part of things, what with all the meetings and trainings you'll participate in. Still, the best part of the day is when you're with your kids, whether it's in the classroom or on the gridiron."

"What subject are you teaching now?"

"Algebra I and II. The tutoring is straightforward, and the grading is easier than teachers who have to deal with essays. That is one thing I won't miss when I become an assistant principal. The grading can be time consuming, as well inputting all the grades into your computer."

Rand smiled. "Enough of that. You need to enjoy today for what it's worth."

"I plan to," West said.

They joined the other coaches, who took seats around the conference table. Coach Markham went over specifics of what he wished to see today in the controlled scrimmage. He pointed out specific players who needed to be evaluated. They would assign players to a depth chart after today's play and while most of the starters would remain the same, West knew the staff would continue to watch players and make adjustments between now and the first game played, usually at the end of August. That's one thing he would need to get used to again, the extreme heat and cold. A third of NFL games were now played in indoor stadiums, and weather conditions no longer factored into the game. The Hawthorne Hawks would take the field and play in the Texas heat, where temperatures on the field could easily be fifteen to twenty degrees hotter than in the stands.

As Coach Markham spoke, West still thought the coach was not firing on all pistons. He grimaced a few times and seemed to be a little short of breath. No one else on the coaching staff seemed to be concerned, but he couldn't shake the feeling that something was wrong.

Markham dismissed them, and West already heard talk and laughter coming from the locker room as players had showed up and were dressing out for today's scrimmage. He got to the door and decided to turn back, catching Coach Markham rubbing the back of his neck, a worried look on his face. West closed the door and returned to stand next to him.

"Coach, you don't look so good to me. I know you've been looking forward to seeing the talent today, but I want you to get checked out."

Frowning, the older man sharply said, "You don't need to be telling me what to do, West Sutherland. It's a privilege, me letting you stand on the sidelines today, not a right. I—"

Markham paused, a funny look crossing his face.

"Tell me what's wrong. Now," West urged, not willing to be shut down.

"It's nothing. I'm just really tired. Been putting in too many hours." He rubbed the back of his neck again.

"Your neck hurts? Any other pains?" he pushed.

"A little. It sounds weird, but my jaw and teeth are aching all of a sudden. And that damned indigestion is roiling through me again. Why, I didn't even have any coffee this morning because of it."

"You're also short of breath. I noticed while you were speaking. Sit down, Coach," he said, gently guiding Markham to a seat and pulling out his cell.

"Who're you calling?" Markham demanded, his voice weaker than usual.

"911, Coach. I think you're having a heart attack."

"I don't have time for a heart attack." Markham sucked in a breath. "Damn, the indigestion is getting worse."

West made the call. He quickly related Coach Markham's

age and symptoms, telling the dispatcher that he believed a heart attack was in progress or about to happen. He listened, getting instructions from the operator, and then ended the call.

"Help is on the way, Coach," he said. "Stay seated. Don't eat or drink anything. Have you had any heart condition diagnosed before? Take nitroglycerin?"

"No," Coach said, looking worried and a little confused.

"Stay here. I'll be right back."

West rushed to the first aid dispensary and removed a bottle of aspirin. He shook out a few tablets in his hand and returned to the conference room, handing them to the older man.

"Slowly chew these," he instructed. "Let's stay calm. Breathe together."

Rand Johnson poked in his head. "Coach, I—" His voice trailed off as he took in the situation and entered the room, closing the door behind him. "What can I do?"

Coach Markham looked at Rand and back to West. "You're going to take over the scrimmage for me, West," he said calmly. "I don't want it cancelled over a little heartburn."

West's gaze connected with Rand's, and he shook his head slightly. Both men knew this wasn't a case of heartburn.

"Are you sure you don't want Rand to do that, Coach?" he asked. "I'd like to come to the hospital with you."

"No." Markham sighed. "Rand's on his way out the door. If this is as bad as the look on your faces says it is, I may not be back to coach." He paused, looking West in the eyes. "This will be your team, West. Step up and be the leader they need now."

"I'd rather stay with you. See that you're okay."

"And I'm telling you the team needs you, West. Understand?"

"Yes, sir." He looked to Rand. "I'm going to clear the locker room. Go to the hospital with him. I'll go find Mrs. Markham and send her over."

"Will do," Rand said.

Before West could go, Coach Markham said, "Wait." He removed the whistle from around his neck and passed it to West. "You'll be needing this."

He accepted it, placing it over his head. He'd never worn a whistle before. It was a powerful moment, this transfer of power. West leaned down and gently hugged Coach.

"I'll come to the hospital as soon as I can."

With that, he picked up the clipboard holding all Coach's notes and left the conference room. He headed to the locker room, seeing that almost every player was already dressed.

"Listen up!" he yelled. "You need to be out on the field in two minutes for warmups. Get moving!"

Those already completely dressed headed for the door. The few left began scrambling, pulling jerseys over their heads or lacing up their cleats. West motioned to the coaches, who all moved in his direction.

"It looks as if Coach is having a heart attack. Ambulance is on its way," he shared quietly. "He wants this scrimmage to continue as planned. I'll be in charge, per his instruction. Any questions?"

"Are you going to tell the kids?" asked the defensive coordinator, his face filled with trepidation.

Quickly, he made up his mind. "Let's go through the pre-game warm-up, and then I'll address them as a team. For now, head out there and keep things as normal as possible."

The staff walked as a group from the fieldhouse to the playing field. West scanned the stands, looking for Mrs. Markham, and found her sitting in her usual spot, ten rows up, behind the home team's bench, at the fifty-yard-line. He climbed the bleachers, shaking a few hands, and arrived at where she was seated. He asked the woman next to her if he could scoot in for a minute, and she moved over.

"Why, hello, West," she said as he joined her. "It's so good to see you again. All of Hawthorne is thrilled to have you back, especially my husband."

"I'm happy to have landed a position on Coach's staff." He leaned in closer and quietly said, "Coach won't be on the sidelines for today's scrimmage. I called 911. An ambulance should be here soon. You should go to the fieldhouse and ride to the hospital with him."

She looked stricken. "It isn't indigestion, is it? He's been complaining of it. He was more anxious, too, than usual this morning."

"I think he may have had a small heart attack or is about to have one," he confided. "Let's go."

West accompanied her down the bleachers, walking with her to the fieldhouse. By now the ambulance had arrived, and EMTs were placing Coach Markham on a stretcher for transport.

"Georgia," Coach said, his voice thick with emotion.

"West told me what's going on," Mrs. Markham said. She looked to one of the EMTs. "I'm riding with you. I'm his wife."

"Then let's step on it, ma'am," the EMT said.

West took Coach's hand, gripping it and walking beside him as they carted him out to the ambulance.

"You'll be fine," he promised.

"Since when did you earn a medical degree?" Coach asked, giving West a hard time.

"Be quiet and do what they tell you, you ornery fool," he said, mustering a smile.

Coach was loaded into the ambulance and it sped away. West returned to the fieldhouse, collecting his thoughts. He emerged once again, going over to the stadium, watching the rest of warmups.

Blowing his whistle, he signaled things had come to an end. He motioned for the team to join him in the end zone. When they had all gathered around him, players and coaches alike, he addressed them.

"Coach Markham won't be with us today. He's had a medical emergency." He paused, letting that sink in.

"What does that mean, Coach?"

It was the first time a player had addressed him that way. The words were sweeter than any West could imagine, other than hearing words of love from Kelby.

"The EMTs believe he might have suffered a mild heart attack. Coach doesn't want any of us worrying about that now. In fact, he'd probably climb off his stretcher and kick anyone's butt if they let worrying about him affect their play today."

He got the chuckles he'd hoped for, wanting to lighten the mood.

"Today is important. A lot rides on it. We need to see how our schemes play out in real time so we'll know what to leave alone, what to tweak, and what to junk. You need to show us everything you've got today because we'll be setting our rosters based upon your play today. I know every player's goal is to be a starter, and that can't happen for everyone. If you become a starter, do your best to keep that role. If you're down the depth chart, then you have a goal to reach for."

West gazed across the sea of faces. "Now, let's go and play some great ball." He thrust out his hand, as did all the others. "Hawks on three. One, two three."

"Hawks!" cried the group.

He tugged on his ballcap, a battered one with the HHS logo and picture of a hawk above the brim. Carrying his clipboard, he headed to the sidelines. Even though it was only a scrimmage, the band was there and started playing the school fight song. The cheerleaders were decked out in uniforms, shaking their pompoms. The drill team was in the stands, doing some kind of hand routine to the band's tune.

Scanning the crowd, he spied Kelby. She waved, giving him a radiant smile. He touched his bill in acknowledgement, glad that seeing her had him centered once more, and then went to the referees on hand.

"Gentlemen, I'm Coach Sutherland," he said, a bit of pride tingeing his voice. "Coach Markham is indisposed today, and so I'll be taking over in his stead."

"Please to meet you, Coach," one of the refs said. "I played against you in the state finals. I was that middle linebacker looking to take a piece out of you on every play."

He grinned. "I recall you quite clearly. I'm just glad I don't have to be tackled by you or anyone else these days. We good to go?"

The refs nodded and took the field.

West raised the whistle to his lips and blew one loud, shrill whistle. The offense and defense took the field and lined up for the kick-off. The kicker, a rising sophomore, acknowledged the ref's signal and kicked the ball. A lanky kick-off returner caught it and headed up the field.

And thus began West's indoctrination into coaching high school football.

CHAPTER

Twenty

Kelby pulled into the familiar parking lot adjacent to the stadium. So many good memories flooded her being back where the Hawks played all their home games. She could still remember every cheer and movement that went with it from her days as a cheerleader. Impulsively, she called Darby, via FaceTime.

"Hey, what's going on, Kel?"

She turned around so that the high school stadium showed in the background. "Look where I am."

"Aw. I kinda miss those days, being a Hawthorne Hawk. I haven't been back to the stadium since we graduated."

"Same." She turned the phone so that Hawthorne High School came into view. "Maybe we should visit our old stomping grounds when you come for the wedding next weekend. If that's convenient for you."

"I will make it convenient," Darby said fervently. "I'm just glad you and West have picked a date. Will it be Friday or Saturday? Either way, I'll come in on Thursday night so I can help with anything that needs to be done."

"I think Saturday. Just at the ranch. We don't want anything fancy. My gut feeling says I'll be able to feel Dad in spirit if we hold it there."

"Indoors or outside?"

"Probably indoors, but Tammy and Mrs. Sutherland will prepare for either. You never know when a quick rain shower might zip through in spring, and I don't want to be soaked while saying our vows."

"Rehearsal dinner?"

She laughed. "Haven't gotten that far, but I would say yes. Again, nothing fancy."

"Then I'll go ahead book a flight out for late Thursday afternoon and rent a car and drive up."

"You can stay at the ranch. The twins have confirmed that they can make it, and West is pleased about that."

Kelby began walking toward the stadium. "Right now, he's on the sidelines for the spring scrimmage. Coach Markham wanted him there even though he's not officially on the football staff yet."

"I'd better let you go then. Lead the stands in a cheer for me."

"Will do."

She slipped her phone into her pocket and went through the gates. Automatically, she headed to the track, where the cheerleaders used to gather, placing megaphones and pompoms. Several girls were stretching, with a few doing back-flips and cartwheels. She saw a woman standing nearby and moved toward her.

"I'm thinking you must be the cheer coach." Offering a hand, she said, "Kelby Blackstone, former Hawks cheerleader."

The blond flashed a smile. "Kay Timmons. And you're right. These are my girls. You're pretty famous around here, along with Darby Montgomery. The trophy case is stuffed with spirit stick awards you and your squad brought home. And you both went on to cheer at UT."

"Guilty as charged," she replied. "I had my heart set on UT from the time I could walk. I just loved their iconic cheer uniforms. The burnt orange called out to me."

"I've met Darby a few times. She's conducted cheer camps I've taken the girls to during summers. I'm not certain, though, if I'll be doing so much longer. I may be moving. My husband might be transferred to Chicago. We're waiting to see now." Kay paused. "You wouldn't be interested in coming to the high school and taking over for me, would you?"

Kelby laughed. "Not a chance. I was a digital communication and media major. I've just started my own company, Social Synergy Creations. I'm working with companies on their social media. Branding. Ads. That kind of thing."

"In case I do leave, would you mind if I passed along your name and number to the next sponsor? You would be a great reference for a new person."

"Sure."

They exchanged cell numbers, and Kay asked if Kelby might be interested in being a judge at the upcoming cheerleader tryouts.

"I have two judges, but I always prefer to have three. An odd number breaks any kind of tie."

"That would be a lot of fun. Text me the info, and I'll check my calendar and see if I can work it into my schedule."

"Thank you. That would be great." Kay looked over her shoulder. "I need to start reining in these girls. Try to watch a few cheers and give me some feedback on the squad."

"Will do."

Kelby glanced to the field and saw players on it now, some stretching, some running small drills. She didn't locate West, though. Other coaches were on the field supervising, but then she noticed Coach Markham was also absent. They must be talking over last-minute ideas in the locker room. She had caught West doodling plays, his mind always on his future occupation.

She made her way into the bleachers, greeting a few others. Mrs. Sutherland waved at her, so she went to join her.

"Hey, Mrs. Sutherland," she said, giving her future mother-in-law a hug. "I'm surprised to see you here. Now that the wedding is a go, I thought you and Tammy would be huddled today, making plans."

"That's for after the scrimmage. And you're about to be family, Kelby. You need to start calling me Meg. Mrs. Sutherland sounds so formal."

"I'd be happy to do so."

Meg smiled wistfully at her. "I can't be your mom, but I hope we can be close."

"I appreciate hearing that," she said. "Tammy's been the only mom I've ever known. It will be nice having two of you in my life."

Dr. Sutherland joined them. "I've been pressing the flesh," he declared. "Just like a politician."

Kelby recalled how her dad had said that in a small town in Texas, the school superintendent, the Baptist preacher, and the police chief were the biggest movers and shakers. They knew everyone and were the three who could get things done. She definitely thought that applied to Dr. Sutherland.

"Joe, tell Kelby she doesn't have to call you Dr. Sutherland anymore," Meg prodded.

He grinned at her. "Honey, you can call me whatever you want. Whatever you're comfortable with."

"I may stick with Dr. S for now," she said, not being able to imagine calling her former principal *Joe*.

Then she spied West finally making an appearance. Coach

Markham wasn't with him, which caused her some concern. Surprisingly, West didn't stay on the field. He headed into the stands, going to Coach Markham's wife.

Kelby leaned closer to Meg. "I have a bad feeling,"

"Same."

They watched West escort the woman from the stands. Most fans had their eyes on the field and didn't notice the departure of the head coach's wife.

"Should I go after them?" Dr. S asked.

"Wait a few minutes. If Georgia doesn't return by then, I'll text her," Meg said, clearly worried now.

Minutes later, West appeared. He blew a whistle, ending warmups, and had the team huddle around him in the endzone. She knew he addressed them because something had happened to Coach Markham and wondered what that meant for West.

He returned to the sidelines and looked up, obviously searching for her. She steeled herself, not wanting him to see her fretting. When he spotted her, she gave him a big smile. That seemed to settle him.

Play began, and Meg slipped out her cell phone, texting Coach Markham's wife. Kelby tried to keep her eyes on the field, worried about what they might learn.

"Coach had a heart attack," Meg told her husband and Kelby. "Georgia is in the ambulance with him now. They're taking him to Decatur. He's alert and talking. Joking with the EMTs. At least that's a good sign."

"We need to go be with them," Dr. S said. His gaze met Kelby's. "Stay here for our boy. He needs your support now."

"I will," she promised, swallowing the lump in her throat. Her dad's passing was still fresh in her mind, and Kelby felt raw hearing this news about Coach Markham. She would do whatever she could, though, to be present for West and comfort him.

The Sutherlands slipped from their seats and headed down the bleacher steps. Kelby watched the rest of the scrimmage, keeping what she knew to herself, even though several people stopped by to say hi to her and talk about West joining the Hawthorne football staff. No one asked about them getting married, and she was glad for that small favor. It was nice to keep something to themselves, especially because so much of West's life—and hers, to an extent—had been lived in the spotlight.

The band played several times throughout the game. She tried to listen to them and watch the cheerleaders as they led the fans through several cheers. It was easy to spot moves Darby had coordinated and the cheerleaders now used in their dance routines. It made Kelby wish her best friend would move back to Hawthorne and be a part of things here.

When the scrimmage ended, Kelby moved down to the track. West was moving about, talking to several players. A few he slapped on the back and congratulated. Others, he took a moment to pull aside and say something personal to them about their play today. By the time he finished with the last player, the other coaches and the majority of the team had already headed into the locker room.

"Hey," she said, approaching him.

He turned. "Hey, yourself."

West pulled her into his arms and held her close for a moment. "I'm drawing strength from you being here," he whispered before releasing her.

"I know about Coach's heart attack. We saw you take Mrs. Markham away. Your mom texted her, and she told us they were in the ambulance, headed to Decatur. It really made me wish that hospital would hurry and be finished here in Hawthorne."

"I need to go talk to the team as a whole. Then I want to go to Decatur to see Coach."

"I'll go with you. Your mom and dad left to go to the hospital before the scrimmage even started."

"Okay." He handed her his keys. "Go wait in the truck. I won't be long."

Kelby made her way toward the fieldhouse, knowing West would have parked near it. She climbed into the truck, her heart heavy for him. West worshipped Coach Markham. If he lost his mentor, he would be in a bad place. She almost wished that she had Dr. Linda's phone number so she could message the therapist and prepare her for what West would need to talk about during his next session with her.

She did text Meg, asking for an update and telling her that the scrimmage was over and that she and West would be heading to the hospital soon. A reply quickly came, telling her that Coach had been taken to surgery and would be there for several more hours, so they didn't need to rush.

Twenty minutes later, West appeared. He climbed behind the wheel, and she updated him.

"I knew something was off about him the moment I arrived this morning. An old, crusty coach doesn't like to let others know he's human, though. He told me nothing was wrong the first time I asked. I'm glad I kept pushing, else he might've dropped dead on the sidelines."

West walked her through what had happened, and Kelby assured him that he had done everything he could.

"I know it was a lot of responsibility placed upon you today. Having to take over the scrimmage was no easy task. How accepting were the other coaches?"

"It worked out fine. I haven't experienced any jealous vibes coming from anyone on staff. They were like zombies for a few minutes after I told them about Coach, almost as if they were moving underwater. I think it was the right thing to do, both for them and the team, by going through with the scrimmage. It helped take everyone's mind off the situation. Besides, Coach would've been disappointed if we'd called things off."

He paused, exhaling a long breath. "I told the team and staff that I was heading to the hospital and asked for them to wait to hear from me before they showed up. That I'd text them the prognosis and let them know if and when visitors could come." He hesitated. "With coach being in surgery, I hope the doctors can save him. That he can come back and coach like before."

Kelby didn't think that would happen. Coach Markham had to be in his mid-sixties or older. When West first told her about landing the assistant coaching position, she'd thought that Markham would groom West to take over for him in a few years. Because of today's medical emergency, Kelby believed the timeline had been accelerated.

Voicing her thoughts now, she carefully said, "Even if Coach Markham makes it through surgery, he will need lots of rest, as well as weeks of rehab. I don't see him coming back to coaching anytime soon, West. If at all."

"But who would lead his team?"

She took his hand. "Let's wait and see how he is. That can be addressed later."

They reached the hospital and were directed to a waiting room. West immediately went to Georgia Markham and hugged her.

"I'm so glad you're here, West," she said.

"All the coaches wanted to come. The team, too, but I told them to wait. To let us see how things are. Coach doesn't need a hundred guys trying to crowd into his room."

They sat waiting with West's parents and Mrs. Markham

and Rand for another three hours before a surgeon in scrubs appeared and asked to speak with Georgia Markham alone.

"Everyone here is family, Doctor. Please share whatever news you have about my husband with all of us."

Kelby could tell the surgeon did a double-take when he spied West, but he introduced himself and spoke professionally and articulate.

"We found two arteries blocking things, Mrs. Markham. Your husband needed a double bypass, where I used a healthy blood vessel from another part of his body to create a new path for blood to reach his heart. The official name is coronary artery bypass grafting. CABG. It's a common procedure, and one Mr. Markham will come back from."

Kelby felt everyone in the room relax at the doctor's words.

"When can I see him?" Mrs. Markham asked.

"He's in ICU now and will be for a day or so until he's moved to a regular hospital room for rest and follow-up care. You can see him in about half an hour."

West had joined her. "How long is the recovery period, Doctor?"

"It can be anywhere from six to twelve weeks. That includes his rehab. Some people bounce back more quickly than others, but Mr. Markham has a decent chance at living another twenty years or so, as long as he continues to eat right and exercise moderately and watches his stress levels."

"What about coaching?" West pressed, clearly concerned. "He's a head football coach. It's his life."

The physician seemed to choose his words carefully. "While many of my cardiac patients return to work, with Mr. Markham's age and the pressures placed upon football coaches in this state, I would advise him to take a step back. Even retire if he's eligible to do so. He can live a good many more years if he takes coaching off his plate."

Turning his focus back to Mrs. Markham, the doctor said, "No decision needs to be made today. Or even tomorrow. Let's see how Mr. Markham responds to his surgery and rehab. I'll have a nurse let you know when you can see him, ma'am."

Forty-five minutes later, a nurse came to the waiting room. "One visit each hour for ten minutes, and only one person at a time," she said.

"Go ahead, West," Georgia Markham said. "He'll want to see you before me. I'll be the one here every day. He's going to want to know about the scrimmage."

"Are you sure?" he asked.

She gave West a knowing smile. "I know my husband and what's important to him. He needs to hear how the scrimmage went today. Tell him I'll be in during the next round."

Kelby watched West as he hugged Mrs. Markham and left with the nurse to go to ICU. No one spoke while West was gone.

When he returned, he went straight to Mrs. Markham. "You were right. He wanted to hear every detail about the scrimmage. How many yards each running back racked up. The passing completion percentage. Number of tackles and who led that."

Mrs. Markham chuckled. "I knew seeing you would be the best medicine for him, West."

He looked nonplused as he added, "Coach also told me that he's done. This operation punched his ticket." Looking to his dad, he added, "And he wants me to replace him as head coach of the Hawks."

CHAPTER
Twenty~One

The past week had been a blur for West. Fortunately, Coach Markham was going to make it. When he had spoken to his mentor after he came out of bypass surgery, fear had filled him, seeing how suddenly helpless and weak the older man looked. But Coach had a core of steel, and he told West that he would be sticking around to spend time with his beloved Georgia.

And no more football.

Coach had said he needed to quit for his health and Georgia's peace of mind, and he would only do it if West promised to take over as the Hawks' head coach. Otherwise, he would continue coaching—and his death would be on West's hands. Even in the ICU, Coach was a jokester, and although West knew the older man teased him, he could sense the seriousness underlying the situation. He readily agreed, saying that everything would have to go through the superintendent. Being that it was his own father, plus the fact that Coach Markham was also the district's athletic director and had final say on the candidate who would replace him, things had come together quickly.

West had reported for duty at Hawthorne High School on Monday morning after a brief visit with his dad at the administration building. Officially, Coach Markham would retire at the end of the school year, about six weeks from now. He had never taken a sick day in over forty years of service, so his accrued sick leave would be used now until the end of the year. In effect, West was a long-term substitute teacher and would earn a slightly higher pay than a sub who came in for a day here or there. Once the school year concluded at the end of May, his new contract as head football coach and athletic director of Hawthorne Independent School District would kick in.

He had asked his dad to have the contract worded so that he wouldn't start his official duties until mid-June. It was important to him to get to take Kelby on a honeymoon, which they would take once school was out. For now, though, he reported daily to the high school. He'd met at length with Blanche Biggerstaff, the principal, going over his duties as Hawthorne High School's head coach. They had discussed everything from budgets to the ordering of athletic uniforms and physicals. Thankfully, Coach Markham had several notebooks in his office which detailed all his duties, including that of the athletic director.

That was a position West had been unsure whether he should assume or not. He would be overseeing all athletic programs in the district, from other sports at the high school to those at the middle school level. He would be the one parceling out money to everyone, and he had no experience in this kind of thing. Again, thanks to Coach being so prepared, as West had gone through things in his mentor's office, he had found notebooks and records of budgets from the past ten years. He would use these to guide him through the process. It made sense for him to hold the position. Football in Texas was always the chief revenue sport, the one which funded other sports programs from volleyball to soccer to cross country. He was actually beginning to look forward to being involved in other sports and working with those coaches.

He had met with his own football staff daily, both as a group and individually. When a head coach was hired, he usually cleaned house, bringing in his own people and not renewing the contracts of the previous staff. Since West had never coached, he was willing to go with Coach Markham's present group of coaches if they were willing to continue in their current positions. He would need to hire someone in place of Rand, whom West had been tagged to replace. A couple of the coaches had suggested names to him, and he had set up interviews with three of them for early next week. More meetings with the other head coaches of various sports would roll out over the next couple of weeks, and then he would meet with all coaches at the middle schools.

From everything he had done so far, he knew he was settling into his new role with ease. He'd always been able to read others well, and the fact that he was an organized, detail-oriented person would be helpful in his dual roles. Kelby had already put together some spreadsheets which would be very helpful to him in keeping track of things.

He had taken over conducting practice while still working with the position players. Of course, Rand was still on staff and helping him in this area. West had pulled files on every single player in his program and read them, taking notes, getting to know them on paper and then in person. Currently, he was working his way through the team, meeting with a couple of players each day. Though he asked about their previous football experience and any other sports they played, he asked them about a variety of topics, such as what their favorite class was and why or what plans they had beyond high school. Discovering who his players were as people was just as important to him as learning about their skills on the gridiron.

In his dual role, he would teach no classes. Though it disappointed him in a way, he realized that the AD part of his job would take countless hours. Already, he was looking ahead, juggling budget items, because it looked as if the HHS baseball team might be headed to the playoffs this season. Playoffs were held away from home, which involved planning transportation, meals, and hotels. West was juggling a lot of balls, but he was having a good time doing so.

For this weekend, though, coaching and anything to do with being an AD would go on the back burner. He had a rehearsal dinner to get to now and then tomorrow's wedding. The next few days needed to be devoted to Kelby. She had been a rock, standing by him as he rode the emotional roller coaster of this past week. They had talked for hours, sometimes long into the night. She was the one he trusted most. The person he would brainstorm with and bounce ideas around. After marriage, she would become a football widow, a term used once the season began and husbands were often absent from home long hours. West vowed to strive for a balance between work and his personal life, but he knew he would be putting in grueling hours come the beginning of the next school year. At least having cheered, especially on the collegiate level, Kelby was well aware of the time invested in preparing and attending games.

He blew his whistle, signaling an end to practice, saying goodbye to his players and fellow coaches. No one knew he was getting married tomorrow. It was something they had wanted to keep private. An occasion just for them and those closest to them.

West hurried home, showering there and dressing in jeans

and a golf shirt. Tonight's rehearsal dinner was extremely casual. Though his mom had offered to hold the rehearsal dinner, he knew she had already put in a lot of effort for tomorrow's wedding. He wanted her to be able to take the night off and not have to be cooking and cleaning.

Instead, he had asked the chef from Bistro Beauvais to cater tonight's affair. It would take place at his parents' house, and Chef Marceau was bringing a couple of his sous chefs with him to help prepare and serve. He'd left the menu up to the talented chef, saying he wanted typical bistro fare—rustic, hearty, and unpretentious.

Kelby had already moved most of her clothes and personal items into his rental. They were still looking for a plot of land to build on, but they had finalized the plans with an architect for the house they would build. Sawyer had said that three was a crowd and offered to move out of their shared rental, wanting to give them more privacy than if they moved to the ranch. Surprisingly, it would be Sawyer who would now live at the ranch. Chance had made the offer, and Sawyer had taken him up on it, saying he wouldn't be there beyond a year because he also wanted to find a place of his own.

He drove to his parents' house now, trying to let go of all the many things still left on his to-do list. All that could wait. This would be the only time he got married, and he wanted to enjoy every minute of this weekend.

Several cars were parked on both sides of the street as he pulled up, along with a catering van. Both the twins and Darby had flown in, and he saw Chance's truck and Sawyer and Kelby's cars, along with a few others. He went inside without knocking, hearing voices coming from the den. Entering, he saw everyone invited had already arrived ahead of him.

"West!" Summer ran to him, throwing her arms around

him. "I'm so happy for you and Kelby. And I'm not kidding. I may write a romance novel using your love story as inspiration."

Autumn nudged her sister aside, and he wrapped his arms around her. "Hey, Autumn. Where's Dr. Flint?"

She pulled away. "I've already shared with everyone else. You'll be happy to learn that Flint and I are done."

His heart skipped a beat. "Done as in completely over?"

"Yes. I'm not ready to talk about it yet. Just know you won't ever have to put up with him again."

He framed her face with his hands and kissed the top of her head. "I'm sorry it didn't work out."

"No, you're not," she fired back. "I knew you never liked him. I finally saw what everyone else did. He's history."

"Will you stay in Houston?"

Autumn shook her head. "This weekend is all about you and Kelby. No sad, depressing talk allowed."

Summer came and slipped her arm around her twin. "Agreed. Let's get West something to drink." She led Autumn away.

Kelby joined him, and he gave her a sweet kiss. "Hey. Everything going okay?"

"I went in the kitchen once. Chef shooed me out. But it smelled marvelous."

His mother came over. "We're eating outside. I hope that's okay. The weather is just too nice not to do so. And Chef Marceau brought a long table and chairs. One of his people just finished setting out all the china and glassware. They brought flowers, too."

"Let's go see," Kelby urged.

They stepped outside, and he saw a long table dressed with white linen. Several low floral arrangements were scattered down it. Kelby took a few pictures.

"It's beautiful," she said. "I'm glad you asked Chef to

prepare the rehearsal dinner. That was thoughtful of you." She grinned. "And he'll probably stay a customer of mine for life now."

"I'll make sure he gets some tickets to a game next season."

"He'd like that," she agreed.

Chef Marceau came out and said, "Everything is ready. Have your guests take a seat, and we will pour the wine and begin serving."

"The table looks terrific, Chef," West said. "I'm eager to dine on more of your food."

"I hope you will be happy with what we have prepared for you."

"I know everyone will love it," he guaranteed.

Once everyone was seated outside, wine was poured by the sous chefs.

West, who sat at the head of the table, tapped a spoon against his glass to gain everyone's attention.

"I want to say thank you for coming tonight and to tomorrow's wedding. I know some of you came from a long way and had to juggle things to be here. Kelby and I appreciate you doing so. We wanted this special time in our lives to be a quiet, intimate affair, celebrating with those we love the most.

He looked at Kelby, wanting to acknowledge her dad. "And thinking of those who aren't with us anymore. Big Jim's presence is definitely missed." West paused. "Thanks for being so special to the both of us." He glanced over. "Chef, any words about tonight's meal?"

Marceau came closer to the table. "Good evening. I am Chef Marceau, a big fan of West's and a client of Kelby's. My sous chefs and I are delighted to have prepared tonight's rehearsal dinner for you. We shall start with a classic French onion soup and crusty bread, followed by rabbit with mustard sauce and bacon, a duck cassoulet, and steak au poivre. For dessert, we shall serve both apple tarte tatin and crème brûlée. Bon appétit!"

He reached for Kelby's hand. "Hope you like the menu. I gave Chef the freedom to prepare whatever he wanted."

"I think he could make a paper bag taste appetizing. Thanks for thinking about using him. I'm surprised he came all this way, especially on a Friday night."

His mom, who sat on West's left, said, "They were in the kitchen all day. I crept in a few times, just to inhale how wonderful everything smelled."

Though the fare was simple, it turned out to be one of the best meals West had ever eaten. He was only able to take a few bites of his dessert because he was so full from everything else. As everyone lingered over coffee, he made his way back into the house to talk to the bistro owner and his small staff.

"I wanted to thank you again for such a special meal. I know you came a long way to prepare it, and everyone enjoyed it so much. Can I give you my credit card number now so you can bill me?"

"There will be no charge," Marceau declared. "This meal is my wedding gift to you and the beautiful Kelby."

"No, we can't accept something so lavish from you, Chef."

Marceau's thick brows rose. "You will do as Chef says and graciously receive this gift I give to you. And perhaps come and celebrate your first anniversary at Bistro Beauvais."

"You are very generous, my friend. We would be happy to do so. I have a feeling we'll be seeing one another many times over the years."

West had everyone move inside so that the crew of three could clear the table and pack up for their trip back to Dallas. Kelby also went to thank Chef after West shared the meal had been a wedding gift.

With the group, he talked about what his hectic week had

been like, including a couple of visits to see Coach Markham at the hospital.

"He's actually looking pretty darn good for a man who almost bit the bullet. I know he wants the stress of coaching off his plate, but he'll be a good resource to me. He also left everything is such good working order, I'd have to be an idiot to screw things up."

"Will you have time for a honeymoon?" asked Summer, ever the romantic.

"I'm tied up through the end of the school year," West said. "Fortunately, I'll have the first two weeks in June free for us to take a honeymoon."

"Where are you going?" Darby asked.

"We haven't decided," Kelby said. "We've both been so busy with work. Thankfully, Tammy and Meg have planned the wedding for us."

"I advise going to a beach somewhere and taking it easy," Chance said. "Maybe an island in the Caribbean. Or Hawaii."

"Says the man who's never been to a beach other than Galveston," Kelby quipped, elbowing her brother in the ribs.

"Just go somewhere," Autumn said. "I never got a honeymoon. You need that time to yourself so you can start making memories."

Chance said he was ready to call it a night, mentioning he usually got up at four every morning. Darby, who was staying at the ranch, also said she was ready to leave, along with Sawyer and Tammy. His parents said goodnight and went upstairs to bed.

Kelby kissed West goodbye. "I'll see you tomorrow at the ranch, Sutherland."

He walked her to her car, leaning in for a longer, better kiss. "I can't wait for you to become Kelby Sutherland, Blackstone."

Her fingers grazed his cheek. "I'm eager for that myself."

He opened the car door for her, waving as she drove away. Then he went into the house again, knowing his sisters would want to talk about Kelby.

"We really are pleased that you're getting married, West," Autumn said.

"And that it's Kelby," Summer added. "We're really happy about that."

"What, you didn't want me marrying some famous model or singer or actress who's in all the supermarket tabloids?"

"You upped your game when you pursued Kelby," Summer declared. "Autumn and I think you are perfect together."

"I think so, too," he said. "I never could see myself getting married. Not until Kelby came back into my life. This is a second chance for us both, and I intend to make the most of it."

They talked another half-hour, Summer an open book as she spoke about work and her life in New York, Autumn closed off, not mentioning her soon-to-be former husband or anything about nursing.

"We better call it a day," he told the twins, yawning. "You've both traveled to be here. I'm like Chance and have been up since before the crack of dawn."

West kissed each sister goodnight and returned home. As he climbed into bed, he thought of Kelby being in it this time tomorrow night as Mrs. West Sutherland.

He couldn't wait to slip his ring on her finger and start their forevermore.

CHAPTER
Twenty-Two

K elby stood in her childhood bedroom, staring into the mirror. She was a bride again, something she had been before, a decade ago. This time, however, the love which poured through her for West couldn't compare to that first occasion. She realized now that she had been too young to wed, only twenty-one and fresh out of college. Though she had dated Bax for two years, she hadn't truly known him. Heck, she hadn't even known who *she* was.

Thanks to West, though, she was blossoming.

Her fiancé had helped her confidence to soar. It had been West who had encouraged her to start her own business, and already, Social Synergy Creations was thriving. Each day would be new and different, something that appealed to her a great deal. Not only did she have his support, but she had his love. Their shared childhoods had built a bond which had proven to be unbreakable, and Kelby felt truly blessed to make something of the second chance they had been given.

She studied her image. For her wedding, she had driven to Ft. Worth and found she was drawn to minimalist wedding dresses, which featured simple, clean lines. She found a flat-tering A-line, tea-length dress in the softest of blush hues, only a hint of color, and fell in love with its silhouette. It was elegant and showed off her curves, and she felt beautiful in it. West would be wearing a dark suit, and she thought they would complement one another.

A light tap sounded on her door, and she said, "Come in."

Darby appeared, wearing a dress in arctic blue, a pale, icy, muted blue that looked soothing and suited her best friend. Her maid-of-honor set down the two bouquets of flowers she held in her hands.

"Hope this is all right," her friend said, running her hands down the skirt. "I also brought another dress in case you didn't like this one."

"It's absolutely perfect. I wouldn't change a thing."

Darby smiled ruefully. "I hope you're not thinking about your last wedding. Or elopement."

"I couldn't help but remember it. Bax rented a tuxedo in Vegas, but he was drunk during the ceremony. His tie was undone and his eyes were glassy and red. I bought something off the rack at a bridal sample place. No time to have it tailored to me. It was too frou-frou. Not my usual style. The ceremony lasted all of two minutes, and the officiant had to prompt Bax to speak his vows. I think he was about to fall asleep."

She shook her head. "It was a disaster from the beginning. Dad was mad that we'd eloped and he didn't get to walk his little girl down the aisle, but Bax didn't want to go through months of wedding planning, not with training camp coming up." She sighed. "I wish we would have waited. Lived together. Instead, we both went straight from a dorm room into a marriage, and then Bax got hurt. It was all downhill from there."

Darby grinned. "I guess it's nice to know I was a better

roommate than your ex-husband." She took Kelby's hands. "You and West just seem to be two halves of a whole. In sync with one another."

"I've known him all my life. Well, we did have a long break where we never saw or contacted one another, but the thing is that we fell right back into a perfect rhythm the moment we ran into each other here in Hawthorne. It's weird, in a way. I feel utterly comfortable with West, as if he's a favorite pair of old jeans. At the same time, he's grown and changed, and every time I see him, my heart quickens. I literally get goose bumps and butterflies in my stomach."

Darby squeezed her hands. "I don't think that'll ever change for you, Kel. You were perfect for each other back then, and you're still perfect for one another now. I know Big Jim is looking down from heaven, mighty pleased with the match you've made."

They embraced, and Kelby said, "You've been with me through the best of times and worst of times. I'm so glad you could be here today and serve as my maid of honor."

"There's nowhere else I'd rather be. Maybe if I'm lucky, I'll find my own West Sutherland, and you can return the favor and stand up with me."

"Are you seeing anyone? You barely talk about that. I don't know who's tighter-lipped, you or Chance."

Darby shrugged. "I'm on the road so much, any guy I start seeing quickly loses interest. I've had a lot of fabulous first dates and several nice second ones. Then I'm gone for work, and I don't come home for two or three weeks. Guys have short attention spans. They want the here and now, not the I'll see you in twenty days kind of relationship."

"Maybe it's time for a change."

Her friend grew thoughtful. "Maybe it is. But today is all

about you and West." Darby glanced at the clock on the dresser. "Looks like we need to get you downstairs."

They retrieved their bouquets, made up of two of Kelby's favorite spring flowers. The plumbago was star-shaped and a bluish-purple, delicate bloom, while the daffodils were the color of bright sunshine. They left the bedroom and proceeded down the stairs. Autumn stood in the doorway of the great room, watching for them. The minute she saw them, she signaled Summer, who was inside the den with a violin. She'd had to borrow one from the orchestra teacher at the high school since she'd forgotten hers in New York, but Kelby was grateful Summer had offered to play for the wedding.

As they approached, anticipation flooded Kelby as she listened to the strains of what Summer had said was Vivaldi's *Spring: The Four Seasons*. The tune was joyful, matching her mood, and Kelby caught herself smiling as Darby rounded the corner and disappeared from view. She followed a few steps later, immediately spying West.

At six-two, he had broad shoulders and a lean, muscular build. His dirty blond hair was beginning to lighten some, thanks to all the time he was spending outdoors at football practice. His deep turquoise eyes focused on her, and she felt adored as she reached him and he took one of her hands in his. She handed her bouquet to Darby and glanced over West's shoulder. Chance, his best man, winked at her.

The same preacher who had spoken at her father's funeral was officiating today's ceremony. She and West had met with him earlier in the week after they had purchased their wedding license. He had asked them a few questions and seemed satisfied by their responses.

"We're here today to join West and Kelby in marriage. Those gathered alongside are happy to share this moment with you. They've known you your entire lives. They've supported you and loved you, and so it's fitting that you share these precious moments with them."

The clergyman paused. "Often, a wedding day causes couples to miss family members no longer with them. I know Kelby is missing her father and mother terribly right now, but others present are here to share in your joy. Remember, marriage is a lifelong commitment, where you will do your best to bring out the best in one another. Today, you embark on a journey of a lifetime. You'll make promises to one another and strive to keep them. Sometimes, things will get rough, but you'll always have the other to turn to, a person you love who can help you back to the good times."

They spoke their vows, their eyes never straying from one another. Both had chosen simple, gold bands as their wedding rings, purchased at the jewelry store on the town square. Kelby hadn't worn an engagement ring, and she wasn't certain she wanted one. For now, the eternal circle of gold would be the ring she never removed.

The preacher offered a prayer, and then he announced that they were husband and wife. West moved in, wrapping his arms about her, giving her a firecracker of a kiss that made Kelby want to forget about the wedding dinner and rush home to tear off his clothes.

He broke the kiss, grinning unabashedly. "You're finally mine. Of course, it's a mixed marriage, with you being a Longhorn and me an Aggie. Hopefully, our kids will see the light and head to College Station."

Before she could protest, he kissed her again, much to the whoops of those present.

West released her, and Kelby went to Tammy, hugging her tightly. "Thank you for being my mom. You have been in every sense of the word. I know you and my mom were good friends, and I appreciate everything you've done for me."

"I love you, baby girl," Tammy responded. "Big Jim would be so proud of you. You got a good one, Kelby. West is like one of those penguins, who mate for life. He's got a pure core of goodness. You're both going to make for terrific parents."

"Wait a minute," she said playfully. "Let us enjoy being married a while before we bring up having kids."

"Don't wait too long. I'm ready for grandkids now. I'm sure Meg and Joe would say the same thing."

She made her way around to everyone who had come, telling Summer and Autumn how grateful she was to finally have sisters after having only Chance as her sibling all these years. The Sutherlands embraced her, both assuring Kelby that she would be another daughter to them. Darby and Sawyer congratulated her and West, and then Chance pulled her aside.

"I can't say that I saw this day coming, but it makes perfect sense to me," her brother said. "I like the fact that my sister and best friend are together forever. It just feels right."

"I think so, too," she said quietly. "I love you, Chance. I hope that you'll find someone who makes you as happy as West makes me."

He snorted. "First, I'd have to find someone to put up with me. I may remain that bachelor uncle to your kids, the one who spoils them like crazy."

"You can teach them to ride. That would be nice."

"Oh, that's a definite, Kelby," Chance promised.

They went to the dining room. The weather had turned breezy today, with sudden gusts of wind, which is why they held the ceremony inside the ranch. The table was beautifully set, thanks to Tammy and Meg. Meg told everyone to grab a plate and head to the kitchen. Kelby had no idea what the two women had decided for the meal and was more than pleased to see Shorty and Marge Bliss, who owned BBQ Bliss in downtown Hawthorne, bustling about the kitchen.

"Congratulations to the bride and groom," Shorty declared. "We've got a little bit of everything for you. Ribs. Brisket. Smoked sausage and chicken. Beans and slaw, and those yeasty rolls you like, West."

They filled their plates, buffet style, and returned to the dining room, where everyone had a story to tell about West or Kelby. The time together was full of laughter and sweet reminiscences.

Meg and Tammy excused themselves, returning with a wedding cake baked by Luscious Layers, the local bakery. It was an almond cake with white chocolate buttercream layers and looked almost too good to eat. She and West shared a knife and cut it together. Meg also brought out Bluebell ice cream to accompany it, which pleased everyone.

Tammy collected Kelby's bridal bouquet, saying she had something in mind to preserve it in a unique way. Meg took one of the slices of cake and said she would wrap it up and freeze it so that the happy couple could taste it again on their first anniversary.

Kelby looked around the table and said, "I want to thank all of you for being here. I know the wedding was small, but it is exactly what West and I envisioned."

West added, "You are the people who mean the most to us. Thank you for being a part of this special day." With a wicked grin, he added, "And now here's the part where we say goodbye to everyone so that I have my way with my new wife."

Everyone laughed. Meg invited those present to come to brunch at ten-thirty the next morning, and then looked at the bridal couple, saying, "You're welcome to show up, but we understand if you can't make it."

Hugs and kisses were exchanged, and she accompanied West to his truck, the others following them outside. The back window, painted in white shoe polish, proclaimed *Just Married*.

Strings of tin cans and cowbells were tied to the truck's bumper.

"It had to be Sawyer," West said, glancing to his cousin.

Sawyer looked the picture of innocence. "I have no idea what you're talking about, Cuz. As my own attorney, I advise myself to plead the Fifth."

Laughing, West opened the passenger door, helping Kelby inside. He climbed behind the steering wheel and started the truck. As they pulled away from the house, he tooted the horn a few times. Then his fingers found hers, closing around them, bringing them to his lips for a tender kiss.

"How're you doing, Mrs. Sutherland?"

"I'm feeling pretty darn good, Mr. Sutherland. Glad that all that's behind us now."

He stopped the truck at the gates to the ranch and before pulling out onto the highway, leaned over and gave her a tender kiss.

"I already like being married, Kelby. Promise you'll hang around for at least fifty or sixty years before you decide whether to keep me around or not."

She laughed, looking adoringly at the man who had changed her life. West had brought a deep, abiding love, and she couldn't imagine her life without him in it.

"I promise. But only for the first fifty years. We may need to negotiate things after that."

"You're on," West said, kissing her again and then turning onto the road, heading to the house they would call home for now.

And moving together into a future filled with love.

Epilogue

AT&T STADIUM—DECEMBER—5 ½ YEARS LATER

West walked into the familiar locker room, one which he had been in many times as a Dallas Cowboys wide receiver. It was the day of the state championship finals. His football teams had won their district five times in a row. The first year, they had been knocked out of the playoffs in the first round. The second and third year, his team had gone to the quarterfinals. Last year, the Hawks had played in the state title game.

And lost.

This year, they were back, chomping at the bit, ready to taste victory and claim a state title. He knew it had been a remarkable run. Very few coaches experienced the continued success West had had, and he was grateful for it. Other athletic directors had come knocking at his door, trying to hire him away to lead their programs in bigger districts, but he had always given them a resounding no. If the day came and the powers that be didn't want him coaching at Hawthorne High School, then he would hang up his coaching whistle and find something else to do because he was dead set on remaining in his hometown.

He had three wonderful reasons to stay. Kate, his daughter, was three-and-a-half now and had him wrapped around her pinky. While she was already starting to read, which delighted his librarian mother, he was excited that her athleticism showed. She could kick a ball with ease, and West could see her playing soccer in the near future. Naturally, Kelby had put Kate in gymnastics, and his little girl was already tumbling and doing splits and all kinds of things he was learning about. Of course, Kelby hoped that Kate would follow in her footsteps and want to be a cheerleader. Whatever his daughter chose to do, be it basketball or the debate team, he was ready to support her.

The twins, Flynn and Quinn, were eighteen months and all boy, into absolutely everything. They were both curious and loved to build with blocks and Legos. They played with trucks and had plastic dinosaurs. Quinn was the quieter of the two, the same as Autumn had been. Flynn was boisterous and loud and loved making animal sounds. His cow moos and duck quacks made his brother laugh hysterically. While it was too early to know what they might be interested in, he hoped they would play some kind of sport.

His kids—and Kelby—were his entire world. Yes, he spent an ungodly amount of hours coaching football and handling budgets, but West was able to let all that slide off him the moment he walked in the door at home. The sweetest word in the world had to be his three kids shrieking *Daddy* at the top of their lungs, rushing toward him, and sticking to him like glue.

He gazed across the room now, seeing the players adjusting a pad or sitting quietly, visualizing a play. These young men knew when it was time to josh around and when to become serious.

David Jordan, the quarterback from his first team five years ago, caught his eye. David had earned a scholarship to Tarleton and started as their quarterback his first two years. A devastating injury had cut his athletic career short, but he had hunkered down and graduated in four years, his goal of coming home to coach with West being fulfilled this year. West nodded at him, and David gave one of his shrill whistles, alerting everyone that their head coach had arrived in the locker room.

West moved to the center of the room. "Gather around."

The team did so, ringed by his coaching staff. He took his time looking at each young man, wanting to connect with them.

"You're about to go out and play the game of your life," he said assuredly. "We didn't get to the championship game with dumb luck. We've worked hard all season long, mastering the playbook, keeping up with conditioning, and our actual game play. What you do out on the gridiron for the next sixty minutes may very well define you, not only as a player, but as a man."

He let that thought sink in a moment before continuing. "You're prepared. That's a given. I want you to go out there and play the best game in you. But I also want you to remember that football is a game. It does teach discipline. Leadership. Camaraderie. It helps you hone your instincts and trust your gut. No matter what the score shows by the end of the game, I'll still love you. So will your family and friends and all the people who live in Hawthorne. Go out and give it your best. That's all I ask."

West thrust out his hand, with players stacking their hands above his. "Hawks on three. One, two, three. Hawks!"

The energy was almost visible now, a humming that carried throughout the locker room.

"Let's go!" his defensive coordinator shouted, and players poured from the locker room.

They went up the tunnel and spilled out onto the field, running through the large banner the cheerleaders held. The band played the school fight song. The drill team shook their pompoms. The crowd roared. It seemed to him as if the entire town of Hawthorne was sitting in the stands.

West headed to the sidelines, looking up. He always found Kelby before any game. She centered him. Grounded him. She was the glue that kept his family together.

When he spotted her, his heart flipped over twice. Spying her in a crowd never got old. Her beauty had matured over the years, motherhood softening her edges some. Yet she was a fierce businesswoman, creative and demanding, managing social media accounts and creating websites and graphics and taglines and a dozen other things for the people and companies she represented.

She blew him a kiss, and he beamed at her. Everything was better and brighter in his life because of Kelby. Flynn and Quinn waved at him, and he waved back.

He glanced down the track to where the cheerleaders now stood, picking up their pompoms. Darby was down there with them, and she waved to him. Kate was in the thick of things, wearing her own HHS sweater and skirt, with a tiny pair of pompoms to shake. Already, she knew every cheer and routine and did them alongside the varsity squad. The fans ate her up.

Looking back at the crowd briefly, he caught sight of his sisters and their husbands. Darby's husband sat with them. So did Sawyer and his wife. Even his mom and dad were there, cheering on their son and his team.

As West turned back to the field, he removed his hat for the playing of the national anthem, placing the ballcap over his heart. He sang it, along with the school song, with pride and gusto. His team stood on the sidelines, watching the three captains head to mid-field for the coin toss. When his quarterback signaled that the Hawks had won, a peace settled over him.

The kickoff team went out on the field, and soon, the game was underway.

Two hours later, West held Kate in his arms, the twins locked to his legs, as he kissed Kelby. One of his teams had finally earned a state championship, and it was even sweeter than when he had quarterbacked the Hawks team which had done the same almost twenty years ago.

"How does it feel, earning your first state title as a coach?" Kelby asked.

"Good," he said, their gazes holding. "But having you and the kids means even more."

West kissed his wife again, knowing how happy the decades ahead would be.

Also by Alexa Aston

HEARTS IN HAWTHORNE

Heartstrings and Helmets

Heartbeat Harmony

Agent of the Heart

Hearts and Hooves

Hoops and Hearts

LOST CREEK, TEXAS HILL COUNTRY

The Perfect Blend

Painted Melodies

Script of Love

Love in Every Bite

Whispered Melodies

SUGAR SPRINGS

Shadows of the Past

Learning to Trust Again

A Perfect Match

A Fresh Start

Recipe for Love

MAPLE COVE

Another Chance at Love

A New Beginning

Coming Home

The Lyrics of Love

Finding Home

HOLLYWOOD NAME GAME

Hollywood Heartbreaker

Hollywood Flirt

Hollywood Player

Hollywood Double

Hollywood Enigma

LAWMEN OF THE WEST

Runaway Hearts

Blind Faith

Love and the Lawman

Ballad Beauty

SAGEBRUSH BRIDES

A Game of Chance

Written in the Cards

Outlaw Muse

KNIGHTS OF REDEMPTION

A Bit of Heaven on Earth

A Knight for Kallen

SUDDENLY A DUKE

Portrait of the Duke

Music for the Duke

Polishing the Duke

Designs on the Duke

Fashioning the Duke

Love Blooms with the Duke

Training the Duke

Investigating the Duke

SECOND SONS OF LONDON

Educated by the Earl

Debating with the Duke

Empowered by the Earl

Made for the Marquess

Dubious about the Duke

Valued by the Viscount

Meant for the Marquess

DUKES DONE WRONG

Discouraging the Duke

Deflecting the Duke

Disrupting the Duke

Delighting the Duke

Destiny with a Duke

DUKES OF DISTINCTION

Duke of Renown

Duke of Charm

Duke of Disrepute

Duke of Arrogance

Duke of Honor

SOLDIERS AND SOULMATES

To Heal an Earl

To Tame a Rogue

To Trust a Duke

To Save a Love

To Win a Widow

THE ST. CLAIRS

Devoted to the Duke

Midnight with the Marquess

Embracing the Earl

Defending the Duke

Suddenly a St. Clair

STANDALONE ROMANTIC THRILLERS

Leave Yesterday Behind

Illusions of Death

About the Author

USA Today and Amazon Top 100 bestselling author Alexa Aston lives with her husband in a Dallas suburb, where she eats her fair share of dark chocolate and plots out stories while she walks every morning. She enjoys travel, sports, and binge-watching—and never misses an episode of *Survivor*.

Alexa brings her characters to life in steamy historicals, contemporary romances, and romantic suspense novels that resonate with passion, intensity, and heart.

Keep up with Alexa
Visit her website
Newsletter Sign-Up

More ways to connect with Alexa